GYNOMITE
Fearless, Feminist Porn

New Orleans, Louisiana

Cover Design: Liz Belile and JoAnn Blohowiak
Page Design and Layout: www.joannblohowiak.org

ISBN: 0966646924

New Mouth from the Dirty South, LLC
PO Box 19742
New Orleans, LA 70179-0742

books@newmouthfromthedirtysouth.com
www.newmouthfromthedirtysouth.com

Contents

Gynomite: Fearless, Feminist Porn
An Introduction

Gynomite isn't just a reading series, a CD compilation, a web site, and a book. It's a forum, and a mission for freedom from anxiety about sex. Not just how anxious we get when we actually *have sex*, but how we get when we—oh. my. god.—*talk* about having sex.

Gynomite gives a voice to the zillions of women out there who just want to feel. Think. Get all hot and bothered. Vibrate. Moan. Fuck better. Come better. Again. Again. And again.

Gynomite is where we share our experiences and ideas with others. Gynomite makes it safe for human beings in general and women in particular to express their true selves, butt zits, saggy tits, wiry nipple hair, jellyroll bellies, knife fetishes, and all.

For this anthology (and for our performances) a few dozen of the best writers around— many of whom had never written erotica before (much less performed it)—spilled their inner sluts in a respectful, sacred, literary setting. What you are holding in your hands is more than a collection of dirty stories, it's a milestone document from an ongoing mission to change the world, one orgasm at a time.

Many of these stories will be jack-off fodder. That's a good thing. We hope you'll find something in here that you can use. There's a wide range, from the subtlest erotic gesture to the most extreme expressions of forbidden rage. Each writer gauged what was *pornographic* for herself; one woman's hot fudge sex experience is another woman's vanilla.

I commend each and every woman who contributed to this collection for having the clit to do it, for daring to express their erotic selves in public. Especially since it ain't all pretty. Yes, there's a lot of violence and rage and non-lovey dovey sexiness here. But that's part of who we are as women, as human beings—and it goes back as far as the eye can see in history. There's also celebration, ecstasy, play, and joy.

Whether the language or imagery is sexually charged or the point of view is unusual, or the subject matter covers new territory, or is still considered taboo, each piece of writing in this book represents an original, personal approach to the concept of "Feminist Porn." Lesbians writing gay male sex. . . straight chicks writing as horny men. . . girly girls getting macha, older broads bucking wild. . . turning stereotypes on their heads. . . giving and taking in equal parts.

Taste the blood *and* the bliss. The spectrum. As the paradigm shifts, so does the axis.

And sometimes that's what gets us off. Even those of us who consider ourselves to be hard-core, radical, academic, grassroots, fuck you, fully-conscious, lipstick and leather, master and slave, post-modern feminists. How great that we can come out at last.

So get on your little pony, boys and girls, and RIDE.

Liz Belile
Houston,
Austin,
& New Orleans,
September 2000

Liz Belile

The Difference Between Erotica and Pornography

I'm at the sink, washing the dishes. I love the scratchy feeling of the sponge scrubber against glass, as it gently removes the food particles. The water is hot and soapy. I've put a dash of Clorox in it to cut through the grease. The smell of chlorine takes me back to summer days at the Westador pool, with the sound of children's squealing laughter and water splashing. "Marco!" "Polo!" "Marco!" "Polo!" And me, resting poolside, with sun-warmed, chlorinated puddles of water under my brown, skinny-girl thighs, drenched in Hawaiian Tropic coconut oil, tiny breasts budding under bright orange bikini top. Scraping skin and bone on steamy concrete while flirting with Ricky and T.C., the older boys, who had suddenly taken note of my growth spurt.

"Wow, Lisa! You're all curvy!" they'd said, making me squirm. To this day I can hear any song off the Eagles' *Hotel California* or ELO's *New World Record* and get instantly aroused. All the mystery. I sigh, back to the present, and I grind my hips against the counter. A deep rumbling starts to build between my legs. It's like a warmth, a spreading, and a tightening. My nipples perk up. Mr. X., my boyfriend, comes up behind me, whistling some Guided By Voices melody and he cups my breasts. Mmmm. He presses his groin into my backside, is fully pressed against me as he runs his soft lips and tongue along my neckline—I love his big puffy lips—and his hot breath on my neck raises the hair there and I'm turned on.

"Make love to me," I whisper. He nods, and pulls my panties down, parting my inner folds with his fingertips, remarking on my intense heat and moisture, then he slides his love into me. We sway and breathe as one, we bite into each other's shoulders, we cry out in sweet painful release. We cling together, panting in the golden glow of our union. And then. . . .

"I'll dry," he says, picking up the towel. We laugh.

II. I'm standing at the sink, doing the dishes. I'm wet. The soapy suds and water have dampened my clothes, which cling to me, so that my tits stick straight out, my nipples rock hard, as cool air moves over them. I reach up with wet fingers to give them a tweak and I moan, grinding my cunt bone into the counter, pouring more water down my chest, fingers moving to rub my clit through tight orange bikini panties. I can feel it swell. I close my eyes and I'm a porn star on a film shoot at a resort in Mexico. Men are lining up to fuck me as I spread myself open for them, rolling around in the puddles of water that have been splashed onto the cement by all the people who are fucking, sucking and having a big orgy in the pool. "Heartache Tonight" is playing on an AM radio in the background and I start pumping in rhythm to it. I'm teasing my clit with one hand and leaning on the cabinet with the other when Mr. X. comes up behind me, whistling.

"Well, well, what have we here?" he says, sizing up the situation. His cock is engorged and hard on my ass and I push my hips back into him, pussy lips parting as he pulls my panties aside to slide his throbbing cock into me with a groan. We rock back and forth against the counter, his hands on my hips, his shaft sliding, gliding in and out of my glistening hole. My cunt muscles grip and massage his huge member as he moves inside me, bending his knees to get a deeper thrust, angling his cock so that it rides to the very end of my love canal. He unleashes his load. We both cum in a loud, shattering yelp, his creamy white jiz drizzling down my thighs. My pussy contracts and releases around his shrinking penis, and we fall apart, slippery, exhausted, sated. He picks up a dish towel to wipe the cum off our thighs.

"I'll dry," he says. And we laugh.

Thing Fer Skinny

When Ann told me about her tattoo artist I knew I had to have him. She was showing me the Rat Fink Big Daddy Roth gearhead designs he'd done on her calves. They looked good, real good. She also had a shitty, homemade tiny anchor on her right bicep (moment of teenage insanity) and half a dragon (her Chinese astrological sign) across her kidneys. Apparently the guy worked in trades, the good old-fashioned barter system. She fixed his bike, he worked on her tats. He was going to finish the other half of her dragon in exchange for a studded Motorhead jacket. I wanted to find someone to do some flames down my back.

"What's he look like?" I coyly asked. Ann was a bruiser dyke who barely ever took notice of what boys looked like.

"Aw, you know. Long-ass dreds. Scrawny. All pierced and tattooed and shit. He used to be a junkie."

My cunt clenched at the thought. Scrawny. Ex-junkie. I had moved back home, to Texas, and was stuck out in the 'burbs. Ann was the first city person I'd met since I got here. At least she listened to punk rock. Both of us had moved back home to the sticks after failing miserably at being rock star drug addict alcoholics in major metropolitan areas. I'd been in San Francisco, she was in New York. We met at an AA meeting (appropriately enough) in

Humble, Texas, just outside of Houston, and had been inseparable since.

"I mean, you can get him to work on you if you want, but his house is pretty disgusting. I always bring my own needles, too. I don't know if you'd like it. It seems pretty unsanitary."

Apparently he didn't even have running water at his place, which he shared with a few other people. It wasn't a squat, exactly, they just had a landlord who was in and out of rehab and jail. The rent was cheap and they had utilities when the guy was doing okay, and they didn't when he wasn't. Shannon, the tattoo artist guy, was sort of the alpha tenant of the house, and had been there a long time. Ann said he had a tattoo chair set up among all his triple-X Japanese anime videos, *Star Wars* action figures and guitars. "Unsanitary" didn't bother me. Nothing could be worse than the 100 or so punk-rock flophouse crash pads I had stayed in all over the country.

Shannon was also in a band, of course, and they were playing that weekend. I asked Ann if she would take me to the show. She said sure, then eyed me suspiciously for a minute.

"You're not thinking of fucking him, are you?"

I didn't say anything.

She howled. "Oh, man. Well, shit. He's a boy toy, but he's been sober for a long time. You never know."

She was right, I didn't know. I was pushing 30 and my divorce had just been declared final. Mexican divorce. The papers had simply arrived, and he had no way to contest it. Typical alcoholic divorce, but fuck him anyway. I found out that the bastard had been having affairs with women left and right since I last left on tour, lying to me even after I begged him to just tell me the truth.

"You're paranoid," he'd say, pretending to be irritated and appalled that I would even doubt him.

Three years with a lying cheater and I was back on the sauce. I needed help. So I left California, crawling on hands and knees to my mom's house. I had sort of fucked up all of my relationships with everyone who had ever loved me, including my parents. Those letters I had written, begging forgiveness and trying to make amends, had only gone so far. I'd even got back a chicken foot and a voodoo curse from one ex-lover in Seattle.

So my mom gave me one year to get back on my feet, then it was out on my own again.

My mom is a smart woman. A bit much sometimes, but smart. I was going on month number four when I met Ann. At that point I was starved for contact with weirdoes and democrats and other people who didn't necessarily wash their hair every day. I needed culture, people my own age. I needed soy milk in my coffee. There were no neighborhood businesses, only giant chain stores where we lived. I was forced to go to Starbuck's for my daily lattes. I got so much shit for my dreds when I first came back that I just shaved my head, which was kind of worse in a way, but now it was starting to grow back. I already stood out like a freak among all the whiteys here, just like I did when I was a kid. I am whatcha call mulatto. I'm actually a Louisiana Creole, kind of a high-yellow in skin tone terminology. Out here in the 'burbs they just call me "nigger." A tattoo artist sounded like a dream date.

I was making a little money writing for zines and magazines anyway, so I set it up with a local shit "alternative" paper to do an interview with him. I knew only too well how many times I had been interviewed by a "rock journalist" who just wanted to meet me to see if I would fuck them.

The tattoo artist's band, Shit Stain, had put out a new CD, *Fudge Tunnel of Love*. So they're a little poo-fixated: I'll take poo-poo/pee-pee over that purposely oblique Belle and Sebastian crap any day. Anyhow, when we talked on the phone, his voice was gravelly and he had a big ol' twang that really turned me on. He also seemed really sweet and we had a lot of music in common. I decided not to tell him that my band, Sucker, was among his favorites. I'd let that be a surprise.

Ann and I headed downtown. She drove. We were decked out in full punk regalia. Ann had shaved her head, and I'd bleached my hair this weird yellow gold. It was like the country girls gettin' to put on their fancy clothes for a night out in the big city. We kept ribbing each other in loud, exaggerated Southern accents.

"There better be some cute girls there," she threatened. "Cos I'm ready fer some serious, tongue twirlin', tittie twistin' ack-shone!!!!"

I joined in. "I'm so horny the crack o' dawn ain't even safe from me!" Ann hooted at that. "That was Tom Waits," I told her.

"Sheeyuut, if I don't get me some Texas poontang tonight I'm gonna open a can of whoop-ass on someone."

And so on, until we finally arrived. Ann went to get some dinner and just dropped me off at the backstage door.

The first thing I saw was his ass. He was down on his knees shoving a dirty pillow into the bass drum. I asked the bald, pierced guy at the door which one was Shannon, and he pointed to this skinny little dude covered in tattoos. Of course.

I used to only like men with bodies like twelve-year-old boys. Flat and muscular, sinewy and hairless. The skinnier the man-boy, the better. Men in their early twenties are sexier to me because they're just starting out and I can wow them pretty easily. Basically, I'm no better than Johnny Depp or Donald Trump. But I'm also kind of a teenage boy myself, stuck at about age eighteen. So I'm a homosexual male pedophile.

"Shannon?" I asked, approaching the stage. He turned to look at me and grinned. He jumped to his feet.

"You must be Marie," he said, extending his hand. His grip was firm. He had the words "I Love" and "Porn" tattooed across his knuckles. I don't think there was a patch of un-inked skin on him, at least not below his chin. Even his neck had lightning bolts and spider webs on it. His eyes were pale green, almost translucent, and big. He had on jeans that were beyond holey, with gray long underwear—you could see the ridges of it poking out of the holes in both knees. San Francisco Bike Messenger Vogue. I couldn't help but notice "Cami was here" scrawled in big black letters with an arrow pointing to his crotch. He had on an AC/DC belt buckle. I reached up and put my finger on it, pressing it into his belly. A bold move. He looked at me with a little bit of surprise, then smiled.

"What's with the AC/DC jewelry, hot stuff?"

He laughed his ass off at that, and hooked my arm through his elbow, leading me to a nearby table.

"Well, hello there. Shall we sit down and talk about it?"

Oh God. I wanted to jump him right then and there. His face was exquisite. High cheekbones, full rosy lips, pierced tongue—mmmmm, be still my throbbing clit!—and dyed bright, rust-red dreds down past his shoulders. Judging from his strawberry eyebrows and pale, lightly freckled skin, he was an enhanced natural redhead. He couldn't have been more than 22, I thought. Gooood. Shit. How lecherous could I get? I'm like a leader of a country or a CEO, a virgin-fucker. I'm a teenage head. I'm lost to the joy of bones.

I asked him questions about his art, his music, his comic book collection. His only vices in life, at this point, were amateur internet porn, cigarettes, and espresso. He had a thriving tattoo and postering business. He did all the musicians and strippers in town, and the punk rockers in recovery. (All of us, of course, addicted to pain, needles, and making a statement.) His band toured pretty much half the year, and had a couple of discs out on their own label. We knew a lot of people in common, both dead and alive. It was a fantastic relief for me in some ways to get to talk about my old life, which seemed like ancient history now. I was a scared, trembly alcoholic who couldn't drink. I had slipped. I'd lost my core self again, and being with Shannon sort of brought me back to life.

Plus there was something sexy to me about a guy who was willing to transform his whole self the way Shannon had. It showed commitment. Ain't no way this boy would ever be working for Exxon.

Ann came back to the club after her cheap taqueria dinner, just in time for the first band to start. I was happy to see her. I would have killed for a beer if she hadn't shown up with sparkly water. We sat through a pretty rockin' girl band called Clit City, whom I immediately hit up for an interview for the same local rag. Then a lame gaggle of sixteen-year-old boys with a lot of attitude, posture and bar chords came on and played for way too long. It was after midnight before Shit Stain went on. It was worth the wait.

You know how you fall in love with bands, like you fall in love with people? It had been a long time for me, not since the last time I saw the Flaming Lips, or Foreskin 500. Weeeell, much to my surprise/chagrin, I fell in love with Shit Stain. And I am not easy to please. Yup. I was mesmerized. Ann kept poking me in the ribs the whole time. Shannon sang "Gimme Danger" and shook his ass and jutted his hips out, kneeling on stage before me, where I stood in the front. The way he played his guitar reminded me of film footage I'd seen of Jimi Hendrix, where he fucks his Strat, hipbone rocking against the curve of it, then bowing before it on his hands and knees.

The crowd went wild for Shit Stain. There must have been 250 people there, many of them horny young girls in halter tops. All of them were clearly there to see Shannon, who oozed fuck-monster, clit-licker, heartbreaker. I had to restrain myself from diving onto as well as off the stage. Some asshole Rollins-neck guy elbowed me in the back and I instinctively cracked his ribs with my boot. It got ugly, but it stayed fun. I hadn't been to a decent punk show in years. It seemed like all the punk bands in San Francisco had either moved to LA to sign big label deals, or gone into rehab, never to be heard from again. The only thing left seemed to be art fuck bands, or kick-ass Oaktown hip hop, which was fine with me, but still I craved the punk. So for the first time since I moved back to my home town, I was happy that the people in Texas were still so unselfconscious that a sorta hardcore punk band would dare to play oh, a Cheap Trick song, and the audience would sincerely love it.

Afterwards, even though Shannon's performance had turned me on in a way I hadn't been since before I met my ex-husband, I'd had enough AA training to know that I needed to get home ASAP. Besides, three long-haired, navel ring Britneys in tube tops were hanging around him, making sure they were the last to leave the club, and I didn't want to cramp his style, so I went up and punched him in the arm.

"Hey, kick-ass show!" He turned and his face lit up when he saw me.

"Marie! You're still here! Thanks, man." He was dripping sweat. Chuck's Angels glared at me from behind their long locks. I smiled at them, giving them the chicks united vibe, which seemed to work. Ann bounded up beside me and grabbed Shannon in a bear hug, lifting him off the ground. He was a little guy. He laughed as she squeezed him.

"Oooh, I just wanna eat you up, Shannon Fry! Mmmm, mmm. You are some tasty chicken, baby!" The Angels were disturbed. Ann ignored them. "Hey, are you gonna do Marie's flames?"

Doh! Shannon looked at me curiously. I hadn't mentioned it to him yet. I was gonna save it for our first date. I was a little covered up for the night and had taken out my more visible piercings. I had a giant phoenix tattooed across my shoulders, and lots of neo-Peruvian style black patterns down the backs of my legs, plus various assorted other images hidden under my T-shirt and jeans. I don't think I had one tattoo that hadn't taken half a day to carve, but hey. As Kathy Acker once said, in being tattooed, she was written. For some reason I didn't feel like being out to him as an illustrated woman just yet. But Ann had sort of forced my hand, so I shrugged.

"Yeah, I was gonna ask you about doing some work on me. But I figured it could wait, see if you like all the nasty mean shit I say about your band in my article first." He laughed at that. The guy was open, easygoing for a local teen idol.

"Sure, I'd love to do some work on you. You wanna tell me what you had in mind?" The girlies got bored, real fast, and retreated to practice smoking cigarettes just a few feet away. Shannon wagged his finger at them. "Don't you ladies go too far, ya hear?" To which they giggled and I burned, suddenly hot. I told him we could talk about it later, that it was no big deal. Ann sighed heavily and stomped her feet. We agreed to hook up the following Friday. In the meantime, I was to email him some design ideas and he'd email me back some sketches. He told me we could work out a "special rate" or a trade, and gave me a quick goodbye peck on the cheek that set my clit on edge.

"His dick is pierced," Ann told me on the way home. I groaned.

"How do you know that?" I asked.

She smiled. "Everybody knows that."

I was a goner.

Okay so, the thing is, this thing for skinny, like I can feel the bones and take the hips between my fingers, laid out flat, and the taut belly drives me wild with desire, but only to have a tight taut belly of my own. See, I'm not what most normal people would call "fat," but I'm not a bone, either. I got titties. I got back. I have been dumped by more than one boyfriend for girls who had bodies like twelve-year-old boys. One time, I even had a guy tell me I was the perfect woman for him, in every way, except that my tits and my ass were too big. Can you imagine telling some man that you would be interested in him, except that he's losing his hair? That his dick is too narrow and pointy? What the fuck ever, man. So I ain't ashamed to admit, I like a big dick and a nice set of ribs. Iggy Pop. Beck.

Boy.

My impossibly soft and female form, so pleasing to the skinny, muscular boy-men, can then descend into its opposite. It's like I'm tightening a string. It is my dream body I am making love to, my body blended into skinny, long femurs, forearms, and shins. Slight jawbones and fine noses. Full lips and hot pine breath. And all the boy-men I've desired can become one sweet cream usa tiger bomb.

So Shannon liked my story. I had painted him as a new Johnny Thunders or something, and he was grateful. I could tell he didn't go out with a lot of girls who read books. We exchanged email and design ideas, and talked on the phone for two days before our date. There was lots of innuendo, but no official flirting. I wasn't sure if he understood what I meant by making an appointment to get tattooed at his house rather than at the shop: I want you to fuck me.

He had been sober for seven years. I was shocked to learn that he was thirty. He looked a lot younger than that. I wondered if the Britneys knew how old he was. Even so, my self-esteem was so shot because of my ex's peccadilloes that I couldn't believe a hot stud like Shannon would like me. Pathetic, I know. But I still couldn't tell if he were interested in that or not. He was just the sort of guy I had successfully avoided for years, those friendly, emotionally unavailable rocker boys I craved as much as any drug. I'd had more than my share. It looked bad on my resumé, I know. But he was also just what I needed, a total slut. Some maintenance.

Our date couldn't get here soon enough.

I went to pick him up, since his van was broken down at the moment, and I had to borrow my mom's car, a giant Cadillac with a "Bush for President" bumper sticker on it. I loved watching the looks on people's faces when I drove past them on the freeway, sticking out my tongue and flicking the little silver ball in it. A brown girl with short, gold hair and cat-eye glasses in a George Bushmobile. My old car, before I totaled it, had a bumper sticker on it that said "Heart Attacks: God's Revenge on Hunters and Meat Eaters." Boy, that would have gone over big here in anti-Oprah country.

I got to his place before dark, and thrilled to see that it was the total hell-hole I'd imagined. He didn't even bother with "excuse the mess." He still gave me the tour. In the entryway, a Sunday school cartoon painting of the good shepherd Jesus tending to his flock hung on the wall, with one lone black sheep in the herd, over which someone had drawn an arrow with the words "You are here" pointing to it. In the living room, on the beat up coffee table, sat the punk household's requisite top half of a mannequin, strewn with Mardi Gras beads and wearing a bad heavy metal wig and mirror sunglasses. The pea-green sofa sagged, and there were dirty dishes and empty beer bottles everywhere. The TV was huge, and there were Nintendo parts piled on the floor in front of it. In the kitchen, the roaches were so brave they didn't budge, even when we waved our hands over them. They just kept right on eating, straight off the half dozen or so plates of dried up mac and cheese, or what-ever that crusted brownish food substance was. There was every manner of band flyer stuck up all over the walls. I laughed at some of the band names: Slow Poke, Velvet Udder, Blue Ball, Dick Almighty, Hissyfits, Catbox.

His bedroom—now we're talkin'!—was large and cluttered. Ann's description was dead on. His sexy bed was a ratty, shiny *Battlestar Galactica* sleeping bag. There were half empty chip bags and plastic Mountain Dew liter bottles, electronics parts, disfigured Barbies, piles of overflowing ashtrays all over the place. There was a giant X-Men poster, and a Christina Aguilera poster with her pants unzipped and her nipples showing and the words "Fuck me in the ass, Shannon" coming out of a bubble someone had drawn from her open mouth. I laughed. I felt like I was back to normal again, after several months of Hotel Mom's ultra air-conditioned, plush-carpeted, marble-floored suburban oasis.

House tour over, I took him out for sushi. Both of us were vegetarian, so we ordered about four dozen cucumber rolls and gorged. We talked about movies for a while and discovered that we had the same freakish taste there, too. *Starship Troopers, Shakes the Clown.* . . I was relationship material and he knew it. But that wasn't what I wanted. I was too raw, and it had been too long since I'd been with anyone besides my ex. I was about to ricochet off the ceiling.

Over dinner I found out that he was a Pisces. I'm a Scorpio, so astrologically we were well matched. When I told him my sign he nearly pissed himself.

"My ex was a Scorpio," he blurted, turning red. Then it hung uncomfortably in the air: I was on the same cosmic footing as an ex-girlfriend. Plus everybody knows that we Scorpios are sex maniacs. In my case this was certainly true. And the best head I ever got in my life always came from Pisces lovers. (My ex-husband was a Gemini.) So I was glad to hear it. But we still had to change the subject fast, to cover up his uncool admission. "So tell me more about this tattoo you want," he said casually.

I had asked him to do some stylized hot-rod flames up and down my spine, starting at my sacrum and blending into the phoenix at my shoulder blades. I told him I needed something to signify the death of my marriage and my rebirth as a single hot chick. I always got tattooed whenever I quit drinking. (I have quite a few. *Ahem.*) He was excited about it, started sketching more stuff out on the paper placemat in the restaurant. I understood that it was going to take a long time to do it.

"We can start on some of it tonight, if you'd like," he said, grinning. Yes. Finally. There is a God.

On the way home, we engaged in a little foreplay: I confessed to him that I hadn't had sex with anyone but my ex in about five years. He was really cool about it. He told me he got tested for AIDS and everything else every six months. In fact, he'd just gotten some results back day before yesterday, and everything was fine. We were both born-again virgins. We changed the subject quickly, back to Pokémon.

We pulled up in front of his place and got out. His housemates were sitting on the front porch, chain-smoking cigarettes. All of them sober, of course.

"What's up," we nodded to one another. One of them, Pablo, his drummer, in fact, was really cute. He was dark, like me, and kinda beefy. Our eyes met and he smiled. Mmm, mmm. Very different from Shannon. Had a yin-yang necklace on. Maybe he was a secret new age hippie punk like me. Down, girl. Satisfy your Thing Fer Skinny first. Tonight. My cunt was throbbing in anticipation. I wanted me some iron cock. We went into his room and shut the door. Yesssss.

"So," he said, crouching in the middle of the room. "You want to get started on those flames or what?" Aaah, he was going through with the tattoo facade, after all. OK. The whole drive over to his house I'd pictured how it would be, and so far it was pretty much what I thought. We were high on Americanos we'd got after dinner, so it was gonna be a while before anyone got some sleep.

He was wearing these skin tight, hot pink vinyl pants and a threadbare Farrah Fawcett baby-T. I lusted after his outfit as much as I did his body. God. His ass was delicious in those pants, like two rose petals cupped against the back of his thighs. His legs were rail-thin and he had on glittery green Doc Marten platforms. The slight muscles in his arms and back were well defined in the T-shirt, and I could see his pierced nipples, too. I almost came just looking at his chest. I knelt down beside him.

"Sure, let's get started," I said. He turned away while I pulled my shirt off over my head and sat down in his leatherette tattooing chair. I wasn't wearing a bra. It was one of those chair massage things you see in health food stores, or even at the chiropractor. You put yourself face down on it, and there's a big round hole for you to fit through, so you can breathe. My nipples had been erect for so long I thought they were gonna bleed. I had on tight black stretch cotton bondage pants, in case he needed some ideas. I pressed my tits into the chair, and spoke from the side of my mouth.

"Okay," I said. He turned around and I could practically sketch the erection I knew he had without even looking. He whistled.

"Nice phoenix!"

"Ahh, you say that to all the girls."

He laughed, told me he was going to start at the bottom, near my booty. Yessss. He'd drawn the outline for the design on thin paper, and began tracing from that, in ink, onto my skin. His fingertips on my hips, as he drew, were too much. From the corner of my eye I could see his thighs near mine, the pink vinyl hugging them lewdly. I could see the bulge in the crotch. I knew my naked skin would get to him. It always works.

I could barely swallow. My mouth felt like Death Valley all of a sudden. I was dying. He was breathing a little heavier than normal, or so I imagined. I caught wisps of it along the fine hair on the backs of my arms, neck and spine. Jesus, my cunt was wet. I thought for a minute I might slip off the chair. Fuck, what if I did that while he was actually tattooing me? It'd be like trying to draw with an Etch-A-Sketch. There'd be a long straight line of ink across my butt cheek. I broke into a sweat, and the fake leather tattoo chair became a dangerous slip and slide. Great. Nothing sexier than sweaty boobs, right? Right. I shifted in my seat.

"Are you uncomfortable? " he asked. What a Southern gentleman.

"I'm fine," I snuffled, my face pressing into the leatherette. He got out a mirror and turned his head (and his stiffy, baby!) away so I could sit up and observe his designs in it. They were really cool, nice even lines of curlicue over my sacrum and hips, and the beginnings of Tibetan-looking flames right at the base of the spine. He was drawing them on me in ink before he put them under my skin permanently.

"Perfect," I said. Now do it.

I always thrill to the buzz of the needle, and that first rush when it burrows its angry white hot ant bites under my skin. Then at some point, maybe seconds into the tattoo, It realize that it hurts like a motherfucker but also that it's not done yet, and this pain I am enduring is something I will have to endure for a long time yet. I'll have no choice but to surrender to it. And it's always like a religious ritual for me then, forcing me to inhabit my own breath. The eyes go inward, the lungs expand, the pain becomes part of me. And I let it go.

My puss was throbbing, throbbing. . . I was straddling the chair and wanted to start humping it right then and there. Then, slowly, way beyond my control, my hips did start to slither.

"Don't move," Shannon whispered, all spittley. Was he drooling? Now that was excitement. I know I have a nice back. Good butt, lots of muscle. Getting a tat on my spine was an excruciating test, but I wanted it. And if I got laid in the process, well, hallelujah for me.

He was blotting the blood as he went. It fucking hurt. Bad. There are a lot of nerve endings near the vertebrae, and they were very pissed off at me now. The pheromones were starting to kick in and I felt that inner peace, along with the life force within me, uncoil. Ahhhh, ecstasy.

Deepen the breath. Surrender. Surrender. Shit, Cheap Trick's "Surrender" started going through my head. *Mommy's all right, Daddy's all right, they just seem a little weird. . .* He worked in silence. I squeezed back tears.

Shannon. I love you, bro. Now fuck me.

Almost on cue, he began to stroke my ribs. Orgasm #1. Finally, his deliberate, sexual touch. I was going crazy. We didn't talk. No way. He pulled up closer. I could really feel his breath on me now. Rose-scented. I'm serious. I started back with my slow, almost imperceptible grind. He kept going. Drill, fill, blot. Ouch. And then the next thing, the freak erotic event that started it all really: He bent down and lapped at the blood on my lower back. My nipples nearly shot sparks. God! What was he doing? I barely knew this guy! And here he was, licking up my blood. But I wanted him licking my blood, my cum, my armpits. . .

He turned off the gun and placed his hands on my hips and pushed the bondage pants down, way below my ass. He groaned just looking at it. His tongue traveled all the way down my ass crack and back. I was writhing now, and he was pushing me deeper into the chair.

"Don't move," he said, and got up to get something from across the room. It clanked, whatever it was. Then "clickclick" and he'd cuffed me to the chair, face down. Hands and feet. The guy had just sucked up my blood, sort of the ultimate act of trust, so I had no choice but to oblige. He pushed the chair down until I was totally horizontal, butt in the air.

"Nice ass," he said. No shit. My pussy was a geyser, just waiting for him to slide his fingers, his cock, his Yoda doll, whatever, in it. I get to this point where I just got to have it. He reached under and around me, cupping my boobs in his hands, rolling the nipples between his fingers, and he brought his mouth down close to my ear.

"Nice tits, too." he whispered. A whine escaped me. A silk scarf came out of nowhere, and he slid it over my mouth, gagging me, tying it around the back of my head. "I want you to let me know if I'm doing something, anything, that you don't like, you hear me, Scorpio?" I nodded enthusiastically in response. "Good," he said, slapping my ass. Orgasm #2.

I heard the rip of the zipper as he undid himself and took his cock out. I wanted to pound my fists into the chair, kick my feet, thrash about. But I couldn't. He ran the head of his penis along the side of my body, my hips, my thighs, moaning, leaving a trail of pre-cum. I could feel the barbell just under the head of the dick, cold on my skin and smooth. He pressed his cock against my ass crack and I could feel it jerk around on its own. I took a deep breath. My pussy was rippling under his gaze and with his hot rod so near. He took off the scarf. I was fucking panting.

Shannon took the cuffs off and turned me over. I drank in his long, lithe body, and just thinking those words made me think of a magazine article about a tennis player or a super-model, but fuck if they weren't true. He had an entire rose vine, complete with thorns, that twined all the way from his back, at the base of his spine, around to his collarbone. Sexy. He also had some seriously stupid tattoos: pot leaves, Betty Page, dinosaurs, and one or two band logos. I was looking for the anarchy symbol, but it wasn't there.

He held his pierced cock in his hand for me to see. I couldn't wait to feel the metal scrape the inside walls and lips of my cunt. He mounted me, just like that. I brought my knees to my chest and he pushed against them with his palms, his slim cock thrusting in and out of my elongated pussy. I gripped him with my pelvic floor and he slowed down.

"Mmm, I can feel that," he whispered. He kept at arm's length distance, his eyes glittering, staring into my face, and he just kept pumping into me.

The door to Shannon's room opened. It was Pablo, the drummer. I panicked for a moment, then smiled. Big. Shannon had me spread eagle on the chair, licking my cunt. He didn't miss a beat as Pablo came over and, without a word, grabbed my arms and stretched them back over my head. I hooked them around his back as he bent to suckle my breasts. I came in Shannon's mouth as Pablo tongued my nipples, staccato. He went nuts on my tits, slurping and nursing and squeezing them together.

"God, I saw these and I couldn't wait to eat them," he breathed. They propped me up. I was happily overcome. Shannon slid his cock back inside me while Pablo held me up from behind. Then I eased Shannon onto his back, not letting his cock slide out of me, and I pinned him down. I outweighed him easily by twenty pounds.

Pablo pushed his wet fingertips into my asshole, which opened greedily, sucking them in up to the knuckle. While I fucked Shannon, Pablo applied even pressure on all sides inside my ass canal, taking me higher. Boom shaka laka. I spread my legs apart, opening my ass to him even further, loving that he was peering into me, and watching Shannon's cock chug-a-lug inside my creamy cunt. I felt a whoosh of warm air, then heard the telltale sign of a man's pants coming off and hitting the floor. My cunt squeezed harder on Shannon's cock, and he moaned. I was all vagina at that moment. And when Pablo put his dick at the entrance to my ass, I nearly wept.

Shannon slowed down. Pablo rubbed several dollops of thick lube into my asshole, hoisted himself over the table and over my butt cheeks, and slid his glorious cock in. For a second I thought I was going to tear open, then we hit that space where it was just me and the rest of the universe.

I felt like a porn star, Debbie Does Double Penetration. Wow. Wait til the kids at home hear about this. But it was more than that. I could feel Pablo's cock rubbing against Shannon's cock inside me, and my whole being was focused on that one place in my body. One false move and somebody gets hurt. They were fucking my vaginal wall from both sides.

I looked down into Shannon's beautiful face. The boys were moving at a tantric pace, and I cracked myself up, thinking that they played music together and obviously knew each other's rhythms well. They were gasping in their excitement. Mmm. A Shit Stain sandwich. Then I saw that they were staring at each other. This was a nice twist. I kindly extracted myself, and wordlessly pointed Pablo toward Shannon, who was nodding his head vigorously. He wanted it. And baby, I wanted to watch it. My cunt was so swollen I couldn't help myself. I sat back and pressed my fingers into my clit, deep and fast, to watch my two fetish boys get each other off. Where was the pseudo-disco soundtrack for this hot boy-on-boy action? This was gonna be good.

Pablo shoved Shannon flat on his back, onto the floor, and went for the nipple rings with his teeth. Shannon threw his head back in ecstasy, his dreds flung back behind him and touching the edges of a bunch of comic books and a banana peel. I loved how Pablo's dark skin contrasted sharply with Shannon's luminous, test tube body.

Pablo's ass cheeks should have been placed on display at the Museum of Contemporary Art. Damn, they were fleshy and firm. I got up and went to place my hands on either side of them and he responded by flexing them and grinding his hips at my touch. Pablo had no tattoos on his body, another contrast to Shannon. I stroked his balls from behind, and squirted more goopy lube onto his dick, and into Shannon's asshole. He yelled out in pleasure, then raised those fine ass cheeks, pushing up on those he-man biceps, lifting his cock all the way til it was poised just over Shannon, then he plunged it in, and Shannon took it just past the cock head.

"Ahhh," he cried out, in some unfathomable pain. Pablo backed up, and plunged deeper. Shannon cried out again, and Pablo lowered himself into him, opening him slowly. I watched the cock slip its way into the hole, and Shannon was quivering. I knew how he felt. Pablo's dick was the size of a small building.

It was like watching a man and a woman make love . . . .only better. I massaged and licked Pablo's entire backside for an hour while he lowered deeper and deeper into Shannon. I positioned myself over Shannon's mouth, face to face with Pablo, who sucked my titties some more, his cock working its way into Shannon, who writhed bit by bit, taking it in, and ate my pussy. We rolled around on the floor all night, oblivious to the porn mags and the guitar picks and the bread crumbs that stuck to us. We covered every inch of all three of our bodies with each other's mouths until the sun streamed in through the dirty blinds. The inch or so of skin that Shannon had managed to tattoo on my back was scabbed over. My blood was smeared all over us, along with pussy juice, cum, and spit. All the forbidden fluids. We collapsed, exhausted, my tongue roaming into Shannon's mouth, over Pablo's magnificent ass, into his armpits, looping through nipple rings, licking barbell and red ink and etched skin and rust-tasting hairline. I was worshipped, I had bled, I had released a thousand bats and doves inside me. I was right where I wanted to be.

Welcome back.

tatiana de la tierra

Dancing with Daisy

I ruined a potential lesbian. I didn't mean to, but I was horny. Her name was Daisy, or so she said. Could have been Concepción, Amy, Elodia, or one of many Marias. I'll never know. This woman, she had been calling me for months. Said she got my number from the bulletin board at the gay bookstore down the street, from a note I'd posted way back: "Lesbian in search of a man or butch to dance salsa with so that I can impress my macha Cuban lover." My girlfriend had already dumped me by the time Daisy called, and Daisy wanted to do more than dance.

She wanted to get down, though she never put it quite that way. She'd call me up, speaking in Spanish, sounding timid. She'd say, "I've never known a lesbian. I was wondering, maybe you can tell me what it's like to be with a woman?" At first I tried to brush her off. It's not like I'm a lesbian hotline or anything. But curiosity got me, and my education in psychology made it sort of like a research project, or an interesting side conversation. And she didn't speak any English and no way was she gonna go to the local tiendita to get the dish on the joys of lesbianism. So I felt a twinge of social responsibility. And hey, why not say it, it was a potentially pleasurable situation. Why say no until at least you've checked it out?

So I told her generic stuff like, "Desire is desire. It doesn't matter who you're with, or what's driving pleasure. It's about giving yourself over." That's not what she wanted to hear. Daisy was forty-two years old, divorced, with three children, touched by men only. She remembered being enamored of a classmate in the all-girl Catholic boarding school she attended in Managua. How she would volunteer to brush and braid the girl's hair, just so she could touch her. How the girl gave her candies and pretty stones every Friday. Then, how the girl had been smitten over a boy during the summer, and how her relationship with Daisy was never the same again. Daisy remembered being obsessed with the nuns, wondering what could be going on between their legs. Surely they menstruated. Did they also tingle like she did? She imagined the stiff frocks brushing their bare thighs, their soft breasts. The sisters belted out orders with stern faces, and she found this exciting. She liked being told what to do.

Which turned me on. I never had a nun up close myself, but my lover—I mean, my ex-lover—that fucking bitch, she was beyond stern. She was the Mother Superior Dominatrix, and I was her sexual slave. Fucker dumped me for a woman ten years younger. Left me, still in love and all hot and wanting more. She had a way of becoming the proprietor of my pussy and every part of me. She'd say "I'm gonna rip you up tonight," and I'd about faint from the pleasure of terror. Pinch my ass, suck my nipples raw, slap my face. Whisper, "Puta . . . cabrona . . . maricona." Eat my lipstick, sniff my cunt. Oh my god, she teased me to the edge of insanity before she'd fuck me. "I'm going to rip you up . . ." She could kill me for all I cared, as long as she was fucking me like that. That's when I would lose my will, become clothes in the final spin cycle, a screaming maniac on a roller coaster, the most urgent pussy in the world. Motherfucker had to get herself another fucking whore.

I wondered if I could get a whore, too. Aren't whores equal opportunity? Could I be a femme with a woman as a sex object? That's where Daisy came in. I could tell she wasn't my type. I envisioned her wearing a gold cross around the neck, cooking white rice, yelling at the kids, watching telenovelas at night, going to church on Sunday, going to bed without any revelations. She had only been in the US for five years, and me, I was born elsewhere but I grew up here. I'm a modern Latina and Daisy was, well, let's just say she was a tacky one. I knew she wasn't meant for me, but I wasn't getting any action, and I had a hot hot cunt, the kind that contributed to global warming.

True, I could have tried to get fucked some other way. But lesbians, most of them, they are just not man enough when it comes to cunts. They have to be in love, they have to know your sign, your whole goddamn therapeutic history, they have to be an ex-lover of one of your ex-lovers, they have to agree with your politics, see themselves reflected in you, they gotta know if your god is male or female, how you light your candles, your medical history, your dietary habits since age seven, the relationship with your mother, how you deal with men, if at all, your first sexual encounter and every one thereafter, your butch/femme or anything-goes identity, and most importantly, details about your past lives, all of them. Give me a motherfucking break! All that, just to get your cunt stroked?

But Daisy wasn't a dyke, so she didn't know any of this. She called every week, asking questions. *Why are you a lesbian?* Cuz women turn me on physically, and because, emotionally, being with women is the only place I feel at home. *Is it true that some are like men and some are like women?* Well, for some of us that's true, but others are androgynous, they look the same and do the same things to each other. Me, I'm a femme, and I have been one ever since I found out I could be a girl and a lesbian at the same time. *How do I know what I am?* Hmm. You're probably a femme, though if you've never been with a woman, how can you be sure? But it's an evolving identity, you don't have to instantly know. *How can you have sex without a penis?* That's easy! With a woman you can fuck nonstop, as hard or as gentle as you want. You can fuck with hands, fingers, rocks, vegetables, Barbies, tongues. And dildos, of course, strapped on or hand-held. Dildos could be made of curved purple silicone, stiff clear acrylic, chunky black leather, translucent pink gel. You can get them in any size you want, and any shape you can imagine, from cosmic swirls to dolphins to penises with simulated bulging veins.

When she ran out of questions, she wanted to meet me. To touch, to have sex, to know a woman in the flesh. "No," I said. I mean, what could I possibly do with another femme?

But like a good femme, she persisted. Daisy was sounding better every day. She was available, she wanted to experiment, and she didn't know any better. And then I started getting ideas. Why did I think that I always had to be on the bottom? Couldn't I expand my sexual horizon? Didn't I have enough experience being in her position to play the opposing role? What would it be like to have a woman under me, to be a bird's beak on her skin, to turn her with the palm of my hand, to whisper crude things in her ear, to inhale her perfume, to tongue the nubs on her nipples, to coax her cunt, to make her please me on command? All right Daisy, finally, you got me. Let's meet.

We drank strawberry daiquiris at an outside café while we checked each other out. There she was, Ms. Middle-Aged Tacky Latina, circa 1975, in the flesh, heavily made up and meticulously dressed. She had just gotten off work in the downtown business sector, where she was a receptionist at a South American firm. Daisy looked at me timidly with cork-brown eyes. Tapped her long acrylic nails nervously on the tabletop. Displayed her cleavage with a partially unbuttoned white blouse that she wore under a navy blue blazer. Showed her wide hips under a matching knee-length skirt, corpulent thighs beneath the flesh-toned panty hose.

Daisy was someone I'd probably seen at the grocery store earlier that day and then forgotten. I had nothing to say to her. And she, she didn't even have any questions for me. We just sat there, watching couples stroll by, avoiding each other's eyes. This woman, this voice at the other end of the phone, this lesbian novice that I knew as Daisy, well, there was not much to her. It was like she'd hung up the phone on me. Hello? Hello? Is anybody there? She was perfect for my Mother Superior Dominatrix ex-lover, who preferred me stiff as a corpse when she was about to come.

"I don't think this is going to work," I told her. Then I paid the bill and took her home with me.

Poured Blue Nun into lead-crystal goblets. She stood at the window, looking out at the water from my ninth-floor apartment. Said something, I don't know what, as I had other things on my mind, like, now what? I mean, there I had some potential pussy in my apartment, and I didn't know what to do! Think, think, think. I put on a CD, Luis Miguel, "Somos novios." Oh no, too romantic. But it's too late. As the syrupy ballad begins, I walk over to Daisy. "Would you like to dance?" She rises shyly, looks me in the eye for the first time.

And then I remember that I can't fucking dance. Okay, I had some private lessons, learned to salsa and merengue up a storm, learned to close my eyes during the baladas and boleros and flow with my lover's rhythm. But lead? Never! So I pretend. Extend my hand, palm up. She takes it. Quickly recall the arm positions of being led, and do the opposite, I hope. Right hand cupped just below her waist, left forearm up, as if waving to floats on a parade. She's trained in this, gets right into place.

And then, I don't move, and neither does she. Of course, we both know, I'm the one who's supposed to make the first move. But there she is, right in my face, and I don't even know her, or for that matter, care to, and I know that this is one big mistake but it's happening and I have to go for it. So I close my eyes, it's the only way, and start swaying side to side.

She's not thrilled, I can tell, she's totally stiff. Then I pull her close until our torsos are touching and we move more naturally together. Our bodies relax, finally, and we are tit to tit. I run my hand up and down her back, press my pelvis into her and think, Yes, I can do this! I am about to get some pussy.

The song ends. She sits down and I go into the kitchen to pour more wine. Okay, now what? I splash liquor on the floor, don't even bother to clean it. Instead, I take a swig of aguardiente from the bottle that I stash under the sink. I place my palms on the counter and let my head hang. I don't know how to make a move on a woman. Fling her down or just make conversation until she begs to be flung to the floor? I take another swig, inhale deeply, do a few arm flexing and releasing exercises. I have to do this. There's no going back. I return to the living room. We toast this time. "To discoveries," I say. "Would you like to go into the bedroom?" She rises, like my question was a command. It seems like she'll do anything I say, and I like this.

"Sit,"I tell her, and she does, at the edge of my king size bed and, once again, she looks out an open window. Luis Miguel is still playing in the other room, the wine glasses are still full, and I still don't know what to do. I fling my glass out the window, straddle her full body between my legs. She gasps, eyes open wide. Maybe thinks I'm a psycho, that I'll be howling at the moon in no time. Regrets ever having called me. "You want to know what it's like to be with a woman? Feel this." Pull up my blouse, let my favorite breast out, tease her L'Oreal lips with my nipple. "Lick it," I order. She hesitates and then, ever so slowly, begins to use her tongue. I feel her breath on my breast, start to feel that cunt fire within.

She's propped herself up with both hands on the bed. I nudge them out from under her, til she's lying on her back. So here we are, me with my tit hanging out and she with her legs spread. And I'm on top? I've never been on top! I flash back to my exploits with butches who know how to handle a woman. They say things like, "Mami, did you get those tits made especially for me?" And I don't know, but I just can't say such smarmy things. Okay, so forget words, just do touch.

My cuticles snag on her pantyhose. How in the world I'm actually going to get into her underwear, I have no idea. And no way will I get on top and hump and grind on her. But I gotta do something. The sooner I begin, the sooner it will end. So I begin touching, smelling, exploring. Polyester, talcum, deodorant, cheap perfume, hair spray, smudged eyeliner, blotchy face powder, shiny lips. It's all so damn gross. You think I'm gonna taste those waxy chemicals on her mouth? I don't think so. How do butches eat lipstick? Her body is soft like mine, but foreign. She has curves, her nipples are hardening, her pussy's warming up. I'm disgusted, and at the same time, I'm getting wet.

Her breath quickens and I visit the thighs again, snake my hand up her skirt, follow the pantyhose to the waist, dig and pull at the elastic, where I encounter a girdle. The type that I thought didn't even exist any more. By now, my right forearm is twisted and suctioned over her womb. Not a romantic moment. It's excruciating, but somehow, I manage to get my fingers on her mound, where it's wet and hairy. It's time to fuck her, I guess. I'm pulling my shoulder out of its socket, chafing my arm on that Playtex rubber, trying to get the right angle. Put my thumb on her clit while keeping my fingers inside, read her body for signs. She moves with me at first and then, who the hell knows why, she stops moving, so I stop fucking, untwist my arm from that mass of elastic, stick my tit back in place.

That's when I see what's become of Daisy. The puffy hairdo is flat, the watery breasts are spilled out, the mauve lipstick is smeared, the forehead glistens with tiny beads of sweat, the flesh-toned mask is beginning to crack. She pats her skirt down, draws her legs together, sits up, squishes all of the breast matter back in, buttons her blouse, puts on the one pump that fell off. Luis Miguel has stopped singing. There are no more words, no more pussy, no more femmes to be had, nothing to do. I drop her off downtown, on the same corner where I had picked her up. We don't even say good-bye. I can't drive away fast enough.

When I got home I fucked my own damn self. Which is what I wish I'd done in the first place.

28 de marzo de 1998, el paso, tejas
revised 28 de julio de 1998, lutsen, minnesota

Celestial Bodies

We arrange to meet at my place, with this condition: I must be on my knees when she walks through the door. She will be taking a taxi from the airport; she has the keys to my house. It's a long flight, from Madrid to New York, and she might be a little tired and agitated. It is my job to relax her, to bring her into her body, to properly welcome her back to the US.

She will be wearing her dick.

I have been waiting for her forever. She always makes me wait and wait. When she is gone I think that I will forget about her, that I will not want or need her, that she doesn't deserve me. But when she phones me from a hotel in London and says, "Hey little girl, how are you?" I forget about all that. "Missing your dick," I respond.

I stay home all day and prepare for her arrival. Clean house, cook, wash my body with sandalwood soap, paint my nails wild berry cream, dust my skin with lavender body powder, burn sage. Put on a skirt and paint my lips pink. I place the pillow on the floor near the entrance to my house. Light a red candle for Changó. Put on some Mexican music and float in the room. Wait and wait for her. Keep an eye on the street, listen for car doors slamming shut, for sounds at my front door.

I start to get anxious. What if the plane is late? What if she doesn't come? What if she doesn't want me? If my need for her dick is too big for the both of us?

I sit on the pillow, on my knees. Close my eyes and wait.

The chill of the night blasts my body when she walks through the door. She is wearing blue jeans, boots, a black leather jacket. Sets her bags down, stands with her legs spread before me, says nothing. I am looking up at her, feeling ever so desperate. She seems distant, like she is still in another country. I can't quite read her. Her looking at me, the silence, it is driving me insane. I want to scream and pounce on her for making me wait. But I remain quiet, expectant. She takes a step until she is right above me. Says, "Come here, little girl." Pushes my face into her cock. "This boy needs some attention."

I close my eyes and brush my face on her stiff dick, feeling hardness beneath the fabric of her pants. I am overcome with emotion and desire. I nudge her dick with my cheeks, brush my nose up her shaft, cherish the moment before she will entrust her most delicate and powerful part to my mouth.

She loosens the button at the waist, pulls down the zipper, and hands me her tool, as if it were an offering and an obligation. I take her cock, solid and heavy, in one hand, stroke it gently with the other, kiss the tip. Make acquaintance, once again, with the pinga that is the source of so much pleasure, its desert-brown shade and bulging veins. If ever I have any doubt about this boy's desire for me, I will find a certain answer in her dick. Always, it wants my mouth, needs a little girl like me who will jerk it and stroke it and lick it and be there for the boy's ejaculation.

I let my tongue travel down the shaft, roll her balls in my mouth. Begin to notice her breaths, am startled by the grip that she has on my hair, pulling, almost ripping the follicles from my scalp. "That was a long flight," she says. "All this pent-up tension." Open my mouth wide and take it, width-wise, between my lips, tapping my teeth lightly while I suck, careful not to hurt her. "Where did you learn to love dick like this, little girl, huh? Who taught you how to please a man?" I continue to service her. I am a servant for her cock. It is my ruler, it tells me what it wants, obligates me to please. I am an obedient blow-job girl.

The boy's voice falls, becomes breathier. "You're doing good, girl, so good. . . " Her grip on my scalp is so painful now. She becomes infused with new energy, with her animal self.

She is the warrior about to plunge a spear through the enemy's heart, the lion that decapitates its prey with one hungry bite, the cock that must be pounded into a little girl's mouth. She rams her pinga into my face, could care less that it hurts, that I can't breathe, that I am gagging. This is what the blow-job girl is here for, we both know this. She comes with a yell, pulls out, smears her load on my lips and chin, fucks my mouth with her fingers, as if coming wasn't enough.

I remain on my knees, wrap my arms around her legs, stay there, her cock dangling at the front of my neck, so vulnerable. I think that this is how I should always be, between her legs, her dick being the center of my universe.

"Come here, little girl," she says. Pulls me up from the floor, kisses my lips, sets me down on the couch. She feeds me marzipan, gives me presents that she has brought from overseas—a black shawl with embroidered red roses, a card with a poised Flamenco dancer, a pair of castanets, and a book, *Beatriz y los cuerpos celestes*. I put my thumbs through the string of each of the castanets, and toy around with them, try to make sounds from my hands.

She begins to love me like a boy, taking control, making me more of a girl with every touch.

I don't know if she knows this or not, but there is a part of me that gets smaller and smaller when I am with her. She has a way of being so sweet, melting me, and then so rough, destroying me. Sweet and sour, delicate and spicy, kind and cruel, these are the keys that she holds, that she uses to enter and break me. I become so small with her, a girl who is barely a woman, one who is thirteen and then eleven and then eight and then five and then three. A girl who is so little that she is always new, always untouched. A girl without language, uneducated and unsocialized, a little animal girl, a hungry hungry girl, so needy and natural with desire. A baby girl, with a little baby panocha and pink pezones. A desperate and dirty girl, one who needs to be teased and punished for being what she is.

The boy sits on the couch and has me straddle her. She drapes the shawl around my shoulders. I am playing with the castanets, trying to make a rhythm with my fingers, pa-pa-ta-ta-ta. My tap-taps are clunky, and I keep trying to make music while the boy caresses my forehead, cups my cheeks, kisses my eyelids. I come up with a little riff, da-da-ta-ta-ta-pa-pa-ta-da-da, and start to hum. This is when she slaps me, making my skin resonate, tingle and burn. Her cock is rubbing my panocha while she licks my nipples as if they were honeyed. Sucks them as if she was giving me head. I am tapping frantically with my fingers. My brain goes on a wild ride. I wish her pinga was inside of me, I wish to be a fuck machine. But that is the boy's prerogative—to decide when to ram a little girl's panocha. The boy suddenly clamps my nipples between his teeth, attempting to sever them from my breasts. I scream, not only for the pain of that moment, but for the pain that is to follow.

Little girls always have to be punished first. They have to be broken down and bloodied before they are loved. I know this.

He pushes me off of him, leads me into the bedroom. Undresses me. I get so scared, completely naked before a boy. The fact that I am a grown woman is impossible to hide then. I am ashamed of being so big and so vulnerable. I wish for complete darkness, I wish I could disappear, I wish I was not conscious of my flesh. I don't want her to see the shame on my face. He looks at me, and I know that he knows, and I know that this excites him, to be fully clothed and in control and to have a girl-woman to do as he pleases with. I look away, focus on the flame of Changó's candle, await my instructions.

"On your stomach," he says. I know what he is going to do and I want to cry. I need this so much. All my life, this is what I have needed. She dangles fat strands of seasoned leather on my back, teases my nerves. Whips me once or twice, twenty or fifty times, I don't count. Black leather becomes a switchblade to my back. It aims to lacerate me, to put me in my place—my place on the bottom. Under any other circumstance, I would probably wrestle for my survival. But black leather is here because I invite it to try, oh just try, to break me.

Black leather always wins, of course. And the boy always stops, after I've screamed, after there's visible damage. During the moments in between pain she trails her fingers on the hot fresh welts. "So red and tender," she says. Her voice is always soft, her words so careful. Somehow, I feel like I am being loved, and that is always when I cry; it is the gentleness that hurts.

The first time I cried with her, she said, "What's wrong, girl? Where are you going inside?" I can never respond intellectually to my pain. All I can do is feel it, yearn for it.

If ever she asks me what I need, I say, "I want you to hurt me." I don't need to be pierced or stabbed or burned, though. All I need is enough to let me go beneath the surface of my skin. This is where I am most me, where I hurt and love, where my power lies. Where I am a little girl, one that gets smaller and smaller and needier and needier. It is the place of everything unnamed, an encyclopedia of dreams, my true self, that which I must hide if I am to live. Going there always makes me cry, makes me break down. Tears are my key to my self.

Sometimes I fear that I will pass out inside of myself, that I will never come back to the moment, to my body, to the room, to her. That I will get lost in my subconscious. That is why I need her and her kind. She opens a path for me, one that leads inside and brings me back. One that takes me to the bottom.

"You're such a good bottom," she says. "Look at you, all wet and sweet." I am in her arms now, my back is throbbing, alive with pain. I am a girl-woman in tears who is about to get fucked.

"Turn over so I can fuck you like a dog," she says. As if I weren't exposed enough already. He knows what he is doing to me, obliterating my self-respect as I get on my knees and spread my ass for him. I hear him remove his boots and pants, hear him tear open the condom's wrapper, snap a latex glove on one hand, squeeze the bottle of lube. He is watching my ass all the while. The latex hand goes right for my asshole, fucks me without any further preparation. "Such a tight asshole," he says. "Gonna have to stretch it out some." He fingerfucks my ass, brings blood and sensation to this forgotten part of me. Makes me wonder if I have a brain deep inside my ass. Me da cerebro. Expands my asshole, has me pounding my fists into the bed. Then he pulls me up by the hair, keeps a finger in my ass, sits me down on his cock, and finally, finally, finally motherfucking fucks me.

How long have I been waiting for this boy to ram his cock into me? How long has my papaya been on fire? How long was my panocha sweet and unfucked? How long have I longed for this boy's big, bulging, brown dick? I become a madwoman, a crazy fucking whore, a cheap fucking whore, a shameless fucking whore, a violent fucking whore. Fuck-me-or-I'll-kill-you, fuck-me-or-I'll-kill-you, fuck-me-or-I'll-kill-you.

I push him down on his back, slap his fucking face. Why did you make me wait so long, cabrón? I take a long fucking ride on his dick. Make him suck my tits just right. Punch him in the fucking chest, bite his nipples until I can taste the blood. Fuck me, asshole, I order, I don't care if I am fucking hurting you. Fuck me, hijueputa, fuck me, comemierda, fuck me, cabrón, fuck me, you fucking dickhead. Fuck-me-or-I'll-kill-you.

He complies because I have my hands around his neck. If he lets up I'll fucking strangle him. Let's see how much power you got now, boy. You think it's up to you to decide when and how to fucking please me? When and how to fucking please yourself? You think you're the only rapist in the house? That you can get away with catching my emotions in your hands, putting them in your mouth, and never letting me see them again? Eso es lo que crees? I slap the fuck out of his face, make sure he keeps fucking me all the while, ride him hard enough to dismember any man.

I used to be terrified of being on top. Now, I think that I am a terror on top, a social menace. I want to violate this fucking little boy. I think he needs to be put in his place. You think a dick gives you all the power? No matter what I do, I say, you have to keep fucking me. This is my command. I wrestle around on top of him, turn, touch the leather straps that keep his dick in place, spread his cunt open. Don't do that, please, he says. The boy has a terrified little voice. Who asked you what you wanted? This is to please me, not you. I push the strap aside, plunge him with four fingers. He has a wet pussy, ripe for fucking. Keep fucking me, asshole, I say, while I pound his cunt, pumping his liquid, raping the little fucker. I'm not certain that he's enjoying this, but I don't even care. In fact, I hope he hates it, I hope he feels exposed, I hope he feels like a girl, I hope he feels powerless, I hope this takes him to his pain.

I take my hand out of his cunt and force it into his mouth. Make him eat his girl cream. He is crying, little boy tears, and I kiss him so soft. It's okay, little boy, I say. It's not your fault. I had to rape you. I couldn't help it. I've always wanted to rape you. You are just so powerful with your cock, little boy, you make a fuckhole out of me. You open me up and make me river and thunderstorm and volcano. You make me so little and scared. I had to punish you for that. You make me cry and you hurt me, and then you don't hurt me enough, you've never hurt me enough, you've never fucked me enough. You always make me so ashamed of my desire, and you leave me with so many images, and I never know when you'll be back. For all these reasons, I have to hurt you. You understand, don't you? I have to cause you pain, take some of your power away from you. Because I want to be a poet, and all I am is a whore, and it's your fault.

I know that this little boy understands why I had to rape him, just as we both understand why I am his blow-job girl, the servant of his cock. We play this pain-pleasure, top-bottom, boy-girl game together. I kiss the little boy and sweetly tell him, I am not done yet, little boy. I still need your dick. Your life is still in danger. You have to fuck me still.

I think that there is an army of women inside my cunt, and they are all getting fucked along with me, and they are all ready to kill him if he doesn't comply with all of our collective desire. I think these women want to get eaten, they want to sit on this boy's face, come in his mouth. I pull out of his cock, kiss it, it is so wonderful, put it in his hand. You have to jerk yourself off, I say, you have to stay hard, because I'm not through.

By now I have no shame, I sit on his mouth while I face his cock, make him suck my asshole first of all, and touch himself at the same time. He is making soft little boy sounds, strokes his dick while he eats me. I position my clit right on his tongue. I kiss the tip of his cock again, suck him while he sucks me. We are in that place of no language, in the moment of truth. The place of death and desire and confession and pleasure. I am gagging on his cock and he is making the entire Amazon nation come in his little boy mouth.

But like I said, I'm not through with him yet. I get off his face, jam my throbbing papaya into him again. He sits up, throws me on my back, bites my head and fucks me like he could give a fuck about the Amazons. Ejaculates inside of me, slaps my face hard, over and over, and holds me so close and sweet that I cry.

20 de noviembre de 1999, buffalo, nueva york

Nancy Agabian

More Intimacy

My boyfriend's head is big. I didn't say it was unattractive; it is a really adorable large head. When he rests it somewhere on my body it can get unbelievably heavy—he has a ton of brains in there. My boyfriend has soft, light brown hair; he calls it dishwater blond. And his complexion is kind of on the orange side—I guess he'd be a summer. And he has a lot of freckles and moles all over his body. When I first met him, I noticed there were two small moles lying right on the edge of his upper lip, and although I was attracted to him, I thought, "I can't kiss this guy with those moles there." This was never an issue once we started kissing. I love his moles—the other day when I was spooning him I found a plump pink one underneath his hair on the back of his neck. It was an exciting new find.

My boyfriend has a big nose, sort of; it's hard to describe. When he smiles, his sizable nostrils rise up into his cheeks and he looks unbelievably cute; I just want to gobble his face off. He has some spaces between his teeth because he was born without those teeth—I forget what they are called—that are between the two front teeth and the fangs. Some percentage of the world population is born without those teeth, just like some people are born without the ability to roll their tongues up into a curlicue and some are. Or some people are born albino—that's probably a better example. My boyfriend is as special as an albino. No offense to albino people; I know they may not want to be considered special.

My boyfriend wears horn-rimmed glasses. He has a dark brown pair and a red pair.

My boyfriend complains that he has the smallest hands and feet of any man he knows. I like to walk with him and hold his hand because he twitches a bit; he shifts his fingers in this childlike way. I like that very much; it always fills me up with love.

My boyfriend is around 5'10", but he slouches so he seems shorter, which is good because I am only 5' tall. He has thin, shapely, muscular legs. He has tiny man breasts and a round belly. He isn't fat, but he sticks his stomach out slightly because he's had hip problems for most of his adult life, and he got used to sticking his stomach out to shift his weight so it wouldn't rest on his hip. Last year he got an operation. The surgeon actually took out the whole hip joint and put a titanium version in. My boyfriend has a big scar from the side of his butt down his thigh. After the operation, his left cheek was gone—it was like the surgeon took some of my boyfriend's butt meat along with his hip. His butt has since filled out nicely, back to its round, cute shape. There is some scruffy hair growing intermittently at the very bottom of his rear. When he is on top of me, I grab his bottom and push him in me, and I love the soft fuzzy feeling; it's very primal.

He has a real nice penis. It's just right size-wise. It leans in one direction when he is hard. I forget which direction. Also, he is uncircumcised, which makes for more pleasure for him and for me, because when he is hard, the foreskin serves as a type of sensitive clit at the tip of his dick.

I was lying on the bed and my boyfriend came sauntering by, naked, so I cradled his balls in my hand like they were those metal orbs they sell in Chinatown. I had never really examined them while he was standing up, while they were hanging. They looked like eggs wrapped in soft brown elephant skin. One was higher up than the other and I told him so. He said, "That happens. And sometimes they change position." I found this disturbing. There is nothing in the female form that is even vaguely comparable to balls shifting around inside a sac; I can't relate.

"You're looking at them with disgust," my boyfriend said.

I changed my face so it would look better and said, "Nice balls." Then, "I don't understand why people say 'You've got balls' to mean 'you're so tough.' I mean, balls aren't tough at all; they're delicate."

Nancy Agabian

"That's where testosterone comes from," he said, smiling.

"I have testosterone," I said. It's true. I know because I'm growing a beard. Not intentionally—I pluck it out.

My boyfriend was naked and crawling towards me on my twin-sized bed. I was fully clothed. We hadn't been in this position before. I mean, I had been clothed and he had been naked plenty of times, but usually it was after he had taken a bath and was sauntering through the house with a faux-sexy look on his face (half-shut eyelids and mouth open, tongue lolling about) and faux-nonchalantly slinging his towel over his shoulder while I was pretending to be oblivious, completely absorbed in preparing the ramen. But now we were in bed, about to make love, which we usually commence both clothed or both naked.

A moment ago, he was sitting in my desk chair fully dressed and saying he needed to get new glasses. "I need a new image," he said. "How am I going to change my image?"

"You could take all your clothes off," I suggested. Immediately my boyfriend put on his faux-sexual look and did a little striptease for me. It was cute and exciting. It got a little clunky when he was taking his jeans, briefs and socks off because he can't move his left leg very freely, but that added to the charm. He was naked, and I cradled his balls, and then he crawled into bed next to me, where he is now.

I ask him if he wants me to do a striptease too, and he says yes, but first I must go pee. When I come back, I suddenly get the urge to look for my checkbook. I have the feeling that he mistook my checkbook for his and I look in his suitcase and there it is. "Good thing I caught that before you left," I say to him. My boyfriend is leaving tomorrow morning. He lives in another city—a four-hour flight away. We lived together during the first year of our relationship, but we have been a long-distance couple for nearly two years now and will be for one more year because I'm in a graduate program. It is really hard. Sometimes I feel like we should break up, not because I want to be apart from him but because we are already physically apart. A voice in me says *this long-distance relationship is a symptom of something unhealthy*. But I don't know what that unhealthy thing is. *Probably because you are in denial about it, bonehead.* Oh shut up. And sometimes I get attracted to other people, which only makes me feel more guilty than attracted. Things get particularly tricky when it's a woman. Did I mention that I'm bisexual? (Long story.) So I think, *Damn, maybe I'm a big lesbian in denial.* No, I'm not, I'm bisexual; it's normal for me to occasionally be attracted to women—it doesn't mean I have to do anything about it. Besides, italics voice,

— *GYNOMITE:*

you are always looking for the weak link, always trying to make sure I'm not making a mistake. I'm not making a mistake, okay, I love my boyfriend. Sometimes I forget all that it means to be in love, to be attracted to him, even though we talk on the phone every single day, pretty much. We share our lives over the phone and we love each other over the phone. But we really have to see each other, feel each other to cement the deal. It just goes to show that you can't be in love just in your head. It has to be in the body too. *Duh.*

I take off my blouse and fling it across the room and then remember I was supposed to be sexy about it, teasing. So I put it back on and try to build some anticipation by rubbing the open panels of the blouse over my breasts, as if my breasts can't wait to pop out. It is turning me on. I remember all the porno images I have seen of women, right before their clothes come off—that is always the most exciting part to me. Finally I reveal my breasts, they are encased in a flesh-toned see-through bra. I undo the clasp and then slowly release my beauties. I like my breasts a lot. There have been studies about how most women don't like their breasts—they are either too big or too small, but I have always felt pretty good about mine except for that one time when I went on the pill and they swelled up to a bigger cup size. My nipples are brown, and I have quite a bit of long, wiry nipple hair. I have to admit I'm not too crazy about the nipple hair. My skin tone is what would be called "olive" in the beauty magazines, but this is a term I despise. My hair is black and my skin is light, even lighter than most white people but I look like a person of color; my skin tone is grayish-yellow. *Oh yeah, that sounds much nicer than "olive."* I am sorry; I refuse to be compared to a kalamata.

Topless now, I shift my hips back and forth, smiling. I feel really silly. But my boyfriend is rubbing his dick, so I must be doing an okay job. I continue to swing my hips awkwardly to some silent sexy music; the whole thing makes me wanna crack up, but I am too far in—I gotta finish so I throw off my pants. Then it's just me and my panties so I slowly push them down; they get stuck on my large black bush that grows down my fat thighs. I experience all the excitement I feel right before me and my boyfriend take off our underwear, after kissing and licking and feeling each other up for a while. I push the panties all the way down and throw them in the dirty laundry basket and jump into bed with him.

"Was that sexy?" I ask him.

"Yes," he says.

"Was it silly?"

"Yes, it was both."

"It was sexy and silly?"

"Yes, it was a lot sexy and a lot silly."

Then I lean onto him and his body is warm and my mouth melts into the nicest mouth in the world and his skin is so soft and he holds me and that is all I'm going to tell you. We both came, if you need to know, but I'm not going to tell how. I mean, I am going to have an orgasm over here writing this and I don't feel like doing that right now. Why do you have to know any more than what I've told you? I've already revealed a lot. Our lovemaking is private. It is an expression of our love for each other. I want to protect it; it is precious; it is not for you. I want to celebrate my beautiful boyfriend, whose body I miss for many months out of the year. I want to show normal people in a sexual context. I want to show me, with my fat thighs, being loved. Because for a long time I never thought me or my body would be loved. There is so much sickness concerning sexuality in this culture. When people try to talk about sex openly, I know they mean well, but before my boyfriend came along, I always felt like a mutant freak in those discussions. I had very few sexual experiences because I was afraid of sex, of intimacy. So I got left out of the discussions and I always hoped no one would notice but eventually someone would. "What about you Nancy?" they would ask. I would shrug my shoulders, about to cry. I don't want anyone to read about me and my boyfriend and feel left out, the way that I did.

There was a time in my life when I would have told you everything. I was in my early twenties and would tell random groups of strangers about my sex life, or more accurately the lack thereof, under the guise of performance art. After years of repressing my sexuality, I unleashed it in a very public way. It was very healing for me to do that. But I don't need to be healed anymore. But I guess a part of me misses revealing everything. Because I love talking openly to random groups of strangers. Is there anything more intimate than that? Well, yes, actually, there is. I could tell my boyfriend what is in this story—that would be more intimate. That would be better. But then, what do I tell you? If I have found more intimacy with a partner, have I betrayed my intimacy with random groups of strangers?

Oh I love you, random groups of strangers. I really do. I just have some love in my life now—it's really good. If I could find love, you can too. Please don't feel left out. *Who says they do?* You know, you are my family.

Carlisle Vandervoort

More

She always begs for more.

"I want all of it," she whimpers.

"No, baby. You know how sore you are the next day."

"I DON'T care, I've got to have you. I need it. I need you to fill me up. I need more and more of you."

"All right, love," I say, and slide my cock out of her, kissing her face. I tell her that I love her. Slowly stroking her wet cunt, I open her up with my fingers. One, two. . .

"More, baby!" Four, as I feel her open up. Her wetness squishes through my fingers. I'm kissing her stomach, licking her clit, mentally bowing before her, calling to the goddess in her. "Hurry, baby!" Out comes my hand. My ring flies off the bed. Back in. I tell her, "Breathe deeply, love. Breathe from your heart and your pussy." She opens more, time slows down and speeds up. This time she's wet, wet, wet. My hand automatically collapses into itself. Lick, lick, "breathe baby."

Whoosh. I push up into her, past the pubic wall, fist inside. She cries out, my heart opens. I am always amazed by this. She takes more. . .opens more. . . Each time I can open my fist wider. Now, here, I can open and wiggle, open and wiggle, push on her wall. Lick, too slick from the lube. I find the spot. In and out.

She arches.

I see God. Feel God. Am God.

Carlisle Vandervoort

It's A Clavicle Thang

What is your favorite body part of a woman? Mine is the clavicle, also known, *en françias*, as le décolletage, the sweeping expanse between neck and breasts. I go weak over a beautiful clavicle. It's so delicate and open, yet structurally strong and sturdy. Something about the duality of fragility and tensile strength co-existing in such a small area really sends me. A beautiful décolletage is a seductive landscape with broad open plains and high ridged cliffs. When I see one I want to roam there, pressing my hands and cheeks against the sweet smelling canyon floor.

The revelation of this particular fetish occurred many years ago. My father had persuaded me to attend a black tie event. I was living in L.A. and had come to Texas for Christmas. It was a big holiday party and I was dreading it. Here I was, gay and single, in Houston at some very straight party at the country club where I grew up, with my father. Dad was thrilled with my presence-you know how parents love to show off their children, even after they've grown up. I cruised the bash wondering just how long a "little while" was, filled with judgment, disdain, and a very dismissive attitude. My impatience and aggravation with the evening increased as the drunk son of one of my father's friends attempted to put the bite on me. (Drunken ex-frat boys who have never left Texas are truly pathetic.) Escaping that scenario, I flirted here and there until I felt I had fulfilled my contractual holiday obligation as a daughter and sailed over to where Dad stood to say goodnight.

My plan was to knife my way into the knot of people he was visiting with, plant a quick kiss and flee. But you know, this is just not possible with a sixty-five-year-old native Texan whose passions include fishing, storytelling, and manners. He insisted that I meet yet another old friend, the friend's son, and the daughter-in-law. "Yeah, yeah, okay, then I am leaving!"

We had to wait, as the couple was engaged in another conversation. Bored, I sidled over to check out their profiles—nice looking WASPs, seen a ton of 'em. Finishing their conversation they turned towards us, smiling in anticipation of exchanging pleasantries. Introductions were made and small talk followed.

Because of the large crowd we were pressed tightly together. After a few minutes the crowd shifted and we all stepped back from one another. Being the evil, lecherous lesbian that I am, I thought I'd give the wife the secret full-body scan. I subtly dropped my eyes to her chest and was dumbstruck. Her clavicle was alive. It was emitting the light of a thousand suns. My entire being wanted to bathe in her blinding radiance.

Suddenly, I didn't want to leave. Frantic to extend my fleeting moments with her luminous décolletage, I grasped onto any shred of conversational commonality that we might have shared. A few precious seconds were granted until social convention required that she move on and speak to others, and I was left with something wholly new.

Carlisle Vandervoort

I Heel To Myself

I am skirting the real issue here in my writing this morning. I am not being honest with myself. I am convinced that I should write about my clavicle fetish; after all, it is the essence of a woman to me. I have fallen in crush over the structural elements of a gorgeous clavicle. It would be a good piece of writing, but it's not what I fantasize about when I masturbate. So there is a split here: Write about beauty and essence and it will be safe, romantic, lofty, and perhaps even high erotic art, or put down what really goes on for me when I need to get off. It is low, too low to speak out about. Not that it's bad or dirty or shameful, but it is somewhat taboo. It is primal and revealing. No lofty John Ruskin, Venus de Milo high-art ideals with beautiful disembodied torsos lovingly placed on pedestals to be worshiped, adored, and swooned over. Nope. You don't have that with ass-fucking.

Yeah, there is for sure a torso: Mine. Grasped tightly by two hands, holding me captive in the most vulnerable position possible: face down, butt up. (I love a good ass-fuck. Some days this is the only thing that will set me straight.) Usually by this point in the fun I have whimpered and begged for it. (Oh, and lest y'all get the wrong idea about me. . . I do not have an open-ass policy.) Take note that the woman who can get me on my hands and knees, twitching with desire, fear and anticipation is a woman who knows herself well and loves to do this. A great ass-fuck is not for the faint of heart, *whichever* end you're on.

My ass lover can deal with the rawness of it all. DEAL WITH IT. Deal with me baby and TURN ME OUT, 'cuz I can't take being strong and in charge anymore.

Goddamn it, my mind runs me. I swear if I didn't meditate I'd be dead. Or your worst nightmare. Some days, meditation isn't enough, and my willfulness exhausts me, until it becomes unbearable and I finally heel to myself. I open up to my need to be on hands and knees with my back exposed and my asshole open. It's a matter of life and death.

I want her hands kneading my ass while she pushes her swollen clit into me, splaying wet lips from underneath the harness straps. Her breasts brush across my back and I hear the titillating squirt and squish of cold lube as she loads her cock. I am purring now—scared and thrilled because it is about to get tricky, real tricky. The butt plug has to come out— an achingly exquisite moment—but I dread its departure. A butt plug is easy. It's in, it feels great, and I don't have to surrender. But now it's gone, and the moment I long for and need *because nothing else will scratch this particular itch* is upon me.

I have begged for, dreamt of, and fetishized this act and now it is time. And yet I wonder, "Does this make me a pussy? Will she think less of me? Will I lose myself?"

Lose myself. Isn't that what this is all about?

Oops, I can't think anymore. She's ready to take the plunge. Her hard prick bumps against my tight ass, straining to get in. Oh God, I love this and yet. . .

"Come on baby, breathe. Isn't this what you want?" she coos in her most commanding and kittenish voice.

A warm palm cups my right ass cheek. SMACK. Ouch! SMACK. *Yummy.* Whispering my name, my lover kisses the tingling red spot. I am swoony. My chest tightens and my heart races. Her fingers caress my wet cunt and trail back to my not-so-tight-anymore asshole, mixing my juices together with the slippery lube.

That's it. I jam my head down onto the bed, reach back with both hands and pull apart my ass. Grasping my hips, she slides into me and slowly works her cock. I tense, breathe, relax, and push back into her, repeating this until we hit our stride. "Baby, you are so beautiful," she says, and lightly strokes my back. The senses become so acute that everything turns to white noise and the air buzzes. My chest tightens one more time and then rapidly expands. Again my head bows down to the bed and I am aware that my heart is higher than my head and that it is exploding. Her hands grasp my shoulders, pushing and pulling me back and forth, feeding me love.

Something happens here for me that I can't explain. Always at this moment. It is as if all the love in the world is present, whirling around us, and her hands on my shoulders are the conduits. My heart opens so widely that I fall into it. She follows me. There is no mind here in this place of the heart. Simply infinite space.

And we float.

Shaila Dewan

Starr Report: The Excerpts

Nov. 15 Sexual Encounter

A t about 10 P.M., in Ms. Lewinsky's recollection, she was alone in the Chief of Staff's office, and the President approached. He invited her to rendezvous again in Mr. Stephanopoulos's office in a few minutes, and she agreed. (Asked if she knew why the President wanted to meet with her, Ms. Lewinsky testified, "I had an idea.")

According to Ms. Lewinsky, she and the President kissed. She unbuttoned her jacket—either she unhooked her bra or he lifted her bra up—and he touched her breasts with his hands and mouth. Ms. Lewinsky testified, "I believe he took a phone call. . . and so we moved from the hallway into the back office. . . [H]e put his hand down my pants and stimulated me manually in the genital area." While the President continued talking on the phone (Ms. Lewinsky understood that the caller was a member of Congress or a Senator), she performed oral sex on him. He finished his call, and, a moment later, told Ms. Lewinsky to stop. In her recollection: "I told him that I wanted. . . to complete that. And he said. . . that he needed to wait until he trusted me more. And then he made a joke. . . that he hadn't had that for a long time."

Nov. 17 Sexual Encounter

Several witnesses confirm that when Ms. Lewinsky delivered pizza to the President that night, the two of them were briefly alone.

Ms. Lewinsky testified that she and the President had a sexual encounter during this visit. They kissed, and the President touched Ms. Lewinsky's bare breasts with his hands and mouth. At some point, Ms. Currie approached the door leading to the hallway, which was ajar, and said there was a telephone call. Ms. Lewinsky recalled that the caller was a member of congress with a nickname. While the President was on the telephone, according to Ms. Lewinsky, "he unzipped his pants and exposed himself," and she performed oral sex. Again, he stopped her before he ejaculated.

Dec. 31 Sexual Encounter

She told him her name—she had the impression that he had forgotten it in the six weeks since their furlough encounter because, when passing her in the hallway, he had called her "Kiddo." The President replied that he knew her name; in fact, he added, having lost the phone number she had given him, he had tried to find her in the phone book.

According to Ms. Lewinsky, they moved to the study. "And then. . . we were kissing and he lifted my sweater and exposed my breasts and was fondling them with his hands and with his mouth." She performed oral sex. Once again, he stopped her before he ejaculated because, Ms. Lewinsky testified, "He didn't know me well enough or he didn't trust me yet."

Jan. 21 Sexual Encounter

According to Ms. Lewinsky, she questioned the President about his interest in her. "I asked him why he doesn't ask me any questions about myself. . . and is this just about sex. . . or do you have some interest in trying to get to know me as a person?" The President laughed and said, according to Ms. Lewinsky, that "he cherishes the time that he had with me."

They continued talking as they went to the hallway by the study. Then, with Ms. Lewinsky in mid-sentence, "he just started kissing me." He lifted her top and touched her breasts with his hands and mouth. According to Ms. Lewinsky, the President "unzipped his pants and sort of exposed himself," and she performed oral sex.

Feb. 4 Sexual Encounter and Subsequent Phone Calls

According to Ms. Lewinsky, the President telephoned her at her desk and they planned their rendezvous. At her suggestion, they bumped into each other in the hallway, "because when it happened accidentally, that seemed to work really well," then walked together to the area of the private study.

There, according to Ms. Lewinsky, they kissed. She was wearing a long dress that buttoned from the neck to the ankles. "And he unbuttoned my dress and sort of took the dress off my shoulders and. . . moved the bra. . . . [H]e was looking at me and telling me how beautiful I was. I was wearing a kind of lacy bra with seamless cups, and he was stroking my nipples through the bra until they became taller than I had even seen them before, just sooo tall it was almost funny, like an inch long, and I started to get really turned on. He was so much more glamorous in real life than on TV, really cute, you know, and very wicked. He spread the dress out around me like a blanket on the desk, and he told me to close my eyes."

Then, according to Ms. Lewinsky, the President tilted her head back manually, and she drew her knees up to her chest, placing her feet on the desk for balance as she lifted her pelvis up slightly so he could remove her underwear. The President then spread Ms. Lewinsky's legs apart, leaned forward until she could smell a faint whiff of "very masculine" Armani cologne, and blew softly on the dampened genital area. "I felt really open and embarrassed, like everyone in the world could see how excited I was, how hungry I was, how desperate, and I just wanted the President to fuck me but when I opened my eyes to ask him, he just pushed my head back again and said, 'Shut your eyes,' so I did and he touched my breasts very slowly with his hands and mouth through my bra, so slowly that I started to cry, and then I could not bear it anymore. Why wouldn't he fuck me? And I didn't think it was sweet anymore, I used to think it was sweet that he wouldn't fuck me, so I drew my knees together and looked up with my *thongiest* look, and he said, 'No, Monica,' and pushed my knees back open and put the bra cups back on as if we were finished, and that's when the television camera burst in. Nobody moves, and I am just there, with the hot light from the TV camera glaring right at my bare cun. . . genitalia, and the TV guy who came in with the cameraman is wearing a dark gray Hugo Boss suit."

According to Ms. Lewinsky, the television reporter looked at her, and looked at the President, and unzipped his pants. The President went around behind the desk and, according to Ms. Lewinksy, said, "Close your eyes, Monica," as the man in the suit approached and exposed himself. "He says, 'This will be for private use only, you understand,' and the President nods and the camera keeps rolling. He's very handsome but kind of steely, and well, unfriendly, you know? 'She looks ready to get fucked,' he tells the President—the understatement of the year. The President reaches out and squeezes my nipples, which spring up and strain against the bra, you know, where the material is worn slightly thin from my nipples anyway? 'Check out her tits,' the President says, pulling them out over my bra cups so they're held up and outward and bare. The TV guy keeps a very stiff, straight face, as if he's waiting for the anchorman to introduce his live report. My eyes are wide open now, and I'm trying to see if he has a big cock, which he does."

According to Ms. Lewinsky, the generously endowed television reporter moved over her into push-up position. "I feel the rough wool of his jacket on my bare nipples, brushing lightly as he takes his cock and starts to put it inside me. I look up at the President, who is watching the horizon of my body intently. I feel like my body is the New World. He notices me looking up at him and he twists my nipples once more, and suddenly my vulva thrusts upward around his cock—the TV guy's cock—and the TV guy laughs grimly, fucking me up and down in this push-up position like he's in boot camp or something. And all I can feel is rough wool and starched shirt and the thin whip and scratch of a shirt and I come, throbbing. I have soaked everything. 'I can't get a grip,' the TV guy says, and from a great greeny distance, a whole continent away, I watch him as he pulls out his cock and puts it between my breasts, and the President spreads his hands wide and pushes my breasts together around the TV guy's cock, pinching the nipples hard with his short fingernails, and I reach two fingers down to my pussy, wet them, and touch my clit very lightly, stroking myself into another orgasm just as I feel a new warmth, heavier than water, spreading on my neck and breasts."

Like Rain

S he stood over him in the bathtub and asked if he was ready. For an answer, he wrapped his arms around her legs and kissed the insides of her knees and thighs. Ceremoniously, he licked all the parts of her that he could reach, pressing his white cheek to the brown curve of her leg, burying his whole head softly in her pussy. Her wet skin tasted sweet and clean. His hair was cut close to his head, and his bangs shot forward briefly and sharply. His otherwise delicate face had a slightly Aryan smirk; she had once thought him cruel and derisive, and very sophisticated.

She squeezed her knees around his head viciously and he turned his mouth up, trying to reach her pussy with his lip while she squeezed tighter. He gasped, wrenching his head free and kissing her thighs once more—a brief, open-mouthed, desperate kiss—before sinking back into the tub and closing his eyes. She had one foot on either side of his white, exposed ribcage, and she put her arms out to brace herself against the tile wall at the back of the tub, lifting up the curve of her ass. A trickle of warm water hit the base of her spine and poured down the crack, split, and coursed along the inside of her thighs quick as snowmelt. She arched her back and raised her heels in order to let the stream moisten her vulva.

Nothing came.

"Do you *want* me to piss on you?" She demanded angrily, as if it were his fault. They had come home early, eager for each other and sick of everyone else. They had sex, usually, in the afternoons in his upstairs bedroom, surrounded by trees, unable to get up and do anything else for their want of each other, their hands kneading each other's flesh forcefully, their secret pleasures falling like the petals of an old tulip: softly, inevitably, singly. I want you to turn over, whispered, I want you to put your legs up here, your finger there, your tongue in this crack.

"I want you. . . to piss on. . . my face," he said, writhing with the effort of articulating such a thought. And hearing his words turned the lips of her pussy inside out and brought her heels down hard.

She closed her eyes and concentrated. She relaxed and stared at the ceiling. Now she knew how men felt when someone walked up to the urinal next to them. Nothing. She attempted to pee surreptitiously, without letting her body know she was trying to pee. Still nothing.

She turned around, and, reaching behind her to cup her buttocks with her hands and spread them apart for him, she gulped warm water from the trickle coming out of the shower. Water ran down her chin and spewed off her chest as if her nipples were spouts. She heard him behind her, whimpering, and felt his hands around her ankles. When she had drunk as much as she could, she turned back around and straddled him again, this time kneeling over him and putting his hands firmly at his sides. Her wet swirl of pubic hair brushed against his smooth, bare chest. Slowly, she pushed her breasts against his closed eyes, and as he opened his mouth to take them in, she stood up suddenly and a hot spurt of piss splished down and spattered once on his chest, then on his face, and then ended abruptly when her pussy spasmed with pleasure. She looked down helplessly. He had grabbed his cock in his fist and was moving his hand up and down with slow, determined strokes. "Do you want me to piss on you?" she asked, and he convulsed, saying nothing, his ass slapping repeatedly against the tub as he fucked his own hand.

As if it were second nature, they had known how much and when to abuse each other. She would wrestle him and pin down his arms, steer his head back with a fistful of hair and whisper that she was going to put her cock inside him, that she really wanted to put her cock inside him, and she would put the tip of his cock inside her, and then she would tell him she was going to go deeper, and she would slide down over his cock, and then she would say softly that she was going to fuck him, hard, with her cock, and she would ride him roughly until they both came, stuck together in paroxysms, screaming at each other. He shaved her pussy naked while she stood in the tub, feet slightly apart, arms crossed over her breasts, breathing deeply as the blade neared her clit. She dreamt that he tattooed her shoulder, buzzing slowly into her skin, while she looked on in the mirror. She wanted to smother him, to burn him, to feed him bits of her uncooked body, elbow and buttock and ear. She wanted to piss over him, wanted him to drink her piss, wanted to piss into his open eyes, and her toes curled and she reared her ass into the air like a feral cat.

She swiveled the faucet hotter, and turned and put her hands behind her, into the shower, and arched her back as if she were bound there. "But you *always* have to pee," he said, teasing her. And she laughed, and something shifted in her and her mind snapped out of focus like a rubber band let loose by a schoolboy and one of her hands came off the wall and slapped her thigh, and she was pissing, a spattering stream so hot it was light as a vapor, splashing all over him, and as her water feathered his head and body with flecks of heat he froze, like a statue in a fountain, a fountain of her, his hair dampened as if by sweat. Then he was moving, stroking himself frantically, and the piss gushed out of her as if the boy had yanked his thumb from the dike, her dam opened, her water broken, streaming and streaming long past reason, and as he clenched hard, gathering the flesh of her thighs up in his fists as he came, white semen arcing into the rainy air, she whirled like one of those rounded stone phalluses that sit upright in Hindu temples, surrounded for eternity by the cosmic vagina, its pouring spout like Aladdin's lamp, spurting out a river of sex that flows all over the universe, sweeping like minnows anything loose into its downward course.

Juice

She hates waiting at the station, watching people file off the bus, wondering whether he or she will be the first to see the other. She raises her eyebrows, purses her lips into a moue, frowns, and is reminded of the Woody Allen scene where he frantically changes record albums, trying to decide which one to have playing when his date comes over.

"Hi!" she says with bright nervousness when he finally appears. "Ready?"

He smiles at her, refusing to be hurried as he looks her over. She is tall, clean, and shimmery, her makeup careful, copious, and applied as if she doesn't quite trust that she's beautiful. Her short, blond hair, olive skin and green eyes seem almost one color, like different parts of the same camouflage pattern. Her hands are clenched inside the pockets of a soft black leather jacket, so new the pockets haven't gotten linty yet, so new that she feels new, luxurious, like she has been shipped from the cosmetics counter at Neiman-Marcus right to this filthy bus depot, with Joey not much cleaner than it.

"You look all rich and shit," Joey says suspiciously.

He's a backwoods Louisiana Italian, skinny—the scrawny one in the family—with fucked-up teeth and a scruffy beard and the blackest brown eyes she's ever seen, each eye like a single, enlarged grain of polished snakeskin. Joey's grandmother bathed him until he was fourteen, he watches midget porn, and once, when his best friend made fun of him in public, Joey took his drink when he wasn't looking, unzipped his fly, and put "a little nut juice" in it.

He holds a fist towards her as if it contained a live goldfish. "Let me see one of those pockets," he says, and when she takes out her hand he slips the goldfish into it. "A present for you."

When they get to the car—his car—he takes her hand from the door and spins her around. He presses her up against the car door so she can feel the metal roof on the back of her neck and he kisses her, and suddenly she is back in that alternate universe, where there is only she, Joey, thousands of lost electrons buzzing like angry wasps, a chattering whisper of dirty words, and at one end a blue blue ocean that is alternately warm and cool. In the alternate universe, she does not care if Joey is not her type, or if he is her type.

Then he is telling her an amusing story about a friend who just tried to borrow money from him to pay another friend to whom Joey also owes money, and they are in the car, where the jawbone of a small shark, cleaned by leaving it in an ant bed, encircles the rearview mirror. He takes one hand off the wheel and slides it up her skirt to where her thigh is soft as rain falling on a field of talcum powder, softer than Joey thinks he deserves, he's a happy man, and it's as if someone slips a warm pat of butter into the crotch of her panties and it instantly melts.

She leans the car seat back, puts one high-heel-with-ankle-strap on the dash, stretches her arms over her head and thrusts out her tits, medium-sized tits that bob forward and crest with the nipples pointing straight up at the sky, and which Joey looks at with raised eyebrows and a peevish expression while she grins and stares out the window. They get to a stoplight and he lunges, gets a mouthful of black stretch velvet, snarls, spits, and guns the motor while she giggles, taunting him. Joey is predictably vengeful, and she knows he will get her for this, and she can't wait.

Before she met Joey, she had never met her ideal lover: one who would participate in screaming, dish-hurling, wake-the-neighbor arguments out on the driveway, then make up by fucking her brains out on a mattress on the floor with a fan blowing, one who could say "I'm going to fuck your brains out" without making her laugh, one who started to drool at the sight of her, a red-blooded man in a white wifebeater with hard, small muscles and snakeskin eyes. An Italian, if someone had just told her, you want a backwoods Louisiana Italian with plenty of nut juice.

Joey hasn't said anything in a while and she knows he is getting properly steamed. She pulls the lever on the car seat so it pops upright and turns toward him, pulling her titty out of the black velvet top and teasing her nipple. He lunges again and she slips it back in her top. He slaps her hard across the cheek. "Bitch!" She leans back, head away from him, breathing hard and feeling the warm sting of the slap like a sprung mousetrap. Her body shudders involuntarily. "Don't have a wreck, baby."

"Jesus Christ, I'm an asshole," Joey says. "When we get home I'm going to roll up something to smoke as big as my dick."

"Why don't you roll up something as big as the dick you're being?" she asks.

"Shut up, bitch." Then he says, "We're stopping at the bar so I can watch your ass while you put money in the jukebox."

She smiles, closes her eyes, is swimming in that blue ocean, feeling the water all over her body, clear as a church window and heavy as hair, swirling with each stroke into soft, wet flames.

Her ass is so hot, Joey thinks at the bar. Look at it, it's like waves. A snowblind ass. An undertow ass. That chick should be making porn movies, he says to Vince, who agrees boozily. We'd be rich. Then he sidles up behind her and somehow manages to be touching her bare behind under her skirt and panties. He gives it a squeeze, his thumb in the crack, right up close to the action. "Joey!" she yelps involuntarily, thinking everyone can see.

"We're going home," he says.

Joey sits in the armchair in the house and, after he smokes a joint that is not nearly as big as his dick, he bellows at her like Archie Bunker. When she comes over, he gives her skirt one yank and lets it drop to the floor. "Bend over here like a good girl," he says, crushing the joint out in the ashtray and blowing a puff of sweet and sour smoke into the room.

And she does, putting her stomach on his knees, her ankles crossed daintily up in the air. He slips his slippery hand up her velvet bodice and fools with one of her tits while she stares down at the floor and wriggles. "Baby," Joey says, "I prayed to God and he sent me you," then he pinches her tits until they're hard little trembly knots and spanks her until his dick gets hard, until her so-fine talcum powder ass is hot and cold at the same time, until butter pats bubble out of her into her panties, until her panties are off and the two of them are rolling on a mattress on the floor, kicking dirty laundry out of the way and tearing their clothes off, her stretching his undershirt tight around his neck as if to strangle him, him slapping her cheeks and breasts hard, like a snake striking, and suddenly she is swimming in cool water, the electrons are dancing, he is whispering that she is a little whore with a juicy cunt and she is diving down, swimming until she comes up for air and the ocean has spread out all around her as far as she can see, and her body is the ocean, her body has turned to water, and she is drowning in herself only because there is no end to it and she is exhausted, liquid, hot and cold and then Joey is saying somewhere above her head "What about your fucking present ? I bought you a goddamn fucking present bitch," and he is frantic, he finds her new jacket and shakes it upside down and until a heavy chain falls out.

On each end of the chain is a clamp that looks like a mechanical dragon's head, and suddenly she is anchored by its teeth sunk deep into the creamy cresting nipple of one tit, and then by teeth sunk deep into the frothy cresting nipple of the other tit, and the water of her body laps up against the dragons, Joey is sliding into her ocean caves and she feels the cold thick chain on her, clear as a church window and heavy as hair, and the lost electrons form two cones and bombard these two points on her body with fizzy electron-ness, and she looks out from the ocean, and down from the ocean, and up from the ocean, and sees two mechanical dragons holding tight with their teeth to either end of a shimmering bridge.

No Satisfaction

I . . . *Can't. . . Get. . . No. . . Satisfaction. . .* she writes when she finds the chalkboard in his kitchen, wanting him to notice that she knows songs from when he was growing up, that she knows what real rock and roll is. Generally speaking, he is her uncle, but technically speaking, he is not, because he is the brother of the man her aunt married. She is from the city and he is from the country, so their ways of being shameful are foreign to each other.

When he sees what she has written, all he says is, "And you never will."

She says, "Why," and he says, "Because you are a woman."

A woman? But she doesn't even brush her hair. She can't even walk in high heels. She still has to remind herself, some days, that she is not a virgin anymore. And he tells her things like, "You're going to break a lot of hearts." And he tells her, "Listen, pay attention to the quiet guys." And she wants to know if he was a quiet guy, but she does not ask.

She tries to remember if she has ever been satisfied, scrolling over her brief history, a document so short it barely reaches from one cylinder of the Torah to the other. She remembers Patrick, who she had a crush on for about ten seconds, before he stood behind her in the school darkroom and whispered, "Girl, you are alllllllllll woman," running his hands over her chest and then plunging them into her pants where, she knew, he could feel her body jerk like a very short movie that shows, for a beat, the moment when water turns into ice, and then, for a beat, is rewound into water, while in front of her she watched Patrick's face in her photograph materialize in the tray of developer. She remembers Cody, the second guy she ever had sex with, right after the first guy, who she didn't count anyway, and how the instant his mother left the apartment he had pinned her down on the twin bed, with his one free hand pulling the condom out from its lair, opening it, and with a motion like plugging his penis into the socket of his fist slid into it and then her, so unhesitating that she could only close her eyes, touch her own breasts, let a gentle panic ride her body as she bucked, an ivory jackstraw unable to extricate herself without disturbing the pile.

At the end, she had believed herself satisfied, and she did not think there was a difference between believing oneself satisfied and being satisfied. But still, she wanted to know if there was more to it.

She twisted one ankle all the way around to the outside, and then all the way back around to the inside, the way she had seen Jennifer Narun do as Daisy Mae in *Li'l Abner*, a role she herself had not even been eligible for because last year she didn't have breasts yet, and she got so distracted by what she was trying to look like while she was thinking that she forgot what she was thinking about. Then she looked at her not-technically uncle and said, in a tone that she believed to be extraordinarily seductive, "Maybe *you* can satisfy me."

Once she had made up her mind on this course of action she did not stop, except when she first saw his chest. It was a mass of curly gray and red hairs, and it looked so alien that she tried not to let her breasts touch him because she was half afraid that chest hair was a contagious condition.

She trembled. She fretted. Not very much happened. His fingers made small, insistent circles just around the mouth of her vagina. Thinking he must be bored, she pushed the palm of her hand awkwardly toward his crotch. Was that his penis? Or the seam of his jeans? The chest hair, actually, felt sort of good once she got used to the idea of it. He was maybe thirty-five, thick, with a heft that high-school boys didn't have. He put her nipple between his lips like something he had just lodged there for a second to free his hands, still making those lazy circles with his finger. She gave up on his crotch and knit her fingers feverishly into his auburn hair. His finger, meanwhile, slipped deeper and deeper and, against her thigh, there it was. She felt everything now. He had no face. He had no language. She closed her eyes.

It was an endless amount of time before she realized she was floating, out at the end of a long, thin tether. The tether was made of all the blood vessels in her body, which he had siphoned slowly through the hole in her nipple and massaged, inch by inch, with his lips and bathed, centimeter by centimeter, in the shallow of his mouth and laid end to end so they formed miles and miles of tensile line, like the rubber casing of electric wire, and it hummed with the hum of electric wire, unreeling from his mouth until she was closer to the moon than she was to earth and closer to her cunt than she was to her heart, and from there she could look down and she could see satisfaction like a lake of marbles, and she could smell satisfaction like a cold bar of ocean-flavored butter, and she could taste satisfaction like tiny crisp beads of pork bone marrow and, in that moment, she declined it all, not wanting to be full.

Slave

The heart kingdom is a fiery place, full of angels with plucked eyebrows and evil creatures carried to and fro in sleds, intricate diagrams to avoid stepping in, and hundreds upon thousands of slaves wearing thin, damp rags and chained in rows all up and down ladders on the hillside. They shovel coal into fireplaces whose burning makes the hillside glow heart-red. It is hot.

And I am nine, burning down to a limber nub, sizzling away into nighttime fritters of flesh. My nipples are nearly indiscernible, circles of soft glint on my chest, which is flat and small as the box for a deck of cards. They have been smudged with burnt wood. They dome up like two soft pouts, aching. There are large iron circles around each of my wrists, as if I am playing dress-up with a lady's jewelry.

I am made to wait, and the minutes inch by like caterpillars crawling along my body toward my secrets. The guards fondle my pear-shaped, hairless vulva with their cracked hands. One takes from his belt a thin iron penis, and they touch parts of my body with it, my lips, my neck, my small asshole, fresh as fruit, which I myself have never seen, the tiny nub in front I think of as my miniature penis. I try to close the lips of my vagina together.

Then they take me and hang me upside down by my feet. I swing out over nothingness and my hair unfurls, rolling down in a dark black tangle almost as tall as I am.

I am being lowered, as slowly as a woman taking a man's cock into her mouth for the first time, as slowly as a lover discovering, with his tongue, the backside of a knee or the damp crease under a buttock. There below me is a huge caldron of bubbling tar, waiting to scald me into a nakedness I have never known, more naked than a sand dune, more naked than a salt-washed worm, more naked than a woman bound and gagged and made to kneel. All around me are the slack, heavy eyes of the people of the kingdom, and they stare as if of one mind, and as I drop slowly down towards the caldron, the eyes burn me like many tiny bulbs of hot light. And the eyes pinch me like thousands of mean baby fingers, and the eyes press me like the dry links of a twisted chain that tightens as I struggle, sobbing as my skin goes white and thin as the throat of a lizard, then red and yellow in the heat of the heart.

Amber Gayle

15 ¼ Nights

350 nights a year

I lay down alone and tuck the blankets between my knees.

Which stories do you write?

I throw out the dull ones.

350 nights a year

don't get published.

"Lube it up," he said—I had a lover like that.

We fucked and we hooted like cowboys

his mouth was rough and careful

he tasted like beer

he gave me nothing else.

Amber Gayle

I lie in my witch's bed
my single bed and dream of smooth hot sex
long blond wigs and go-go boots
I dream of naked bodies
I wake up myself
beneath my nun's quilt
I carry out the day.

"I want to fuck you," he said, he spelled it on my tongue—
I had a lover like that.
He came in late from his office and pushed dinner back from the table
to reach my hands my mouth my legs
he didn't have much time to waste.
Anger and sex go together
I've known it intimately
my aggression and the men who feed it
go hand in hand in hand
(I like to bite.)
A lot of men can't even fuck.
Did you know that?
I keep a lot of secrets.
They lose it and then they don't know what to say
and they go home and go to sleep calm and do not dream
while you wander

around the borders
of your city
fury
ricochets
against the borders of your skull.

I want things that don't seem to exist
(like sex)
fucking is so peaceful
they're so rare those moments of sweat and saliva and limbs
I am calm
sweet and calm
it's so rare
350 nights a year
I lay down alone and tuck the blankets between my knees.

"I got this for you," she said,
and pulled a four-foot sunflower from behind her back
(blushing)—
I had a lover like that.
In the blur of way-too-drunk-to-fuck
I opened my eyes to get a glimpse of her face above mine
and her eyelids
in the blur
I etched that on my memory:

One lucid moment

with the texture of her tongue and fingers in my cunt

and most of all my heart

whispering in my ear, "It's her! She's kissing me."

That's all, over and out

but the story is worth a month of words

with nothing else to tell

and you always have to wonder if it's understood

that you know about the telegraphs that got sent through our confidantes'

confidantes

or if I should try to be innocent of all that?

I'm too scared

I'm too scared

all I can think about is everyone leaving

and she and I on this couch

sitting this close

even if it weren't a crowd

all I can think about is her kissing me

kissing me

kiss me.

It's not a story if it didn't happen,

if it doesn't

it didn't.

Nothing ever happens

350 nights a year
and of those remaining fifteen and a quarter,
five are blacked out with gin or meaningless numb on beer
or you paid so long and so hard for the pleasure
you wonder what made you want it.
Where do you get yours?
How much do you pay for it?

"Do you know what you do to me?" he asked
and placed my hand on his heart—I had a lover like that.
Where did he go to?
I watched the shadows where his eyes might be until dawn
I listened to him start and stumble
his hands make
his hands made
the whole world come
rising up around me.
Just catching his fingertips in a crowded room
the bottom of my belly
drops to the floor.
Behind closed doors
while the rest of the planet sleeps or suffers
is so good too good real good mad good mind gone good.
Lover, lost him.
This planet is so damn big

but nights like those when I felt my heart stretched out taut on a rubber band
with his
are why I bother.

I lie alone
I lie in my bed
I watch the ceiling
and tell myself stories
I tell myself secrets
I remember everything even the things
no one else saw
no one else heard
no one else felt.
I know every cell of my own flesh
I know the taste and the smell and the longings I don't publish.
Witches win
nuns learn
—lovers leap—
girls who think too much
don't get laid
all that often.

L.J. Albertano

Screw Sex
... a kind of rant

Y eah. Screw sex. I mean it. If sex is so inherently fabulous, how come everyone has to be drunk or stoned to do it? Would this be considered a bad attitude? Or does my anti-sex position have more to do with being raised by screaming fundamentalist fruit-loops who convinced me early that Jesus was scrupulously observing my every thought and every deed at every so-called private moment? That lovely sweet-faced man. Hovering. Just saying "no" whenever my innocent fingers wandered near my pubic area. Whenever I so much as considered reading *Peyton Place*. By the time I was an adult I had to enroll in a masturbation class just to find out what the fuss was about. Even so, I was kicked out of the course for not doing my homework.

In all fairness, however, I'm sure I'd like sex a lot if I could do it just like a man.

Let's say you're a planet-beating industrial giant of a guy who regularly has his way with the world. You've got big dough and a slick auto. You put out an all-points bulletin to find the most gorgeous female carcass in the vicinity. So far so good. (Me personally? I favor *male* beauties. Show me where they feed and I'll sneak up and put salt on their tails.)

Anyway, back to you. You're tracking voluptuous babes. Hey! Intelligence is even a plus if not *too* overwhelming. No doubt she is younger, shorter, less financially sound and infinitely more succulent than you are. She is less of just about everything that counts but curves and looks. Because if she is *more* than you of anything else, it's gonna cause friction. And *not* the kind you're angling for.

So. You're the guy. It's your turf, your friends, your movie. You're definitely in the driver's seat. Rush Limbaugh would be proud. The cameras are churning as you squire her into, let's say, Lucques for dinner. "Check it out!" you think as all eyes swivel in your general direction. "I'm with this Claudia Schiffer lookalike and you're with Tammy Faye Bakker!"

Later you do the deed in your impressive bachelor's lair and you dig it. She's in love! You send her home in a taxi with a promise to call. But you don't. You're too busy fighting crime, righting wrong, wreaking vengeance, prowling the skies in your Batmobile and all those other Chief Executive sorts of activities that leave precious little time for romance.

Yes! I'd love having sex like *that* kind of man!

I'd find myself a pretty little construction worker looking good in his tattoos and his torn T-shirt. Then I'd lie my fucking head off. "Oh, Rocco!" I'd scream at the perfect moment. "You oinking animal! It's never been this good. I love how your huge, hot, hard and probing member *yes!* thrusts in and out, in and out like a wild sinewy, sensuous, relentless python yes! relentless, I said, relentlessly throbbing in and out, in and out. . . not unlike a familiar hamburger joint seen on countless bumper stickers around town. Oh, the smell of your manly spunk! The taste of mustard and secret sauce!! You're my kind of guy. I think I. . . love you."

Unfortunately, that's probably not how it's gonna happen for me. I lack the necessary prerequisites. A huge portfolio. Wheelbarrows full of money. And a red Jaguar.

Oh well. As an inveterate hater of rude copulation, I should probably mate with a gay male. Everything up front. I'd never have to hire a detective to discover that my boyfriend has a boyfriend. Perfect platonic harmony. He'd be beautiful. Clever. Thoughtful. Quite social. An exquisite chef. Creative of home and garden. Fascinating conversationalist. And he'd always feign a headache at bedtime. Just for me.

Then again, perhaps Madonna had the right idea: Cruise the avenues after midnight in a stretch limo. I'd do Santa Monica Boulevard. I'd choose a stellar male prostitute with smudged eyes and translucent skin. I'd have my chauffeur lure him over and learn his name. *Ramon.* Splendid. Step right in, *Ramon.* I'd pique his interest by implying I'm a transvestite, and that I was packing a pretty impressive appendage that I'd love to show him if it weren't taped up between my butt cheeks just now. Then, once I'd gotten his attention, I'd ask him to give me what I've been aching for body and soul all these years: *Complete and avid understanding.* Sympathy. World-class listening. Oh, I'd make it worth his while. Long green etchings of General Grant and assorted portraits of other notables.

Then it'd be *oh, baby!* You understand me so deep and hard. *Oooh,* you have the longest, most beautiful comprehension I've ever seen. Mmmm. Listen to me, Daddy! *Listen* to me all night long—oooooooh—with those great big wet and throbbing ears of yours. You take me in so deep, Daddy, all the way. I love how I feel inside your head, licking along your powerful, rock-hard dendrites. Juice up my neurons, Baby! *Oh god*! You sensual oinking he-beast, ignite my synapses with the heat of your flaming empathy! Do it to me. Deep in the medulla. Uhn! Uhn! Squeeze my corpus callosum. Make me scream "sweet *Jee*-sus!" Fill me with your sweet and sticky similes! You got my limbic system shivering on the pelvic bone of language! Don't stop 'til you hit the reptile brain! 'Til you hear a rattle and hiss! 'Til you feel my forked tongue! You got me by the brainstem, Daddy, and you're twisting 'til it feels sooo good! Uhn! Uhn! Do it to me, Daddy! Uhn! Uhn! AAAAAAAAH!

oooooooo. mmmmmmm. hmmmm. sigh.

Care for a cigarette?

Or is this a smoke-free conversation?

One last thing, girls.

Remember (to quote Laura Kightlinger). . . If you're faking orgasm, it's because your man is faking foreplay.

La Vieja Loca

"Hot-blooded heterosexual females are sick of picking up after their slovenly mates," Barbara Bush said, kicking open the door of her 1957 Cadillac Eldorado convertible with its seventeen coats of hand-rubbed cherry-pink paint. I figured Babs—that's what I call Barbara Bush, I call her Babs—I figured Babs meant George. I figured she meant George's awful boxer shorts. And those hideous little garters he wears to hold up his silk socks. But then Barbara is so strange. She once told me she's aroused by the sight of a potbellied man in stupid underwear and black knee garters. She likes young meat, too. But more about that later.

In college, George was a profligate slob. His dorm room was a hellhole of fetid tennis shoes and gooey condoms. We called it the "abattoir." Barbara, of course, was in her medium. She bloomed like a hydroponic tomato. Always the bohemian.

In case you hadn't guessed by now, me and Babs go back a *long* time. We've put away a brewski or two in the land of muchas cervezas. You probably never thought about it much, but I'm here to tell you, Barb's a real down-to-earth, regular kinda gal. And one hell of an exotic dancer. She does a routine with a feather fan and a pair of pink pasties that'd make a stiff sweat golf balls. Clockwise, counterclockwise. She can really shake her booty! And nobody knows about it but her and 150 disadvantaged kids from San Bernardino. Does she give of herself, or what? I'm telling you, the woman has a heart of pure Kruegerrands!

San Berdoo's been her home away from home since back when she rode with the Angels. And weren't *they* the meanest cowboys ever to do a wheelie on a Harley! They used to set each other on fire for the simple joy of watching a pal writhe and shriek like a girl in a porno flick. But Babs had her way with them. She was the baddest mama they ever did see. She got them to time their initiation with her moon cycle. Half the guys in the California chapter earned their red wings when Barbara Bush had her period. But hey, don't mention it to George, OK? He's so easily threatened.

It was through the San Bernardino disadvantaged youngsters benefit that she met this particular simple sociopathic teen she basically destroyed last summer. She took her wanton pleasure and thoroughly roasted his mind, leaving him with no prayer of hooking up with her again. But Barbara's like that. You couldn't keep her down with a steel straitjacket.

It's a little-known fact that Barbara Bush is a Golden Homegirl, conceived and produced in the proud heart of Venice of America. Swear to God, if she wasn't able to slip away from the secret service once a month and jet back to sunny southern Cal to hang with her buds in V13, *that* little lady would be *one hurtin' unit*. Ow! La Vieja Loca!

But about this kid she met. If he were a fifteen-year-old girl, and if Babs had been Roman Polanski in a pair of expensive shades, she'd have peeled back his lurid vaginal lips and done things so startling there that Howard Stern would've blushed. But she's the ex-president's wife, and he's a reprobate teenaged degenerate whom I thought she honored when she called him "young man."

(How anyone could label a putrefying mass of garbage, pizza, undigested chili-dogs, and belched-up beer "young man" is beyond my meager power to comprehend. But there you have it.)

He was a swaggering, bragging, locker-room kind of guy who hoped to seduce Barbara in her hotel, and then lay waste to her credit card. Ordering up room service, flushing lobsters down the toilet, stuff like that. But once he'd crossed her threshold, he was doomed. Babs told me she waited for him on a fake-fur bedspread like a patent-leather anaconda. He approached her hot-pink shrine with less confidence than he'd imagined. With her fingers, she touched his teeth. She simonized them with her tongue. She gave him a kiss that revved his engine so bad, he wanted to park his Buick in her garage then and there.

Barbara, however, had other plans. She handed him a smooth wooden object shaped like a fat Oreo cookie. But where the cream should've been was a tight little axis with a string wound round it. Yo-yo inferno. Rock the cradle, Baby! Ooooooo. Make that yo-yo sing! She made this poor sap strut his stuff. She got him to do *everything*. Walk the dog. Loop the loop. Around the world. Sex and yo-yos. Yo-yos and sex. He ate so much crinkly gray hair that day he had to brush his teeth with a pocket comb.

Oh, they got room service, all right. After that it was *lobsters* and yo-yos and sex. If she had been Bob Guccione or Hugh Hefner, and if he had been a fifteen-year-old girl, she'd have taken Polaroids so deep into the fleshy folds of his meatflower, you could've seen what he'd eaten for breakfast that morning. And many years later, when the lad had reached man-hood, and was about to be crowned, say, Mr. America, or about to be appointed, maybe, Attorney General of the United States, she'd publicly pop out porno pix of his pubic parts to be published in *Playboy* or *Penthouse*. Wow! His nomination would be withdrawn faster than you could say "Vanessa Williams" or "Lani Guiner." Coitus Interruptus Politicus! To put the cherry on the sundae, she'd have gotten him to give her a rim job in the taxi on the way to the airport.

But she's the ex-president's wife, and he's a putrid beer-bellied adolescent. So she washed her hands in the hotel and took a limousine.

One thing I will *never* understand about Barbara Bush. . . . Hot-blooded heterosexual females are still sick of picking up after their slovenly mates. So at the end of every sum-mer, how come she always goes back to George? Could it be her simple recurrent need to tag the entire architecture of Kennebunkport with black cholo letters three feet high? La Vieja. La Vieja Loca. Viva! Viva La Vieja! Viva La Vieja Loca!!

Arriba, George.

Melissa Hung

Good Clean Fun

O livia had been on the job for three months, and as far as she could tell, she was the only Asian with the company, which made her much sought after. Not that it surprised her; she was often one of only a few Asians anywhere she went, this being the Midwest, and most certainly she'd been the only one at her previous places of employment. She had become, she realized, a scarce commodity. But she thought by now, management would have hired another one, the way they were always reminding her that she could work more hours if she wanted. Then again, maybe few Asian American women rebelled so fervently against their strict upbringings the way Olivia did.

Besides, there were only so many hours a week one could spend naked without the nudity losing its specialness, its feeling of freedom. When Olivia first saw the ad, she thought it was a joke, which was why, of course, she called. "Earn big bucks! Do you love being naked?" the ad asked. Well duh, Olivia thought to herself. "Do you have a fun-loving attitude, a pleasant outgoing personality?" Yes again. "Do you like being naked and clean?" Olivia didn't know how to answer that one. In retrospect, she realized it was a badly worded question. Did it mean to ask if one liked being naked but the opposite of dirty (as opposed to being naked and doing dirty lascivious things). Or did it mean literally if one liked cleaning, naked. Because that's what she ended up doing.

As a maid for Good Clean Fun, Olivia undertook household chores completely naked. She'd arrive in a company-issued robe, cut of thick terry cloth. Which, she figured, aimed to conjure the scent of towels, showers, and hence cleanliness into the minds of her clients. Her first act always was to tuck the check into her pocket. She resented the robe; it made her feel silly, like she was gift-wrapped, and she disrobed without grace, as if she were stumbling into her own home after a night of bar-hopping, tossing the robe onto a chair as she walked by. Then it was off to get the Ajax or whatever. (Her clients provided the cleaning supplies of their choice.) She worked in this order: dusting all the rooms first, kitchen next, then bathroom, and floors last. For this last chore, she wore slippers. But other than that she was one nude maid.

Being naked on the job required a certain upkeep of one's looks. Olivia had to shave regularly. She began to tweeze her eyebrows and the stray hairs around her nipples,which she usually didn't bother with. And then there was the quagmire about her pubic hair. Should she shave it all off, do the Brazilian triangle thing, or what? She opted for a simple trim, nothing that required too much maintenance.

For the most part, the men behaved themselves. Management made it quite clear over the phone that they were not sending out strippers, dancers, or whores. Just maids. Naked ones.

What bothered Olivia most was the knowledge that her clients (all older single men, of course, with the exception of one couple in their thirties, Josh and Laura) had picked her, as if she were a mail-order bride. The agency asked what sort of physical attributes clients preferred. Olivia tried to get into her clients' minds. Surely they all had O-fetishes. Maybe they had a sick desire to see an Asian woman cleaning, scrubbing away at the floors on her knees, her breasts wiggling subserviently. Little miss lotus blossom geisha girl bullshit. Inevitably, one of her clients would confide that he once had an Asian girlfriend, or a whole string of them.

The men thought she was beautiful because she was Asian, and maybe, she tried to reason to herself that, was OK. In the course of cleaning bachelor pads, she grew to understand a distinction in what it was exactly that pissed her off about guys with yellow fever. After all, anything can be fetishized: feet, glasses, big toes, detached earlobes, whatever. If someone thought her sexy because of her looks, well, good.

But if someone thought she was good-looking and smart and charming and exotic because of the fact she was Asian, well, she was going to have to recite to them her rules on how not to treat an Asian American woman. 1) Do not call me Oriental. I am not a rug or a salad. 2) Do not take me out for Chinese or Japanese food. 3) Do not expect me to take you out for Chinese or Japanese food. 4) Do not ask me where I am from. 5) When I answer Texas, do not ask me where I'm really from. 6) Do not tell me I'm cute. 7) Do not expect me to know how to do math, especially in my head. 8) Do not expect me to know what the family structure in the Philippines is, or what sect of Buddhism is predominant in southern China. I've never been to either of those places. 9) Do not ask me where I learned to speak English so well. 10) Fuck off.

If clients could choose her, Olivia was choosy right back. She refused, many times, to return to slimy customers. Her client list streamlined, she could work without disturbance. In the beginning, though, just about everything disturbed her. Some of her clients would sit in one place and watch as she crossed their line of vision now and then. Some followed her from room to room. Both actions creeped her out, especially the latter. But she got used to it, and it became fine by her as long as they kept a certain distance. Some of them pretended to read the newspaper, or watch TV, but she knew they were looking at her. Olivia liked being watched. It turned her on.

The first time Olivia arrived to clean a house, she rang the doorbell somewhat nervously. She had driven by in her Saturn twice before she finally parked. Didn't want to knock on the wrong door, not in a bathrobe. The house seemed newer than its neighbors, a red-brick and white-trim one-story, neatly surrounded by azaleas. Keith came to the door, an equally neatly-kept man with blond hair, a square face that seemed too easily at rest in spite of its sharp angles. In his forties, Olivia estimated. She smirked and introduced herself, "Hi I'm Olivia from Good Clean Fun Maid Service. I'm here to clean your house and only to clean your house. Don't get any ideas I'll kick you in the nuts." She drew her line at the threshold before she crossed it.

Keith laughed, and smiled broadly. His laugh had been too loud, putting Olivia on guard. He seemed a prodigal brat, the kind of man who placed an ad proclaiming himself a sugar daddy. She could see it now: "Sugar Daddy 4U. Romantic, wealthy, man seeking financial arrangement with clean, attractive, slender woman. Me 45, you younger. Meet my needs and I'll meet yours. College students, single moms, bored housewives. Virgins OK."

Olivia undressed with an eye on Keith. Her breasts were small and nearly flat, her ass two perfect melons. Olivia's ass had quite a devoted fan club. Among its members were her current boyfriend Jacob, ex-boyfriends, waiters and chefs at various restaurants where she had waitressed, a blonde lesbian she once met at a bar, and a roommate's out-of-town friend. And those were just the people who had voiced their admiration directly to her. Olivia also had a bit of a belly, which had defeated her in every attempt to reduce it. So many wasted sit-ups. As she stood naked before Keith, brushing her bangs out of her eyes, Olivia noticed a salient bulge in his pants. Men, so easily amused and aroused. Sluts. Did their dicks ever discriminate?

Keith showed her where he kept his cleaning supplies, by the washer and dryer. As Olivia visited each room with a ridiculous feather duster, she wondered if maybe this was a bad idea. A friend had dared Olivia to take the job. She fluttered the duster over a row of books. She couldn't decide if the whole thing was creepy or silly. It reminded her of a *Seinfield* episode, the one where Jerry was discussing the kinds of naked. There was good naked, like hairbrushing naked. And bad naked, like squatting. Cleaning could lend itself to some very bad naked. So Olivia thought ahead in an attempt to prevent any bad nakedness. Vacuuming, that was probably good. Doing the dishes, that was OK naked. Scrubbing the bath tub, she didn't know about that. Was there a graceful way to do that?

Olivia turned to proceed to the kitchen. She saw that Keith had been sitting in a living room armchair the whole time, his legs akimbo, face flushed, one hand on a cheek. He didn't look away but continued to study her. Staring was too harsh a word. He looked at her as if he were contemplating a piece of art. And that look, that faintly studious, wholly quiet, lambent look made Olivia blush. When men looked at her like that, with such dreamlike awe, Olivia could not help but blush. She felt herself growing moist between her legs, not because she was at all attracted to Keith, but because of the way his head tilted just a degree and his eyes blinked but never took themselves off of her.

Then Keith ruined it. He winked at her. From that point on, Olivia referred to him as The Winker.

In spite of The Winker's blatant display of sliminess, Olivia did not feel threatened by him, and after she finished polishing his house, she agreed to return in two weeks.

Then she drove straight to Jacob's work at the bookstore and made love to him in a bathroom stall. Standing—one of her favorite positions—often taxed Jacob's endurance. But the matter of his girlfriend showing up unannounced in a bathrobe was different.

Leaning against the wall with her legs slightly apart, she grabbed his crotch, fumbled at the top button, and undid the zipper with one hand, while holding his head to her face with the other. His cock, already hard, sprung toward her as she lowered his jeans down from his waist. She squeezed him there, held his hardness close to her belly. Slowly, deliberately, she kissed him, and in her hand, his cock grew even harder. Her tongue tingled, a flickering light in the wet cave of his mouth. She leaned her head back, exposing the slope of her neck. Jacob bit her at the junction of neck and jaw line before untying her robe, tasting her breasts. He thought she smelled vaguely of Comet, or maybe it was coming from the restroom. Holding his cock with a hand, he teased the lips of her pussy, dipping in her wetness and drawing circles across its slippery surface. Then he pushed his hands onto the back of her thighs. Lifting her against his hips, he pushed her back into the wall for leverage. She crossed her legs. He entered her, thrusting impatiently. Her body seemed to be gliding in an atmosphere of its own.

He looked at her, her mouth was ajar, her eyes sleepy almost.

Jacob couldn't stand the thought of other men looking at his girlfriend. Olivia had come into his life just as he was trying to figure out what to do with it. She had steered him back to school after a four-year hiatus. In return, he tried to remain supportive of all her pursuits, but this job made him nervous. He thought she would tire of it, but three months later, Olivia remained a naked maid. It disturbed him that she should return from work so hot and bothered. He felt threatened by it. In particular, he hated The Winker. Jacob wanted to know about The Winker's habits and home, the type of clothes he wore and his degree of cleanliness. He wanted to know what was in his fridge. Olivia said she had no reason to open his fridge, but she did offer Jacob this fact: the man owned one of those superfluous wooden banana hangers, placed on his kitchen countertop, from which he hung bananas. They speculated on the types of women The Winker dated (the miniskirt), how lucky he got (slightly more than half the time), and if he had a steady girlfriend (no). They also wondered if any of the women had discovered his choice of cleaning services. Would they—or she—dump his ass? Olivia thought about it. If Jacob hired a naked maid, she would become enraged, then upset. Now here she was, the Other Woman—a maid of the most untraditional sort, not like the hotel maid or the office janitor, sweeping while you're absent and bringing every little thing back to order, but a nude maid, perhaps the subject of arguments between males and females, or of barroom fodder among Keith's buddies. Jacob wondered what The Winker said about his Olivia.

The Winker, Olivia also revealed, did not wink every time, but did it often enough to re-inforce his name. Olivia and Jacob began to bet when he would do it. As the months passed, their bets became more specific. Jacob guessed that he would wink after Olivia cleaned the kitchen, or as she was returning the mop and bucket to its place. Whoever lost the bet had to perform the sexual act of the other person's choice. In this way, Jacob came to suck Olivia's clit for over an hour with an index finger up her asshole.

A little jealousy, it seemed to Olivia, was healthy.

One September afternoon, after Olivia had been working roughly five months at Good Clean Fun, she arrived at The Winker's house to find a carefully folded note taped to the door. "Olivia, had to run some errands. Be back later. Key in the mailbox." He had left the check on the dining room table. Olivia disrobed and grabbed the duster. What did he mean by later? What an odd choice of words. Most people would write "be back soon." If he was going to show up later, she would start in his bedroom first. Olivia wanted to snoop.

She pulled the top drawer of his dresser, which rolled out smoothly toward her. Black and white socks. Boring. She shut that one and pulled out the next, which stored boxers, some in assorted colors, some plaid, a few in zebra print of unnatural colors, one with dogs and cats on it. Then Olivia found a few briefs. She snapped the drawer back. The bottom drawer held T-shirts.

Olivia was beginning to lose hope of finding anything remotely telling. She surveyed the room and spotted the mahogany-stained night stand by the bed. On it was the digital alarm clock, touch-sensitive bullet-silver lamp, and square box of tissues she had dusted many times before. But she had never opened the drawer. She rolled it all the way till it stopped. A box of condoms, a notepad, and beneath that, a magazine folded open to a spread of young East Asian guys touching their massive cocks.

Olivia could not believe what she was seeing. She had seen the chopsticks, the green tea, and the kanji books, and suspected The Winker was a rice king. But actually, he was a rice queen. How could she not have noticed it before? The sixteen pairs of shoes, the hair care products, his collection of Broadway musical soundtracks?

But why would a gay man hire a naked woman to clean his house? Olivia stood by his bed with her hands to her face, trying to figure it out. And swiftly, her frenzied brain came to one conclusion. Maybe she looked like a boy to him with her nearly flat chest and short hair, bringing new meaning to the stereotype that "they all look alike." Horrified, she had to leave the house right then. She left the magazine on top of the condoms in the drawer and locked up the house in a rush.

That afternoon, Olivia quit Good Clean Fun. It was starting to get cold anyhow, and she had not looked forward to wearing leggings with the robe, and then a coat over that. How ridiculous would that look? As she stood in the company offices, emptying the pockets of her robe, she found The Winker's check for the day.

Olivia had not finished any housework. She cashed it anyway.

Translation

I cannot read this sentence. I don't know what it says. And it lays unread by anyone for years, unseen inside me. Sometimes I am able to make out a word: clit, cock, fuck. Sometimes I think they might be other words: self, sleep, hurt. I am walking through the streets on a heavy afternoon with these unwrapped words loose within when I meet you. Months pass before we stare into a kiss, a careful construction of angles, flickering tongues, slow wanting tugs.

In the evenings, in the coolness of your house, you ask what I'm thinking as I lie on my back, the unblinking ceiling above us. You, on your side, your face so close that your stubble brushes my cheek, that the moisture of your breath dissipates into heat across my ear. I wonder, for an answer, if images count. But I say nothing. Your hand has not stopped moving, gliding across my breasts, pausing in my navel, squeezing my thighs, lingering. Teeth on a shoulder. Lips to a hardened nipple. The smooth, flat top of my foot rubbing against your foot. The perfect curves of your ass; my hand a waterfall, passing over and over them.

You take my body in your arms and pull me as you sit up, unfold me. We sit facing each other, tangled arms in each other's laps. The crease in your thigh like a road. The curls on your belly, a patch of warmth. The head of your cock, so smooth like a rock shaped by moving water. Lightly, I run the barest of my fingertips there, delicately following the ridge. A whisper of a touch. Not like the way your fingers press down on my clit, drawing circles, then spinning. Not that firm stroking pressure, your insistence.

I close my eyes and imagine we are touching each other like this in public. At the symphony, with the swell of orchestral triumph floors below us, the musicians reduced at this distance to black specks, to movements. But the rumbling of the tympanum, the plaintive yearning of strings, just as pure. And up in the mezzanine, your fly open, my skirt hiked up, we masturbate each other, your fat cock in my hand.

(Dick is a weak word, limp, flaccid.) But your cock, your cock right now pointing at me, pulsing. My hand moving rapidly along your shaft. Your fingers inside me, my hand wrapped tightly around your cock. Our bodies rhyming.

Without warning, you push me flat on my back, and enter me. Everything becomes warm. Everything becomes an verb. Your mouth buried in my neck, exhaling as you thrust, stirring a sensation so rich, like a rainstorm forming on my throat. An energy gathering momentum. My jaw my arm my toes my clit tingles beneath you.

The alphabet spills loose.

And I think I might come close to reading the sentence now.

Michelle Glaw

A Surprising Sexual Fantasy

How many of you folks out there like Holly Hobbie? How much do you like her? Well, I like her. *A lot*. I discovered this when I was trying to decide what to write about, and an epiphany descended upon me like a large parrot. It arose from my unconscious mind quite ferociously and wouldn't go away. I have concluded that there can only be one reason for this: I must secretly want to have sex with. . . Holly Hobbie. Yes.

And now that I think about it, she is my ideal girl. I love romantic-looking country girls. . . Anyway. Here's how my fantasy goes:

First of all, I imagine that underneath her large bonnet she has a huge strawberry afro. I think afros are so sexy.

Then I imagine that I would find her basking in the shade, on top of a hill, eating an apple and some cornbread. I would approach her, introduce myself, sit down beside her, and I would slowly remove her bonnet. I would play with her afro, her head in my lap, us looking up at the sky for shapes in the clouds.

Then I would close her eyes with one of my fingers, and kiss her freckled face, and her mouth. She would tell me silly things like "I love you!" and "Come play with me!" You know, Doll Talk. Only she's flesh and bones.

And while she whispers these things to me, I take off her pinafore and touch her nipples through the fabric of her thin calico dress. Her breasts are surprisingly large, so I can see why she always wears a pinafore.

Then Holly Hobbie puts her arms around my neck, moving them down slowly and firmly across my spine and finally to my ass.

She is sweating, so I unbutton her dress, and take it off over her huge 'fro. I am already naked. I've been naked since the beginning of this escapade. She is sweating, I am sweating. Not from the heat—it's actually a little windy—the sweat is from the tension between us.

By this time we are really making out on the ground beneath the tree. I pull off her pantaloons—which are actually pretty dorky, now that I think about it. Anyway.

She has a nice pussy. It is hidden behind a small patch of blond hair. It is typical of every pussy that most people have in their fantasies: tight and childlike.

I'm actually at this point disappointed in Holly Hobbie as a lover. She is not reciprocating at all, but I eventually go down on her, my tongue snug inside her, and I wiggle it around and poke it in and out. She tastes very bland, kind of like sawdust, only wet.

I move my tongue up and lick her clit until she's about to climax. It doesn't take long.

Then I stop. I sit up. She is still laying down, languishing, and I tell her to lay across my lap on her stomach. She has a groggy look on her face; she is panting like a little puppy.

And she obeys.

She lays across me with her big tits squished into my thighs, and her little freckled butt is in the air.

I happen to have a switch from the tree, and I use it on her. I spank her so hard she gasps for air and screams. Weak doll screams.

She's crying pathetic little fake tears. I know they're fake because her perfect cunt is throbbing and dripping onto the grass.

Her ass is red now, and I keep on spanking her, occasionally gagging her with a half-eaten apple, which she bites into. The switch makes sharp swishing noises.

I like those sounds. And I want to keep hearing them. This is what I do to bad lovers, because this is what they want. They want and deserve more punishment. They want more attention of any kind.

I notice that her little cries have turned into moans. Slow groans, so I stop, and spread her legs wide open and stick the wide end of the switch inside her. I shove it up there good, and I make her crawl about thirty feet, to the edge of the hill, with the switch sticking out of her cunt like a Doberman's tail.

I stroke her spine and her sore ass one more time, and pinch it so the switch moves in and out. Then I pull it out. I like watching that.

I push her and I watch her climax violently as she rolls down the hill.

And in the end, I'm surprised she did all this.

Michelle Glaw

An Essay on Sex and Music
(Notes from an Improvisational Live Performance)

A lot of people turn music on when they have sex. I don't. It bugs me. Music and sex are a corny combo. It interferes with the natural rhythms of your body when you are fucking.

One of two things usually happens when the music is on: 1) My stupid partner starts singing along and moving in sync with the song, or 2) I get distracted by the music and start just listening to the words and I stop fucking. I just lay there. (Or both things happen simultaneously.)

I love music, don't get me wrong. And I like sex. Sure, it can be fun—if the person knows what they're doing. I just can't stand it when someone thinks they're really hot and they put on cheesy jazz, like Kenny G. Or worse, Loggins and Messina. I hate that. Cheesy.

For instance, this one guy I fucked enjoyed doing it to that song "Time After Time" by Cyndi Lauper. It was so tacky. I mentioned it to him, told him how it bugged me, and he said he "respected how I felt." Of course he did. The asshole was getting laid for the first time in years. Dork.

The pseudo-Beatnik guys (speaking of jazz) will try to impress me with Coltrane and their knowledge of coffee beans. Usually, this kind of fellow likes to concentrate on poetry rather than on getting me off. Then, after sex, he'll turn on his stupid, cerebral KTRU public radio crap and write a poem about how he fucks like Henry Miller or Bukowski while I'm trying to get the hell away from him.

These boys become the ex-boyfriends who try to win me back by "serenading" me on their guitars with some out-of-tune babbling and weak chord structure. The whole boy-meets-girl-girl-dumps-boy thing comes into play here, but these sorts of guys are not really human, they are just goateed aliens from the planet Kerouac.

Or I'll be over at some Gen Xer's pad, and he'll try to seduce me by showing me his vinyl collection. Oooh! He has the Beatles on vinyl! He's so cooooool! Ha. Whatever. This courting ritual is silly, and unnecessary, because the only reason I'm over there is to fuck him. He knows that. I know that. He just wants me to think he's "with it."

When I was a teenager, before I started having sex, I made out with a few guys my own age. My tastes tended toward the geeky sci-fi types who were crazy about bands like Pantera and Metallica. The scenario was always the same: I would go upstairs to their room and we would lay on the bed. I would stare at the Pamela Anderson/Kathy Ireland posters on the ceiling, while "he" would be pretending to play the drums to Mötley Crüe. Then suddenly, he would lunge at me and try to attack one of my small, secondary sex glands. It was like a game. Then they would maul my face with their tongues, and pull back at a pivotal point in the song to lip sync an innuendo to me. It was usually some corny ballad, like "Give Me Something to Believe In" by Poison.

This was supposed to make me put out.

Sometimes it would almost happen, but we'd get caught. It was a bizarre ritual. If the tape stopped, the boy would freeze up, then turn the tape over and go back to business as usual. It never got beyond heavy petting with these heavy metal guys. And they were so virginal. It was like the music gave them a sense of vicarious virility.

And speaking of near misses, not too long ago there was a certain fellow I almost slept with. . . . He was a cute guy, but he was on all these meds and he was a big loser, a recovering drug addict who still did drugs and abused Ritalin. Did I mention he used to be a skinhead? Anyway, he was still cute.

He was crashing at my place, and we decided to fuck. I asked him for a rubber but he didn't have one. So I suggested that we go get some. Of course I bought the damned things, and they were twelve bucks. At that point I'm thinkin': "This better be good."

But it was problems from the get-go. First of all, he had trouble getting it up because of the meds. Then he wanted to hear some music. So I turned on the radio, but it was BBC news, which depressed him. I just wasn't thinking about it. I didn't care. Then I noticed that his dick had started swirling around of its own accord. That bored me and turned me off. Way off. So I kicked him out of my room. I mean, that's too much trouble for one lousy fuck.

So I guess I just like things quiet. Not even a radio. Stark.

Sassy Johnson

Fucked-Up White Trash Porn Flick, Part One

If the trailer's a rockin'
don't bother knockin'
just step on up the cinder block porch
throw open the screen door
and don't do no talkin'

I t's a humid July evening, around dusk. The air is thick with mosquitoes. I park my car on the side of the gravel road; the ruts were too deep for me to continue driving. Other people must have had the same problem, I realize. The roadside is littered with brightly-colored low-rider trucks, windows tinted.

I'm in Mississippi, visiting my family. Earlier I had run into some old high school buddies at the 7-11. They were on their afternoon smoke break and invited me to a party. They didn't give me an address, just said, "keep on drivin' down Red Bird Road past the detour sign, and keep goin' until you see the PARTY TRAILER."

So I'm walking, and as I walk the air gets thicker, and the mosquitoes get so dense that I don't even notice them anymore, except when one makes it into my nostril or down my throat, if I open my mouth. I'm sweating and panting and smoking my mom's Virginia Slim Menthol Light 120s (that's all I could find lying around the house) and I'm wondering exactly why I decided to come to this party, held by friends I hadn't seen in six years. Curiosity, mostly. That's why. I'm listening for music, for the party. I hear crickets chirping. Eighteen-wheelers on the highway nearby. Dogs barking. An occasional gun shot. . . hunting. It's something season. I don't know what. I could never keep it straight.

I notice a light up ahead to my right. Finally. I turn into the driveway, which is really just tire tracks through knee-high grass, and sure enough the trailer fits the description I was given. It's one of those short, white ones with a thick, dark-brown stripe running the length of it. There's a mangy dog chained to a tree out front, a swing set rusted orange and black, and a pickup truck with tires taller than my waist and a Confederate flag for the back window. The trailer is dark. The light I saw was coming from the bug whackers, one on each side of the cinderblock porch, meant to ward off the mosquitoes and water bugs attracted to the property by the small stagnant pond nearby. A wooden "Home Sweet Home" sign with hearts and little black children painted on it hangs over the screen door, crooked. What was I *soooo* curious about that made me come here? But it's too late to turn back.

I walk around to the back of the trailer, avoiding the dog, who doesn't move anyway. Maybe he's dead. My friends are all there. Two of them are in folding lawn chairs, one's perched on a five-gallon bucket, another's on the doorstep, and there's one person I've never seen before, straddling the keg. They are all drinking beer out of Dixie cups, and the guys are spitting their snuff onto the ground in long, brown streams that cut through the dust.

"We've been a-waiting fer ya!" they say when they see me. "Let the festivities begin! YEEEE HAW WHOOOO!!"

There is a scramble of lanky, hairy bodies and drunken yelps. Wayne gets up to move the truck around to the back so we can have some music. Bubba goes into the trailer to fetch me a Dixie cup. Tammy follows Bubba (he is her stepbrother/lover) and Missy points to a shed fifteen feet from us, just on the other side of the barbed wire fence, and whispers, "That's where we grow our weed." She sneaks off to get some. This leaves me alone with the person straddling the keg.

I can't tell if it is a boy or a girl. The person has not yet spoken, and after a few awkward moments I brilliantly say, "So," in my usual way of lacking small talk. She looks up, and I know that she is a she when I see her eyes. She looks me up and down, smirks, and stands up just as Wayne makes it back around the trailer with the truck. The headlights shine directly on her for an instant. She's tall, probably six feet, with short, stringy, blond hair poking out from underneath her Marlboro hat, and she has the clearest green eyes I've ever seen. She's wearing cut-offs, a Metallica T-shirt, no shoes. I look at her, wondering which trailer park she came from, and reveling in the fact that my small Mississippi hometown had indeed birthed another lesbian. She sees me looking at her.

"Wayne, I'm. . . uh. . . gonna give her a. . . uh . . . tour," she says, motioning for me to follow her into the trailer. Naturally I do. We step onto the orange and green shag carpet, which is littered with stale Fritos and beer cans. Over the wrestling match on the TV, I can hear Tammy and Bubba fucking in the back room.There is no door, just a dirty flowered sheet hanging in the doorway.

I follow the Metallica girl into the kitchen, where she shoves me on top of the plastic kitchen table. This movement startles a few roaches from their sleep, and they scurry up the wall, some onto the ceiling. She puts my hand between her legs and says, "You want some of this?" SHIT!! I thought she was a she, but she's don't have long, hard things inside their shorts (usually). I am completely speechless.

She must sense my panic, because she laughs and drops her pants. "Thank God it's not a dick," is all I'm thinking when I see the harness. She pulls a case of Spam over to the table and stands on it, making her crotch eye-level. In the harness is. . . a corn dog. Now I'm wondering how she knew that I liked corndogs so much. . . Then all questions of how or why disappear when she touches my lips with her corn dog dildo. It's still warm. I take small bites as she gently thrusts it into my mouth. She moans as if she can feel it.

Wayne has turned on some Guns N' Roses outside the trailer, and pot smoke drifts in through the cracks in the boards covering the window above the sink. It's dark now, except for the light from the bug whackers. I take my time with the corndog (as much time as I can, seeing that I love corn dogs so much and all) and after I take the last bite, I pull the stick out of the harness with my teeth. She gasps and exhales in sheer pleasure.

I look around the kitchen for something that will enable this strange scenario to continue. My eyes come to rest on a can of EZ Cheese, and as she is removing her harness, I am removing her shirt. I grab the EZ Cheese and squirt it all over her chest, push her to the floor and fall on top of her. We are ripping each other's clothes off, like the guys wrestling on the TV, rolling around on top of each other, covered in EZ Cheese, licking it off of one another to the sounds of "Sweet Child O' Mine" and the bugs frying outside.

Fucked-Up White Trash Porn Flick, Part Two

Y ou know that saying: the bigger the man's nose, the larger the pecker? Or how a person's shoe size reflects the size of their wiener? I always wondered what the size of a person's truck meant in relation to their genitalia. . . .

Mississippi. Summer 1991. I am visiting with my family before I go away to college. It just so happens that my visit coincides with the annual Monster Truck Show held at the county fairgrounds. This is quite a coincidence, since the annual Monster Truck Show had always been a yearly bonding session for my stepdad, stepbrother and me.

After a quick dinner of fried chicken and macaroni and cheese, I found myself wedged between these two men—father and son—in my stepdad's rusty gray pickup truck, setting out on a thirty-mile journey to the fairgrounds, accompanied only by KKK 94.5! *Nonstop Country*! and a pack of sweet-smelling Red Man chewing tobacco. For comfort, I tell myself that the ride there will be the worst part of this excursion. I am sticking to my sweaty, obese twelve-year-old stepbrother as he breathes through his nostrils, heavily, and sings along with the radio in a scratchy falsetto voice. The drone of the monster truck engines will be a joy compared to that kid's voice.

When we arrive at the fairgrounds, I jump out of the truck, not even waiting for my stepbrother to exit first. I land in a sea of hairy, bare, beer bellies hanging over tight-fitting Levis. The three of us enter the makeshift stadium. We have front row seats.

"WE DON'T HALF-ASSED DO NOTHIN'—NO SIREE! IF WE'RE GOIN' TO GO TO THE MONSTER TRUCK SHOW, BY GOD, WE'RE GOIN' TO BE DEAF AND COVERED IN MUD WHEN WE LEAVE, BY GOD. WE'RE GOIN' TO DO IT RIGHT! YESSIREE."

The show got started shortly after we took our seats, and it was just as I had remembered. . . or had tried *not* to remember. I spend half the time vibrating in my seat from the ungodly amounts of engine power and testosterone, and the other half of the time making runs to the concession stand to get chili dogs for my stepbrother, a corn dog for myself, and Pabst Blue Ribbon beers for my stepdad and me. When I got back from my final concession stand visit my stepbrother is whining about someone's autograph he wants to get after the show. "I WANT HER AUTOGRAPH, DADDY! THAT LADY'S!" I assume he is talking about some washed up country singer that he had seen in the audience and I ignore him.

When the show ends, my stepdad slips me a twenty and asks me to take the kid to get his autographs. "Great. This is doing *great* things for my image," I think. "Leading around this prepubescent boy by the hand through a herd of monster trucks through knee-deep mud to get autographs from their half-drunk drivers." I'm glad that I am half-drunk too.

We are wading through the mud when my step brother releases my hand and runs ahead of me screaming, "THAT'S HER! HEY LADY! HEY LADY! THAT'S HER! THAT'S HER!" I stop. The woman turns to face my stepbrother. She is signing his program. I scurry up to them, scolding him. "Don't run away like that again, Johnny Wayne, you scared me! You might get lost. Are you OK?" I look up at the woman. It works. She has stopped the autograph mid-sentence and is meeting my gaze. Suddenly monster trucks become my passion, my drive, my sole purpose of existence. She asks if we want to see her truck —the winning truck, I might add. We both nod, smiling big . Really big. Both in awe of the Monster Truck Madonna.

She walks slightly ahead of us through the mud to her truck. She is small and boyish— short brown hair, blue and yellow coveralls—and has her helmet dangling from her hand. WOW. She tells my stepbrother to stand underneath the truck (He's short; it's a big truck) and to watch what happens when she starts it. Then she winks at me, opens the door, and asks if I would like to take a look inside. I don't even answer, just jump the six feet into the cab of the truck and plop down on her front seat. She starts the truck and closes the door. Then she slides over me and sits in my lap, facing me. No words. She kisses me. Softly at first—then harder and wetter—harder and wetter—as she unzips her yellow and blue coveralls. They fall to the floorboard. Naked underneath. No clothes. She stops kissing me as she backs up a little bit and sits on the gearshift."OH MY," I'm thinking. "OH MY. WOW. UM, WOW." I watch as the gearshift disappears and reappears. . . disappears and re-appears, to her rise and fall.

"UH. . . WOW." While she is fucking the gearshift she *somehow* manages to undress me. I don't know how. I am in awe, my eyes glued to her. She uses my shirt to tie my wrists to the gun rack in the back window. And she teases me. Rising up and down on that damn gearshift. Slipping her foot over to rev the engine to keep my stepbrother entertained under-neath the truck.

She is torturing me, making me watch her get off on that piece of metal, when I am certain that I could do a much better job; though the noises she makes when she comes are from the gut of a beast I have never before heard. I think maybe this is the end of our little encounter. She has gotten off, I have served my purpose.

I don't know how long we have been in the truck. The noises from the crowd have died down a bit. I am hoping that my stepbrother didn't hear her. I am hoping that he hasn't gotten mangled on something underneath the truck. My mind is racing. Then she rises like a phoenix off that gearshift, everything in slow motion, in a haze. She reaches down and picks up a Budweiser longneck from the floorboard. I am feeling thirsty myself. I'm sure she could use some refreshment too. But then she slips the bottle between my legs, and. . . she puts it in me. Yes in me. I was tied to the gun rack, so what could I do? I'm thinking, "What if it BREAKS? SHIT!! What if there is still some beer in it? SHIT! How long has it been on the floor? Who else has used this bottle in this manner before? SHIT. . . SHIT. . . SHIT!!" But like I said before, I was tied to the gun rack, what could I do??? Just relax and enjoy.

I hear my name crackling over the PA system. Guess my stepdad is ready to go. She unties me and I throw on my clothes, jump out of the truck, and grab my stepbrother, who was still entranced by the inner workings of the truck (just as I was). She honks and drinks a beer as we walk through the empty bleachers into the parking lot.

My stepdad beams ."You kids have a good time?" he asks. We both smile—big smiles—and I smell of stale beer.

Fucked-Up White Trash Porn Flick,

Part 3

S mall-town Septembers bring cool breezes at dusk, family fish frys, locusts singing in the night, the final garden crop, school buses. . . and hayrides.

As a member of the First Baptist Church of Pascagoula, Mississippi, I had quite a lot of religious duties. My mom was a Sunday School teacher and church pianist until I was in the fifth grade. When I was eleven, I won the annual Bible Jeopardy trivia competition, beating all of the high school students with my zeal for memorization of the Holy Word. I sang in the adult choir. I directed the children's Christmas pageant. I performed the morning gathering to the summer Bible School students. AHHH, yes. . . In the summers of my childhood I could often be found sitting around the campfire at church camp, singing Christian songs to a broken-down guitar. . . eating homemade cookies for snack time at Vacation Bible School. . . enjoying Sunday afternoon potluck lunches following a sermon I didn't understand. I developed an obsessive-compulsive disorder that demanded I count the number of bricks in the wall behind the pulpit while the pastor spoke.

I witnessed firsthand the music of Christy Lane ("One Set of Footprints in the Sand,") and heard the story of the deadly car wreck she miraculously survived; how she spent years learning to walk again. She called the children forward to sit at her feet while she serenaded the sanctuary. My mom bought a copy of her book and I got an autographed record.

All of these activities were good to pass the time, but it seemed that every church function was just another ordinary gathering, just another event paving the way for. . . the annual youth hayride. See, the youth group was taken on a hayride every September. This was my favorite part of belonging to a church. I began to calendar my year in relation to the hayride: Christmas pageant, nine months until the hayride. . . Lent, five months more. . . Vacation Bible School., three months. . . summer camp, two months . . .and so it was until the day arrived.

September 1991. Seventeen years old. My senior year in high school. My last year as a member of the youth fellowship of the First Baptist Church of Pascagoula, Mississippi. My last hayride. Since college had not yet started for the fall semester, I invited a few of my friends who had graduated before me to attend the annual hayride. Two girls, Tammy and Sherry, had gone away to an all-girls Christian Community College in Alabama. Sherry was my favorite. She had the biggest blue eyes in the county, and was probably the prettiest girl in the world. I had once heard the youth director talking about her as being "unnatural," but I just didn't see how that could be possible. She was the sweetest and prettiest girl I knew.

Both Tammy and Sherry agreed to come along. We all piled into the back of the dump truck (The pastor also ran a gravel business on the side.) and began the drive to the country. Me, Sherry, Tammy, and eighteen other God-fearing youth. Someone had brought along a guitar. Someone else, a jam box and an Amy Grant tape. We were to drive to the pastor's gravel yard in the country, stop for a cookout, then return to the church to be picked up by our parents. As we drove, it began to get cool out and people started digging seats for themselves in the hay. I saw John and Laura holding hands, even though it was against the rules. Sherry had almost buried herself in the hay.

"Make your seat so deep that your butt is on the metal," she told me. So I did. I did everything that girl told me to do. The metal was cold on my butt. "Do you feel it?" she asked.

"Feel what?"

"The truck vibrating," she answered, and pushed her hand through the hay to touch my thigh. OH YEEAAAHH. It did feel kind of. . . funny. . . on my *private*s.

"Yeah," I replied.

"Where do you feel it?" she whispered in my ear. But I couldn't tell her THAT! How improper! My mother taught me never to discuss matters concerning my *privates* to anyone. . . ever. "WHERE?" she demanded.

"I dunno," I said.

"TELL ME!!!"

"No."

She grabbed my hand. "Well, I feel it here." She put my hand between her legs. I could feel the fabric of her skirt bunching up around my hand, which was trembling, by the way.

"Um. . . me too," I admitted.

She then put her hand between my legs. Where no man had ever dared to venture, as my brother used to joke. "Lift up my skirt so I can feel it more," she instructed. I did. Her panties were silky, and wet. "Now just do what I do," she told me. "Follow me. . . like in that Sunday school game we used to play, 'Follow Jesus.' Pretend I'm Jesus," she said.

She slid her hand inside my pants and into my panties and twirled her fingers around in my pubic hair. I did the same to her. I could feel myself blushing. I was glad that there were no street lights in the country. She began rubbing me in a slight circular motion. I could feel myself getting wet down there. I was worried that I had peed on her or something, I was so wet. We had just stuck our fingers inside each other when the dump truck stopped moving.

I told Sherry to pretend she was asleep, and I did the same. Everyone got out and I heard the guitar playing start and I knew that we were safe.

Sherry said, "I'm hungry, but I don't know if I can wait for the cook out. Do you have anything I can eat?"

"I have some left over Skittles in my pocket," I said.

"You don't know, do you?" she said, laughing. "That's not what I meant. Just do what I do." I was puzzled, but I agreed.

We lay down in the hay, pushing it up all around us so no one could see inside. She took off her skirt and her silky panties. I did the same. She kissed me and stuck her fingers inside me, this time moving them in and out. I did the same. Then she got up and moved so that her head was at my feet , with her feet at my head. And she lay down on top of me. "Now this is what I want to eat," she said, and she pressed her lips to my *privates* .

I did the same to her, modeling my licks and strokes and nips to hers. It was unlike anything I had ever done. She was dripping all this wet stuff on my face and I didn't even care.

It didn't taste like pee at all. She felt so soft and slimy on my tongue. When she started to gasp, so did I, and our tongues moved faster, around and around, until I just couldn't take it any longer. I didn't know what was happening to me. With a couple of moans and a soft scream, we collapsed into each other. The guitar was still going; they were on the last chorus of "Onward, Christian Soldiers" and they were calling us together for a pre-dinner prayer.

We quickly got dressed, knowing if we were not present for the prayer our absence would be noticed. The pastor asked our guest Sherry to pray. "Thank you Lord for your food, fellowship, and friendship. We feed one another through the love you give us. . . " she squeezed my hand amen.

"Thank you Sherry, and the first burger is yours!"

"No thanks, I'm not hungry," she replied with a smile.

Fucked-Up White Trash Porn Flick, Part 5

Well, it's rodeo season again. . . and, as usual, I've been under much financial strain. So I got me a part time job up there at the rodeo, like I have every year for the past three years—even though after each rodeo season I promise myself I won't go back. I figured I could work myself to death for three weeks and then take it easy. But I didn't make it this year for more than two days. . . .

I was on lunch break on my second day of employment, waiting in line for my daily corndog. The transaction had just been completed, and I turned to the condiment bar to drench my corndog with bright yellow mustard. And then I saw her, head and shoulders floating just above the top of my corndog. The distance between us gave her an elongated oval body of greasy browned cornmeal (which made her all the more intriguing to me).

So I stood still and nibbled on my twelve-inch corndog, each bite revealing a bit more of her body, until the dog was gone and her red cowboy boots were visible and she stood in front of me some twenty feet away, a vision in tight cowgirl black.

She wore black jeans, a black tank with a heart cut out on the chest, just above her breasts, like any good cowgirl would wear. Normally I find those shirts completely hideous, but this was an exception. She also wore a black belt with a blinding silver buckle the size of a CD and earrings to match, peeking out of her frosted shoulder-length hair, topped off with a black cowboy hat. When our eyes met, a hush fell over the crowd and the only sound I could hear over the swoosh of her tight jeans rubbing together as she approached me was the voice of the glittering thirteen-year-old singing Patsy Cline's "Crazy" on the karaoke stage.

The crowd of cowboys—barbecued turkey legs in one hand, other hand in the back pockets of their sweethearts' blue jeans—parted as she walked towards me. As she neared, I noticed a crown around the brim of her hat, rhinestones gleaming in the shape of hearts and the numbers "1999. "

Oh yes, I had heard tell of this girl. Straight out of Pasadena, she won the hearts of everyone at the 1999 Houston Livestock Show and Rodeo, crowned "Miss Sunshine Cow Patty Sweetheart of the Rodeo 1999, Early Twenties Division." Her name? Betsy Rae Rayburn. We met halfway, wedged among cowboys whose dicks were bulging, packed tightly into Wranglers that were three sizes too small. I spoke up.

"Hi, Betsy Rae. I met you last year. Remember?" I was lying. "I work at the Pro-Pork booth. Last year I gave you some earrings made out of crystallized pig anus, er, anii. . . hell, whatever the plural of anus is," I laughed nervously. (Actually, this was a gift that our booth dedicated annually to the winner of the rodeo pageant).

Let me clarify quickly that I am not a rodeo woman. I am not a cowgirl, though in my childhood I did dream of competing in the barrel races and traveling with the glamorous rodeo circuit. But my stepdad broke his arm one winter and the truck line laid him off, and we had to sell all the cows and the horse, too, so my barrel-racing dreams left with the last of the rusty cattle trailers that pulled out of our gravel driveway and turned right onto Highway 62. So, no I am not a rodeo woman, and no, I do not personally agree with the Pro-Pork booth's mission, which is to find innovative uses for every part of a pig possible for human enjoyment, but I needed the money. And I can do a damn good imitation of a good ol' cowgirl when necessary.

Betsy Rae and I spent the entire day together. My boss at the Pro-Pork booth figured that if one of her employees was seen with THE Betsy Rae Rayburn, then it would boost our business. We ate funnel cakes, and rode the mechanical bull, had our pictures taken with the rodeo clowns, and watched the barrel races and viewed the 4-H livestock show. Betsy Rae was a celebrity judge, and because of my extensive knowledge of pigs, she let me pick the winner of the "Pig Most Likely To Taste Best As Sausage" category. It was truly an amazing day.

As the sun set over the fairgrounds, Betsy Rae and I headed to the carnival, while most of the rodeo-goers made their way inside to hear Billy Ray Cyrus sing. Betsy Rae had to make an appearance at the concert, but not until the intermission, so we still had a good hour together. We ate cotton candy and rode all the rides that would normally make me sick. I wasn't sure if the feeling in my stomach was nausea or lustful excitement, and I didn't care. We rode the Gravitron and the Tilt-A-Whirl and the ride that is a circular train of cars that goes like 90 mph in a circle and over little hills with a strobe light and blaring loud rock music. (It happened to be Poison's "Talk Dirty to Me" while we were on it.) Our bodies were crammed into one six-inch space towards the interior of the cart as we spun round and round and round. She screamed laughter, holding tightly to her rhinestone hat with one hand and gripping my thigh tightly with the other. I knew that after this ride, it would be time to make my move. Time to take her to the double Ferris wheel.

See, I learned all these picking up cowgirl tricks from the redneck boys who tried to woo me in high school. I knew something good would come of that somewhere down the line, and if there were ever a time when I would secretly thank those nasty, pimply-faced, greasy-haired redneck boys, it was now.

I led her in stumbly dizziness to the double Ferris wheel, which we immediately boarded. "Miss Sunshine Cow Patty Sweetheart of the Rodeo 1999, Early Twenties Division" didn't have to wait in line for anything at any rodeo event for the duration of her reign. We quickly ascended into the thick Houston sky, looking down onto the fairgrounds. . . onto the cattle trailers and four-wheel-drive trucks filling up four parking lots. . . at the carnival-goers, the cows and the cowboys and the security booth and popcorn-eating children and the litter that results from a crowd of hundreds of thousands of people. . . we were looking down onto a seemingly distant culture from which we had momentarily been separated.

Our creaking cart rocked back and forth as I nervously shifted my gaze between Betsy Rae and the small bolt that connected our cart to the larger machine. These cheap carny rides had always frightened me. We came to a sharp halt when our car was directly on top of the upper Ferris wheel, while others boarded the cars on the lower section of the ride, hundreds of feet below and a world away.

"I have some candy. Do you want some candy?" Betsy Rae Rayburn asked from her ripped red vinyl throne across from me.

"Sure," I answered. She reached inside her cowhide purse and pulled out a sucker.

"Shit, I only have one. I guess we'll have to share."

"Sure," I said. She unwrapped the crinkly plastic with fumbling fingers, nails painted fire-red and glossy.It was one of those torpedo suckers—know what I'm talking about? One of those long, pointy crystally rainbow colored suckers? She leaned forward, aiming the torpedo at my mouth, offering me the first lick. I could see her black bra through the heart cutout of her tank top. I took the sucker deep into my mouth, sucking out all the flavor out that I possibly could, my eyes focused downward on her boots, her fire red fingernails in the foreground. I thought I was going to gag.

"And this is yet another reason I have never given a blow job," I thought.

She giggled, as if my thoughts had appeared in a cartoon bubble above my head, and said in a faux male voice: "Ma'am, you sure are good at that. . . but I'll wager a pack of Red Man and my best hog that you've met your match." At which time she leaned forward and extracted the torpedo from my mouth with her teeth and somehow managed to fit the entire length of it into her own mouth.

I reached over and pulled the torpedo out of her mouth a bit, genuinely concerned with the well-being of her throat. She didn't need to do that to impress me.

"Oh. . . I get it. You like it like this, huh?"she said as she cupped her lips around the narrow tip of the torpedo and turned it round and round inside her mouth. I blushed. Like I have never blushed before. My cheeks hotter than a branding iron. She leaned towards me and put her free hand on my belt buckle, snatching it open, and with one swift motion the belt and the button of my jeans were both open. Yep, wide as a barn door. Not once did she take her thick-lashed "maybe she's born with it, maybe it's Maybelline" eyes off of mine, not once did she take her lips off the tip of the torpedo, as she unzipped my jeans and motioned with her tiara cowgirl hat for me to stand up. And I did stand up, jerking the cart so that I had to steady myself by grabbing on to the bar across the top of it. Before I knew it she had my jeans around my ankles and my belt wrapped around my hands which were wrapped around the bar.

"I used to lasso," she explained.

"Looks like you still do," I replied. I was concerned that our lost rodeo colony below might be able to see what was taking place in the rusty cart, but only for one bronco-buckin', cow-tippin' second, because Betsy Rae said, "Oh my. . . I have such a dilemma. This sucker tastes so good. . . but I think I might like the taste of this better," and she stuck the torpedo inside the elastic waistband of my cotton underwear and pulled them down to my ankles.

"Uh. . . hu. . . um. . . maybe you could have both," I half-joked, half-pleaded.

"Now that right there's good thinkin', little missy," she said, in the faux male voice again. And right there, in the rusted yellow cart of the Double Ferris Wheel, overlooking a crowd of now gaping-mouthed rodeo-goers, Betsy Rae Rayburn—"Miss Sunshine Cow Patty Sweetheart of the Rodeo 1999, Early Twenties Division" fucked me with her crystally rainbow colored torpedo sucker while keeping her mouth to both the sucker and the places it touched.

And the car *jolted* into motion. Literally. The Ferris wheel started again. Betsy Rae glanced at her rhinestone watch; time for her to be at the Billy Ray Cyrus concert.

"SSSSSSHHHHHHHIIIIIIIIIITTTTTTTTTTT!!!!!!!" she screamed, so loudly and for so long that by the time she shut up, our cart was almost to the exit platform of the Ferris Wheel. She quickly untied me and helped my get back into my pants. When we stepped off the cart, she handed me the torpedo and said, "We'll finish the sucker later, cowgirl," and galloped to the Astro Arena, like a mare to the apple orchard.

I followed after her slowly and watched from the entrance as she was summoned to the stage to perform her self-choreographed clogging number to Dolly Parton's "9 to 5," the talent entry that had helped her take the title of "Miss Sunshine Cow Patty Sweetheart of the Rodeo 1999, Early Twenties Division." I slipped out of the arena before she could find me, knowing that we could never finish that sucker. The moment had been too perfect to taint with the expectations of another meeting. And I wanted to remember Betsy Rae Rayburn just as she had been on our first encounter.

Besides, I sold the torpedo for twenty bucks to the ride operator.

Diana Wolfe

Kiss and Tell

Do I contradict myself?
Very well then. . . I contradict myself;
I am large. . . I contain multitudes.
  —Walt Whitman, "Song of Myself"

T
he strangest advice I ever got when I was about to kiss someone was from Alexa. We were at camp, lying as rigid and close together as bowling pins in her bottom bunk. When the moment was about to come, when the dampness that had started in my armpits suddenly spread to every bend and crevice on my body, when our eyes painfully met, swollen with desire, she said, "This will only work if you forget who I am." And for those next two or three momentous minutes, I could think of nothing but who and what she was: my best friend, a girl with long brown hair and deep brown eyes, with the lingering scent of horse manure in every fiber of her clothes. I wrecked my lips on the totality of her.

We were in bed together, for the first time, and there I was, holding the kielbasa that was his penis. I had no earthly idea what to do with it. It was so much bigger than the only other one I had ever held. His English had given out, and my French was about as sharp as a kindergartner's scissors. I was having visions of how he would leave me. And so. He rolled on me, hopelessly assuming the position. I pushed on his chest.

"It's not that I don't like you," I whispered, "it's just that I don't want to get hurt."

He pulled back a few inches from my face and said, "Well, just tell me when it starts to hurt and I'll stop."

After softball practice, Laura and Donna and I drank Pepsi in Randy's kitchen while she told us stories peppered with vagina jokes. She prided herself on knowing more about you than you yourself knew.

"If you're ever with a girl and you don't know what to do," Randy said, "just do the alphabet with your tongue. Like this." She demonstrated on her Pepsi can, swirling her fat pink tongue around its opening: a, b, c. . . . "Half a grapefruit works, too."

I rolled my eyes and said, "Gross." Laura and Donna said nothing.

Randy went into her room, came back with an 8 x 10 Sears portrait of a blond-haired, blue-eyed girl in my English class. A girl rumored to be Randy's girlfriend. "See this," Randy asked, flapping the picture in my face. "Pretty, isn't she?" Her breath was quick and close.

I looked away, shrugged.

"Well, she's history now."

Then, in what I would later discover to be typical Randy melodrama, she held a cigarette lighter to the photo and burned it as far as the girl's nose, while we watched, sipping our sodas.

I left right after he developed the habit of saying, "Suck it, baby. Suck it."

Everybody got their periods at the same time that summer. The bunk talk at night was filled with wild rumors and gross-out stories about this new phenomenon.

Suddenly, our little pee-pees had grown up. We were women. We were cursed. We broke out the hand mirrors and studied the Tampax pamphlet. So many people talk about holes.

You hole, they call you, *Stick it up your hole, you ho.* But a hole is only an opening until you realize you can fill or empty it. I suppose that is why Stacy Levine thought it perfectly reasonable to insert a tampon up her rectum. All day long, a white string hung from her behind while she bled unencumbered on her mint green shorts.

I have heard so many things, so many alternatives to the simple and underrated, "I love you, too." One earnest boy shook me by the shoulders and said, "I don't believe in saying I love you, but I feel, I feel, *I feel.*"

The second time I lost my virginity was with a kiss at 3 AM. Even though I knew all about passion, lust, love, and sex, I was unprepared for that kiss, in that car. Even though I was cursed, unable to forget who I was kissing, I tried to empty that car of heat by rolling down the windows. Then she flipped my seat back and laughed. The moment our lips met, my body burned and fell away, my heart and mind exploded, I spun, drifted, and died. Approximately twenty-three seconds later I came up for air, squeaked, and pushed myself into the empty street, under the circle of light from the street lamp. The only movement in the world was the shadows of trees stirring on the pavement. For the next twenty-four hours, I thought of Randy and her soda can lessons and screamed a little every time the phone rang.

In high school, a cute short boy named Stephen who looked a little like Eric Roberts invited me over to lift weights with him. He slunk around like a creeping vine, schmoozing his way across the cafeteria. It was about a fifteen-minute bike ride to his house, and it was misting, so I looked like shit when I got there; sweaty, my hair flat and damp. He let me in and showed me to the basement where his equipment was. He switched on some music and put on workout gloves. Then he began doing bench presses. I spotted him. Then it was my turn. I lay down on the bench under the chrome weight bar and he straddled me, facing me, so I couldn't move. He had me pinned there and then he pushed up my sweatshirt and rubbed my tits and told me he wanted to eat me. Then he unzipped his jeans and pulled his dick out (like he was going to piss, I thought). It was hard and veiny. Thick. Large. A cock. I didn't have any desire to touch it, and I still couldn't move. He got up off me, knelt in front of me, pulled my shorts and underwear down and slid his cold tongue up and down over my pussy. I wanted to enjoy it, I tried to put myself *there*, but things were going too fast, and I was afraid of how I must have tasted—sweaty and unwashed—so I wriggled away from his mouth, sat up. We made out for a little while, and I was relieved to taste myself on his tongue and find that it wasn't putrid, but I was still not as turned on as I had hoped. Eventually, we went upstairs and startled his mother. He introduced me to her and she gave me a look like I was a turd she'd stepped in.

"She came over to work out with me," he explained, and then she turned to me and said, "So you're one of *those*." Then we all sat down and had a snack. His mother offered to put my bike in the trunk and drive me home since it was raining hard. During the ride she talked about the obscene phone caller she had bothering her. "Finally one night I was fed up and I told him, 'Why don't you just come over here right now?' That scared the shit out of him."

When we got to my house, Stephen lifted my bike out of the trunk, and said *See ya!* in a way that I knew he was not thinking of the future. I called him later that night after television and we chatted for a little while. I was playing the usual tough guy, thinking I had his number and that he was just another overcompensating short guy. He told me that he and his father liked to pick up blondes together and they preferred their women to wear lacy black lingerie. I cringed, remembering the faded pink cotton bloomers he had pulled off of me. In the middle of our conversation he was called away and when he returned to me he said, "That's my *real* girlfriend on the other phone, so I gotta go." I don't recall speaking to him at all after that.

The townie dyke bar in upstate New York always had plates of celery sticks out. *Why*, I asked Margaret, on our first date there. "Because celery makes the cum taste sweet."

I picked celery strands out of my teeth for a month.

I made sure our first date was for Jones Beach. I wanted to prove that I hadn't imagined his beauty in the drunken dark of the club, with the strobe lights providing only intermittent clues. He was two hours late, but as soon as I saw him again, leaning on the doorjamb, Vuarnet sunglasses practically his only coverup, I forgave him. I couldn't understand his thickly-accented English too well, but I learned what I needed to know during the ten-minute ride in his vintage Chevy—no AC, no seat belts, but a fine radio. He wore a white tennis shirt, dark blue trunks, sneakers without socks. The hair on his body was distributed perfectly. And later that day, lying on top of him on the sand, kissing him, being held in his lean, ropy arms, his hard cock against my bikini, I discovered my favorite part of a man's body: the hollow just under his hipbones, where his torso gives way to the nether regions.

The thing I love about kissing a woman is how soft her mouth is, how soft the skin around her lips. The face bones are less obvious than a man's, the soft flesh covered with a tickling of down. Sucking and pulling at a woman's lips, rubbing my tongue inside her mouth, tasting her, running the sharpened tip of my tongue along the ridges of her teeth, finding the rhythm of the kiss, then opening, thrusting, licking, sucking, closing off, opening, taking that tender bottom lip and nibbling it, sucking it harder, drawing the blood to the surface. Then kissing that sweet and smooth neck, no Adam's apple, no razor stubble, just more and more of the same sweet flesh, running seamless down to her collar bones, her chest. Hearing her breathing faster, pushing her down on the bed to get at those breasts! Knowing and not knowing what to expect.

If I had to describe the perfect male body, for me, it would have to be that of a young nubile boy, approximately seventeen to twenty-two years of age, tall, lean, but not skinny, and as hairless as a man can get away with. A man who could almost be mistaken, from the back, in the dark, with enough of a buzz on, for a girl.

In third grade, Denise and I used to dry hump each other in her narrow twin bed, pretending that I was Tony and she was Karen, the most popular couple at Shore Road Elementary. Once, "Raindrops Keep Falling on My Head" was playing on her record player just as I came.

I was furiously in charge of these encounters, always on top, always initiating the ritual. She was so bony, and her front teeth were large and yellow. And her face was too narrow, and her eyes popped out of her head, but I was in love with her. So grateful to her for letting me wrap my legs around her sharp hipbone and fuck her until I came, gasping, red-faced, always pushing off her before the last little pulsations had ceased. Grateful to her for never refusing me, for never turning me in.

In fourth grade, I moved on to a more glamorous girl, a pretty rich girl with a huge bedroom, her own TV, and a subscription to *Dyn-o-mite* magazine. She required more persuading than Denise, more elaborate story lines to get her in the mood, but she played her part well. It didn't last too long, though, as she was unaccustomed to being told what to do.

My foreign fetish lasted years. After the Dutchman fucked my brains out he asked me if I felt guilty. The Irish guy wept a lot and sung to me. The Frenchman was scrupulously clean and possessed not one iota of sentiment or romance in his soul. The Hungarian had a wicked Oedipal complex and kept pictures of his bikini-clad mother under his bed. But my greatest weakness by far was for men with English accents, almost no matter what they looked like. No question that I put up with more from Englishmen than I would have from any American. But when Ian said, *Do you want me to take your trousers off?* and Nigel joked, *Are you sure you don't have any English in you? No? Would you like some, then?* and even when Colin said, *I'm really sort of aching with regret,* my clit stood up at attention, the honey flowed, and I wanted to fuck my way through Great Britain.

I had tried for years to get a tampon in, but the flesh would not give way. I was petrified, figured maybe my hole was only a quarter of an inch deep after all. I had received instruction from many different girls, from books, from the Tampax brochure, but nothing worked. Then, one summer day, I was at my friend's house, hanging out, and I got my fucking period. I was getting ready to go fool around with my boyfriend, so I was completely pissed off. I asked if I could borrow a pad. She shook her head. "I only use tampons," she said. "You have no choice. Just go put it in." I took the tampon from her outstretched hand, went into the bathroom, and jammed it home like I'd been doing it for years.

What I love best about kissing a man is the taste of the inside of his mouth, warm and secret, something from the back of a closet, not unpleasant, but not used to public exposure. I can feel myself giving in, inch by inch, semi-swallowed up by his lips, his working tongue swirling over mine like a wave, the tickle of stubble under his bottom lip, the strong chin and jaw bumping into my face, almost enough to bruise me. Being held fast in his arms, his hands knowing me, leading us in a dance.

For some reason, making out standing up has always turned me on more than any other position; perhaps it's because I know that all our attention will be focused on the kissing if we can't just as easily start to screw. I like mashing my breasts against his chest, knowing I am responsible for the swelling in his jeans, the vigor with which he tightens his grip on me, releasing my mouth at last to go for my cheek, my neck, then back to my face, maybe even breaking contact just for a moment to stare longingly, as if to say *Are you ready now?*

After many torturous nights of massages through silky pajama tops, I just couldn't stand it anymore.

"Lila, I have to kiss you. I have to kiss you more than I have to take my next breath!"

It was pitch dark inside the bedroom of the B & B. We were far from any familiar landmark or face or voice, and my impassioned words had all the pain and huskiness and urgency of a blue-balled teenage boy's, and she consented. She let me kiss her and it was like hot honeyed butter melting in my mouth. I kissed her and kissed her, and ran my hands under that goddamn pajama top once and for all and found her two hard titties and I sucked at them and licked them, knowing she was getting the sex of her life, and I straddled her soft thigh and came without even trying to. She said nothing, but she moved against me, moaning and like panting a bit, and she drank all my worshipful saliva and swirled her tongue around mine and in the morning, we didn't speak of it. Instead, she told me long boring stories about her ex-boyfriend, the actor she'd met in AA. We took the plane back to NY. She ran her hand up and down my thigh the entire eight-hour flight, and I was so fucking wet I was like savage and speechless. We parted at the baggage claim, and back at the office on Monday, she avoided my eyes. On Tuesday, she invited me to spend the night, but she had more resistance on her home ground and broke it off entirely after three weeks, despite coming all over my grateful face many, many times.

The best date Malcolm and I ever had was at the beach. He taught me a trick with a matchbook while we waited, outdoors, for the "bus" (actually, it was a car service). He would pull a match from the pack without breaking it off, then flick it across the strip with his thumb and light it up. It was so cool-looking because it was one-handed. I practiced and got good at it, too. He smoked and smoked and he held me, and he kissed me. It was really hot out and I clung to his thighs.

Once we were in the car, he outright groped me while I sat on his lap, which I didn't like, but I was into him being into me. Then we got to the beach, went onto the sand, and put our stuff down together. We went into the water. It was romantic, salty and slurpy, and we made out and dodged waves. I can't explain it, but Malcolm looked better wet than he did dry. His looks literally improved when he was soaked in water. His eyes were liquidy blue and red, and his skin seemed to melt off a little and become softer. He would whip his wet head around like a dog and his flaxen hair would spike up to one side, twisting around his skull like golden seaweed. He was a water god and I fell for him big time, for that one suspended moment. It started to disintegrate as soon as we were back on land.

Malcolm was always frisky, always horny—even for a seventeen year-old he seemed a little too randy. It had an edginess to it that made me feel not only that he wanted me, he *needed* me. We were walking back to the bus stop, and he grabbed me and threw me down on the shady cool grass surrounding the Boardwalk Restaurant.

There we were, rolling around on the grass, just underneath a row of floor-to-ceiling tinted windows. I had the sense that we were being watched, but I went along with it; I didn't have the struggle in me yet. We were making out, lying down, legs intertwined and working, arms interlocked, etc., and when I finally got him off me after what I considered to be a sufficient amount of time, I looked up and clearly saw the silhouetted figures of the diners behind the smoky windows. Hundreds of them, a colony of dark creatures, above me, looking down and laughing. I threw him off me and wiped my mouth. We left, and after that I never felt that he was more powerful than I was. Anyway, he looked better to me in the ocean than when we were standing at the bus stop because he didn't own a car, and he was wearing tube socks and I was feeling cheap. Ashamed.

All roads lead to the same place eventually. The kiss starts it, the kiss ends it. In between is anybody's guess. But no matter how hot the sex is, finally what you remember most vividly is the beginning and the end.

A man and a woman are eating spaghetti in a mediocre Italian restaurant. They do not speak to each other. He sips milk, she twists her yellow hair and jostles him every now and then, as if to kickstart a conversation. The way they hug in the parking lot later, it's obvious that it's over.

You never love someone so much as the very last moment that you are lovers. All the tenderness in your soul swells like a boiling river, sometimes spills out of places like your eyes, and a thousand fractured moments push into your brain at once. You may smile helplessly, you may shake your head and laugh and wipe your nose and say things like, "I don't know what to say." And then, whoever is suffering less reaches out and catches the other as easily as catching falling milk. That embrace, that silent, too-long embrace, the moment before the moment you let go, for good, forever, is what gives shape to the life you leave behind. Just as a kiss isn't a kiss until the four moist lips separate.

Andrea R. Roberts

Andrea R. Roberts

Reconnaissance

I.

I have grown a garden of contempt
despising the disposable,
so it stands to reason I would loathe my new self,
contained and quiet,
passive and moving
on wheels

II.

Losing my car made me re-think public transportation. Traveling New York's subways, and Atlanta and Washington DC's public transportation was not half as unsettling as being back in Houston, my city of origin, riding the bus line, known to many as the ghetto limo. There are just certain things my pride does not allow me to do, like being seen waiting at a bus stop downtown. Call it internalized classism, or the American love affair with aristocracy that I had allowed to set up shop in my spirit, but I wasn't feeling empowered by this type of alienation. I just felt alienated.

I am mourning the freedom to rove the flat, widespread expanse of the city.

III.

Nina and I boarded a bus after hours of flirtation and desperate snatches of intimacy. She was greeted by stares, me, by the quick once-over and the "I sized you up in a second" look. I had to cock-block. I wear an invisible dildo at times. When men glare at her bosom and her large hips, something protective arises in me. Today was no different. We both got the look. She dared to be more than a girl, and I more than a curiosity. She, the shaved-head femme, with ample bosom embraced by the soft translucence of a pale-blue peasant blouse.

"Why are you looking at me that way?" her voice high-pitched and deceptively coy. Then she got that "Oh yeah!" Kool-Aid smile because she already knew I'd found myself praying to an image of her in my mind, bare and legs spread. I thought better of speaking the feeling aloud. It would be blasphemy. So instead I played along.

"What way is that?"

She knew mine was the look of covetousness. The sick joy of desiring the unattainable. There was a neo-blaxploitation, Marquis de Sade pleasure she preferred to the harshness of German S/M demands. I dreamed myself a Left Bank-styled Shaft. But the most I could offer her was the chivalrous walk home or, in this case, to the bus stop.

We braved the jerky stops and starts and got off at a transfer point. I followed her around the street corner.

"I just want to wait with you at the bus stop, to make sure you're safe," I told her.

"I'll be all right. What time do you need to get home?" she asked.

"I don't have to be home at no time. You want me to wait with you or what?"

Let me steal another moment. Just another moment with you, your scent, and the feeling you give me. Strong and secure. Vulnerable only to my need to please you. The insecurity I cherish, wondering if I am pleasing you enough.

"OK, walk me then," she smiled.

Andrea R. Roberts

This corner was home to department stores once, now it is the route to "The Tre" (Third Ward) and the address for two-for-ten motels. This is where you never want to go. This is where you want no one to know your name.

I gazed up at the Hotel Montague sign at the end of the block. I recalled my own nights of waiting at that corner, handing out change and cigarettes to petty thieves and crackheads. Most of them were too drug-crazed or ill to realize they had asked the same person twice for a guilt grant, a secular tithe. They walked up and down the downtown city blocks dodging mounted and cycling men in blue.

Tonight the corner was deceptively quiet, like Nina.

"Can y'all help me with my bags please? I'm trying to make the next bus," asked an old black woman, shrunk by age and calcium deficiency. Gout-swollen legs wobbled underneath the weight of her and four white plastic bags filled with dollar-store silk flowers, household plastic and paper goods.

We obliged her. She offered to pay us and we declined. Common courtesy should not be for sale. "You owe us nothing. No, ma'am. Please. We'll just set your things down here."

Nina and I lay each of her bags down and walked to the end of the block where bus riders—mostly men—asked for cigarettes, when the bus was coming, and the questions anyone with breasts and two legs grows weary of hearing from the X chromosome. I leaned against the wall. Fronting control and aping butch, I prayed inside for my lady to turn me to butter again with spontaneous touch, giggle or smile.

I pretended we were in London or Prague or somewhere—anywhere an alleyway or street corner would welcome female-female affection. I imagined we could fuck right on the street corner as if we were lovers in Rome, where even old ladies in black lace would walk by with wise and chaste "Oh, young lovers" smiles. . . .

But it was just my imagination, running away with me.

"That man's staring at us," I told her mischievously, glimpsing a brother with his window slightly cracked. He gazed at us the way tourists watch big window peep shows from the streets of Amsterdam, more judgment and voyeuristic interest in his eyes than anything else. I did like to think he was watching. She knew I did.

"You wanna give him a show?" she asked.

"Yeah." I hate it when my lips lie. My desire to shock, to be felt up under city lights against the backdrop of an abandoned building, was liminal.

So her hands began to graze my nipple. I looked down her blouse like a pirate seeking hidden booty. Her breasts hung full and inviting like an eighteenth-century wine wench as she reached for my crotch. She caressed the hot tip of my clit as my eyes rolled back.

"Is he looking?"

"Yeah, he's looking."

For a moment my eyes raced between his stare and her deep brown opals. Then running, running, running, my eyes fluttering, the breathing heavier. Her hands running the length of a hard clit, sweating honey pot, my warm, damp crotch.

"You're not even looking at him. You don't know if he's looking at what we're doing or not," she laughed and backed away.

"I know, I'm too obvious."

"Yeah, you are," she said through stifled laughter. She moved closer and grabbed my ass cheeks without warning. "You like that don't you?"

"Yes," I replied weakly.

She laughed at my femininity. The bliss came to an abrupt end.

A voice emerged out of the darkness. A man in a Montgomery Ward jogging suit, with braids and the speech of a man who likes his drink strong and cheap approached us. "Hey, are you two freaks? Are y'all freaks?" We stayed close and ignored him.

Good Christian girls always learn not to look back, but we are never prepared for the invasion, the confrontation. Us versus Them. The definer versus the designer.

Nina left my side to answer the inquiry of street cleaners who decided two black women in downtown, late at night, were fair game. Behind the roar of passing buses all I could make out was, "Naw, man, she's got a boy friend and I ain't seeing nobody." I was quaking, trapped inside my head, no longer light, but whimpering. *Healthy, soft black arms, please anchor me in the truth we created, not theirs.* Now, I could not protect her or myself from, "What's your number?" and "Is y'all lesbians?"

But her number was up, emerging from the darkness, blocks in the distance and approaching quickly. My dreams and I had another corner to defend.

How do white men ask the same questions and still seem so clean?

Why are you a lesbian? Why are you a lesbian? Why, why? Freedom is drowning, drying my wet places. The voices in darkness, the white eyes out of brown faces, the look.

I look back: "Yes, those are the headlights of the bus."

She boards and I wonder how people know which light to walk into when they die.

Pam Ward

A Clean Comfortable Room

Sally had been driving long and hard for eleven hours already. When she saw the blue glow of the deadbeat motel she decided to pull in. She'd seen the Blue Star Motor Inn's giant sign from the highway. "Clean Comfortable Rooms for $16.99." Sally turned off the exit and drove to the squat stucco building. It had about ten units connected under one slim roof. Nothing but road dirt and concrete. A loud Coke machine sat out front.

She got out and walked quickly to the office. As soon as she stepped in she was hit with the harsh scent of canned meat cooking. The office looked more like a living room. There were two TV sets, a small black-and-white and one color stacked together. There was a small stove and a giant, brown refrigerator with a big dent in it. There was an ironing board and a rotary phone hooked to the wall. A hefty man in loose-fitting overalls sat in a Lazyboy covered with duct tape. He looked about sixty-five. His bald head gleamed from the neon. His numb eyes were glued to the set. The man broke into a wide smile as Sally walked in.

"I'm comin'," he said, walking laboriously to the front desk. He had one of those beer guts that hung like a sack of rice. His breath was heavy. When he got close, Sally noticed a gray possum wrapped around his neck. Its wet eyes were watching her.

"What can I get you?" He grinned, revealing a gummy row of gapped teeth.

"How much for a room?" Sally had left in the middle of the night and only had twenty-eight dollars in cash on her. She needed a room before she could hit the ATM in the morning.

"We got some go for thirty-five and some that go for seventeen. Depends. You by yourself?"

"For now."

The man chuckled to himself when she said that. His double chin jiggled. "Well, I guess I can let you take the cheaper one." He sighed deeply. He seemed disappointed he wasn't getting a bigger sale.

"Can I see it first?" she asked.

"Sure, sure. Wait a hot minute. Let me get the keys." The man ducked behind a torn curtain.

Sally leaned across the front desk while she waited. She tapped her long fingernails across the wood. *I hope he doesn't take too long,* she thought. She wanted to hurry up and get to her room so she could lay down. She opened her purse and took out her lipstick. She smeared the deep red on. Sally looked toward the blue glow of the television. *Rosemary's Baby* was on. Rosemary was struggling down the street with a heavy suitcase. She looked pale and worried.

Suddenly there was a horrible racking cough, coming from the dark corner of the room. Sally leaped. It sounded like a hyena. She squinted to see. There, next to the stove, was a wide-shouldered man in an undershirt. Sally hadn't noticed the man before. He blended into the dim corner of the room. He couldn't have been more than twenty. Was probably the older man's son. Sally watched him bring a bottle of whiskey to his lips and drink a messy swig. He licked around his mouth and watched her. He was staring at Sally's large breasts. His gaze never rose above her neck.

Sally was wearing a jean jacket over a thin black slip. She'd just shoved the flap inside her pants. Her bare feet were in pink thongs. To avoid the man's gaze, Sally walked outside toward the Coke machine. She wasn't going to stay in there with some wild-looking fool drooling at her.

She slipped in three quarters and the red can came rumbling out.

"Oh—there you are, darlin'," the older man said, walking outside. "I'm fixin' to get that room ready."

Sally leaned against the hood of her car. It was a warm Arizona night. You could see every star from here. Sally heard a rattling sound behind her. She jumped. It was just a corn chip bag stuck in some weeds. Sally was dead tired and her nerves were shot. She hoped he wouldn't take too long.

The man was back in less than ten minutes. He was carrying an old bucket.

"Well, its all spic-and-span. Got it real nice for you."

Sally hoisted her large purse over her shoulder. She followed the man to the room.

"Here we are, little lady." The man stood firmly in the doorway. Sally had to brush past him to get in. He smelled like hard liquor and farm animals. As soon as she stepped in the room the fumes hit her. It had that rank smoke smell. A scent so thick it was embedded in all the walls, rugs, and drapes. Smelled like it would never go away. Like somebody smoked in there year after year and never once opened a window. The wallpaper was peeling off, the bedspread was a hideous floral orange and the corners had cigarette burns. "I'll take it," Sally said.

The man had her fill out a tiny white slip asking her name and license plate number. Sally fumbled around with her purse and finally counted out seventeen dollars. She handed it to him.

"Now, my name is Edmond. Let me know if there's anything you need, sugar." He leaned over to hand her the room key and his huge body trapped her against the doorjamb. Sally fell back and dropped her purse. The man bent down slowly and handed it back to her. "Watch yourself now. Looks like you need some shut-eye."

Edmond walked outside to the lot. He looked hard at Sally's car. It had about five layers of dirt on it. "I can wash that car there for you, if you'd like. Have it looking real nice. Real sweet. I know how to suds a car down. It's all in the motion you know. Got to go in a circular rhythm, keep your hands rubbing round and round and round. Don't have to press too hard to get a shine." His bald head looked hideous in the lamplight.

"Sleep tight," he said walking off. Sally watched his lumbering stride go back through the office door. He looked back at her before going in.

Sally shut the door. *Banjo-playin' motherfuckers,* she said to herself. She slid the extra lock across the frame. She took off her jacket and lay it on the bed. Sally was beat down. She'd been driving for half a day already. She pulled the blanket all the way back and examined the sheets. They seemed clean. She took off her shoes and pants, then peeked through the drapes.

The road was real quiet now. It was 11:45 P.M. There was only one other car in the lot. She walked to the small bathroom. Some of the tiles were missing. A shower curtain hung limp on a metal rod. The toilet paper roll was half gone. Sally took a hot shower and wrapped herself in the thin, frayed towel. She sat on the edge of the bed. She wished she had one cigarette. Something to take the edge off. She clicked on the TV. *Rosemary's Baby* was still on. She watched the set while sipping the rest of her Coke. She looked around the room. There was a small refrigerator in the corner. She pulled it open. There were four beers strung together on a pale vein of plastic. The last person in there must have left it and the owner hadn't noticed it.

Sally didn't drink. She didn't even want to be tempted. Not now. Not after everything that had happened. Sally hadn't tasted liquor for three years straight. Not since that rainy night long ago. She dialed the front desk.

"Hello, ma'am. Room all right?"

"Yes, it's fine, but I found a six-pack in the fridge. I really don't want it."

"That's all right, ma'am. I'll send Leon down to pick it up."

Sally put the receiver down and put her pants back on. Leon must be the fool who didn't have the decency to look me in the face, she thought.

She was buttoning the front of her jacket when she heard a soft knock on the door.

Sally peeked out the small hole drilled over the doorknob.

It was Edmond again. "I'll just take that beer off your hands myself. Leon's busy right now." *Busy?* Sally thought. *That man wasn't doing nothing but jackin' off to* Rosemary's Baby. Edmond crossed the room, looking around it quickly. He walked over to the refrigerator and jerked the handle. He snatched the cans away as if Sally might change her mind. They clanked against his wad of keys. He stood next to her for a moment. She could smell the sour seeping out from his pores. She had emptied a few things from her purse, and a pair of black four-inch pumps was standing erect next to the TV set. He stared at them too. Sally put one hand on her hips.

"Well, I guess you have everything," she said, using that fake sweet tone she reserved for work. She sure didn't miss Sizzler. Only thing she got from that job was a handful of bad steak knives.

"Yes, ma'am I reckon I do. I'll just take this on back to the front. Let me know if you need anything else, hear. You be safe now, pretty little thing like you got to watch herself. Lord knows what's out on that road."

Sally started closing the door slowly. He could see her red lips and giant cleavage through the crack. The man took two steps but didn't leave. He reeked of cheap booze. Sally saw a dirty ring around his neck where the possum had been. She inched the door further in and accidentally touched his hand. It was hairy and rough. He looked down at her. His forehead was sweaty and large. Slowly, the corner of his lips curled up into a crooked smile. "I'll take this on, now," he said stepping out. "Call again." Once his feet cleared the door, Sally closed it shut and locked it tight. *Country fools*, she thought to herself.

She waited a moment before taking her jacket off. She went into the bathroom and washed out her slip and hung it on the shower rod. If she left the window open it ought to be dry by morning. Sally lay on the bed naked. Damn, she wanted a cigarette. She searched the room. Nothing. She thought about the last smoke she'd had with William. It was right after they'd made love. Damn, that man was good. He sure knew how to serve it up. She remembered how he cupped her breasts and sucked both nipples at the same time. How he begged her to climb on top of him, plunging himself deeper and deeper. How he tugged her hair just enough, just until her body was one huge arch. Until she felt like pure steel. Like one hot metal rod. Like she might just snap. Sally loved the way he screamed her name when she violently came. Yeah, she'd sure miss her some William.

Sally began playing with her breasts. She slid her hand down to her thighs. Damn, it was hot. Buck-ass naked and she was still sweating. Sally thought if she got off she could get to sleep. All that road coffee had her fried. She tried and tried but only ended up in a frustrated knot under the sheet. Her long hair was glued to the back of her neck.

She yanked the sheet back and thought about Leon sitting in that office in the dark. There was something peculiar about him. Something backwoods mixed with wild. *Too much inbreeding, I bet.* But there was something else too. Something simmering like a pot of hot greens on the stove. Sally thought about the cigarette pack rolled up in his sleeve. His thick muscular arms and that tight six-pack stomach. The way his eyes ate her breasts. The way he leaned in his chair with his legs cocked out wide. The worn look to his jeans. The hard tips of his boots. The boy looked pure country. A bona fide hick. All wild-eyed and wooly-haired too.

But, it wasn't like she was in the backwoods. Flagstaff was just five miles away. Sally remembered what the gas station attendant had told her. "Be careful on them roads honey," she'd said. "Some of these small towns are more common than the Deep South. Watch out."

Sally took a bag of pretzels from her purse. She was hungry. Besides the Coke, it was the only thing she'd had in hours. She opened her wallet. She only had eleven dollars left. Her tank was already close to the red line. She had to get some cash fast.

Edmond walked back inside the office door and opened the cash register. "Sure is a pretty gal up in thirteen." He counted the money and put it back inside. Leon didn't even look up. His eyes were fastened to the set. He watched Rosemary's naked body being shoved against the long table. She was struggling frantically. The men were holding her legs down.

Edmond slumped his large body back in the Lazyboy. It was stuffed with old copies of the *Phoenix Gazette*. The newspapers filled the deep hole in the seat. "Yes sirree. A real live citified gal. Should have seen them patent leather hoofers she had up in there. Um, um, um." Edmond wrapped the possum around his neck, but it squirmed so much he let it loose on the ground. It ran to a dark corner of the room. He pulled a handkerchief out and patted his sweaty brow.

"I don't know what a lady like that is doing out here in the middle of the night. Did you see her clothes? Look like she just shoved her nightie in her jeans and took off. Must be another one of them women had a fight with their boyfriends. You see she wasn't carryin' nothing but the clothes on her back. Man oh man. If it wasn't for boyfriend fights and city folks cheatin', we'd be out of business."

Leon didn't say anything.

Sally laid across the bed. *Rosemary's Baby* was still on. She watched as Rosemary's slender body moved crazily against the hard table. The men pounded her down, took turns thrashing away, while naked old ladies chanted and held both her legs. Sally clicked the TV off. "Demonic shit," she said out loud to herself. She slid under the sheet and got a whiff of the dank smoke lodged in the bedspread. "Damn," she said. "I wish I had just one cigarette. Something to take the edge off." Sally dug around in her purse even though she knew there was nothing. She wished she hadn't dumped her ashtray out at the gas station. Probably was one butt she could have gotten a good toke from.

Sally scanned the tacky room. It reminded her of all the lonely nights in that hard apartment with William. All those dinners alone. All that waiting and waiting. Looking through windows for hours. All the cars going by, her ears straining hard. Waiting for his rumbling engine. Staying up half the night, smoking pack after pack, wondering when he'd pull in. She thought about all the crazy fights they had in that room. All the broken-up dishes, her clothes ripped in half, the big plates of food that got tossed at the wall. She played back the scene of their last blowout.

It was right after she let him move back in. She'd come home early and found him in the apartment with her coworker. They'd looked like two little kids, stuck in a crosswalk, right before a bus mowed them down.

"Shit," Sally said out loud. "I could sure use a cigarette now."

Suddenly there was a sharp rap at the door.

"Excuse me miss, but I just wanted to see if you needed anything before me and Leon closed the office down for the night. I'm fixin' to go get some fish up at Rusty's. Wanted to see if you wanted some. You was looking kinda hongry when you checked in."

Sally peeked from the hole. Edmond was right there. She could see the hard hairs poking from under his dingy shirt. She could hear Leon's thick, angry cough.

"No thanks," she said through the door. "I need to get some rest. I'm really tired. Thanks for asking." She checked the knob to make sure it was locked. She could see them both step back.

"Well a little shut-eye never hurt nobody. But you sho' don't need no beauty rest." Edmond laughed real loud at that. Leon stepped forward. Sally noticed a pack of Marlboros bulging out from his sleeve.

"Cigarettes," she said under her breath. The nicotine pull yanked her beyond the point of caution. Sally cracked the door. "Mind if I have one to puff on?"

"You can puff on two." It was the first thing Leon said. He said it really slow. It sounded so sexy. His body was young. Strong and well built, but his face looked like twenty miles of bad road. He snapped the box open and shook the pack until one slid toward her. Sally pulled it out slowly as Leon brought a flame up to her face. His whole hand was a spider web of black tattoos. He had a fresh scar across his brow.

Sally didn't want these two men inside her room, so she stood in the doorjamb and eased the door closed behind her. "I don't like the smell of smoke while I'm trying to sleep," she said, stepping further out. She leaned against the door, facing her car. Her huge breasts gleamed under the moon.

"Where you from?" Edmond asked, taking out an old pipe and pushing some tobacco in it.

"Los Angeles," she said, blowing her smoke out rapidly.

"I knew it! You can always tell city folks. Spot y'all a mile away. Y'all stay in a hurry. Where you headed?"

"The Grand Canyon," she lied. She figured they'd make her out to be a tourist passing through.

"Yeah, I reckon we get a lot of folks wantin' to see that. Been out here nineteen years and ain't laid eyes on it yet. Ain't nothin' but a big hole, I hear. Lots of red rock. Folks line up for it all day. Standing there in the hot sun. Taking pictures and whatnot. Yesterday they said a lady fell the whole two hundred feet to the bottom. Got knocked straight off the trail by one of them loose rocks. Said her scream ricocheted for miles."

Leon almost smiled at that.

"So where are you from?" she asked, bored. Her eyes were on Leon.

"Why we from right here," Edmond said. "Never been nowhere else. Never wanted to go." Edmond adjusted the straps on his overalls and looked over at Leon. "He don't talk much."

Sally tossed her butt toward her tires. Leon flipped the pack open again.

"You might want one for later," Edmond said slyly.

Sally pulled two cigarettes out. She put one in her front pocket. Both men stared at her heavy chest. She tried to close her jacket but she was so top-heavy, it flapped open again.

Leon jerked one of the beers from the six-pack. He handed it to her.

"No thanks, I don't drink," Sally said, waving the can away.

"Why not? Nothing wrong with a cool drink every now and then," Edmond told her.

Sally was trying to finish her cigarette. She wanted to get back inside. "I don't touch it now. Did though, had a little problem with it."

"Yeah," Edmond said. "If you keep messing with the stuff, nine times out of ten some kinda problem will come up."

Sally remembered her last episode. All the horrible crashing of glass. She watched Edmond drink huge swigs and follow it up with Wild Turkey shots.

"Never learned how to keep away from it myself," he said. "You married?"

"Kinda."

Edmond laughed heartily at that and even Leon, who looked like he never smiled in his life, looked at least less mean.

"I guess I'm kinda married too," Edmond said laughing, stealing a quick glance at Sally's wide ass when she bent down to pick up some matches lying in the street.

"You can have my lighter," he said. "I got a bunch of 'em at home." Sally glanced up at him. She could see he was torn up now. There was a hint of delirium to his eyes.

"Listen, it was nice meeting you both," she said, stepping back.

"Wait now. . . you want some of this?" Edmond took a small package of crumpled foil from his back pocket. "Best weed around. Y'all can't get this in the city." He handed the package to Leon, who carefully rolled three fat joints.

It was really getting late now. Sally didn't want to spend one more minute with these two. And she wasn't about to blaze up in a parking lot in the middle of the night with some hicks. But Leon took the large joint and lit the shit up, right there over the hood of her car.

"Well, I'm goin' on to Rusty's," Edmond said. "Whatchu want boy?"

Leon held up two fingers and said, "Kaafish."

"Catfish sandwich and fries?" Edmond looked at Leon a long time.

"Umm hum," Leon said.

"You be careful boy out here, boy. Don't want nothing like what happened last time, you hear?" Edmond walked toward a gray pickup. He hoisted his large body inside.

Sally got up from the curb, taking her last cigarette with her. She'd only planned to talk a few minutes to be nice. Her feet were getting cold now. She was ready to go back inside.

"Well, good night," Sally said to Leon, getting to her door quickly and slipping the lock shut. She watched him from the peephole. Leon was blowing the smoke out real slow.

Sally finally breathed out easily. She washed her face and hands and got into bed. She tossed and turned but couldn't sleep. She tiptoed to the door again. Leon was still out there. He was stretched across her car. One leg hung over her rims. His hand was rubbing his flat stomach. *Oh hell,* she thought to herself.

Sally cracked the door open. "You want to come in?"

Leon smiled and walked inside. He closed the door behind him. Sally sat back on the edge of the bed. Leon sat right beside her. He handed her the lit joint. She inhaled it deeply. It was some strong weed. Leon leaned over and picked up one of her black heels. He was rubbing his fingers over the shiny smooth leather. "You want me to put these back on?" she said sweetly, touching his wide arm.

"Um hum," Leon said. *Must be the quiet type,* she thought to herself. Sally got up and went into the bathroom. Her black slip was almost dry. She pulled it over her head and wiggled out from her jeans. She slid the pumps back on. When she walked out, Leon was standing just outside the door, waiting for her. His shirt was on the floor. His slick chest was nothing but muscle. He picked her up and pressed her against the wall. She wrapped her legs around his slender waist, and he kissed her crazily, carrying her to the bed. He gently laid her down, covering her neck and breasts with his mouth. He was so tender and sweet. Sally ran her hands over his huge back and through his thick black hair. She could feel his belt buckle against her navel. He was grinding more rapidly now. With more fever. Sally playfully moved away. She wanted this to last.

Leon pulled her back toward him. He straddled her and started kissing her down her legs. When he got to her shoe, he pulled it off and tossed it across the room. He smiled big, and lavishly sucked each toe. Sally moaned inside his bushy hair. She grabbed a handful and bit into his earlobes. Leon was bucking like a wild bull now. He pulled her slip over her neck. He grabbed her panties with his fist and snatched them from her leg.

Leon got out of his jeans fast. "Slow down, cowboy, I'm not going anywhere," Sally grinned at his naked body. He had the ass of a twelve-year-old boy. She squeezed it while he put himself inside her. He rode her a long time. Real slow. Groaning and going strong. He was breathing faster and faster. Suddenly he yanked it out and burrowed his head between her thighs. Sally thought she would die. Her whole body was hot. Her thighs were pure steel. Leon put it in again, slapping her wide hips until she couldn't hold back anymore. Her whole body jerked into a maddening spasm. Leon was making a guttural sound. The next thing she knew she was asleep.

Sally was half awake when she found him thrashing away again. He had entered her from behind. He was breathing real heavy, almost wheezing against her. He had her doggy style and she could smell the hard whiskey from his mouth. She went to grab his head and found he was totally bald.

It was Edmond. He was fucking her like a mad dog. She flipped over and all his weight fell against her chest. His heavy gut made it difficult to breathe. He pinched her breasts until she screamed. Sally tried to squirm from under him. She tried to roll over but she was pinned down. His wide thighs held her legs apart. Edmond bit hard into her flesh. Sally yelled in pain.

"Shut up!" he screamed.

He wadded a washcloth and shoved it in her mouth. She dug her nails into his huge back.

Just then, the front door flew open. Leon came across the room and grabbed Edmond off of her. "Sta. . . Sta. . . Staaaaaaap!" he yelled. But Edmond socked Leon across the face, tearing open his new scab again. "You trying to tell me what to do? After I raised your lil' ass! Your own mama don't want ya." Red blood poured down Leon's brow. He threw a punch at Edmond but missed. Edmond smiled wickedly at Leon and smacked him across the mouth. Leon looked like he might cry. "Sta . . Sta. . . Staaaaaap. . . . it," Leon stuttered.

"That's right, start bawlin', you big baby! Ha, ha! What's that you say boy? Huh?" Edmond laughed in his face. "Look at you. Got the body of a man and the mouth of a two-year-old. Stammering and carryin' on. Can't say one sentence to save your natural life." Leon's lips started quivering. He was starting to drool on one side.

Sally looked at Leon. She had figured him for the quiet type. She didn't know he was simple.

Leon ran up and rammed Edmond with his head. Edmond snatched the lamp from the table and bashed Leon's skull with it. He fell to the floor and didn't move. Edmond looked crazier than ever. He came over to Sally and slammed her back against the bed. She squirmed with all her might and they both rolled to the shag carpet. The TV was right there in her face. The news flashed a story about a man found with his throat slashed in Los Angeles. An unidentified woman was shot with him.

". . . killed in his own home. Police are looking for. . . "

Suddenly Edmond's foot caught the TV cord and he ripped the set right from the stand. It crashed down and went black.

Edmond was laughing crazily and licking Sally's face. It was then she turned her head and she saw it, her black purse right next to her forehead. He wasn't holding her hands, so Sally stretched out her right arm and rummaged through the contents. She finally felt the cool steel. She took the gun out and blasted him in the face. She fired four times, until he slumped over.

Suddenly it was dead quiet. Sally held her breath. She could hear her heart beating. Her whole chest heaved up and down. Suddenly there was another sound, a scratching from behind the TV. She looked down and saw the gray possum dart underneath the bed. Sally grabbed her clothes and got out. She took Leon's Marlboros and both men's wallets. Combined, they had seventy-eight bucks. She snatched the large key ring and went to the front office, opened the cash register, and found another hundred and a half. She took all the candy bars and bags of chips. She got back in her car and roared off. Sally clicked the radio on.

"Manhunt for possible female murderer. Sally Jones has been missing for two days now. Her husband was found murdered in their Compton home."

Sally punched the lighter in and headed up toward the interstate. *Damn,* she thought. *In two days, I killed three people already. There has got to be a better place to live.*

Maggie Estep

Joe

One day Joe woke up with a headache so violent it made a red curtain hang in front of his eyes. He blinked several times, but it wouldn't go away. He sat up. He moved his head. He opened the newspaper, even though trying to read any of its print made the red curtain throb.

> LOS ANGELES (AP) - Children were greeted with hugs, love, and performing clowns today as they returned to the Jewish community center that was a place of terror just six days earlier.

Joe was glad he didn't live in Los Angeles. He lived in Chicago, near Rogers Park. The neighborhood was home to rehabs, furniture moving companies, people on SSI, gangs, and women who worked for tips.

Joe thought about the performing clowns cavorting around the murder scene. Which made him remember Susan's clown outfit, the one with bright red suspenders holding up a red garter belt and white fishnet stockings.

Thinking of this gave Joe a hard-on in spite of the now-blinding headache. He dialed 911. Joe briefly marveled over having a hard-on in spite of the fact that something was obviously very wrong with his head. This was the last thought he had for a long time.

When Joe came to in the hospital three days later, a nurse was there at his bedside, emptying a tube full of his urine. "They removed the tumor from your brain. It was the size of a grapefruit."

Joe wondered why it was that tumors were always compared to fruit. He wondered if the nurse liked to have sex with fruit. Susan did.

Joe met Susan at the rehab where he worked as a janitor. No one really knew how Susan had gotten to the detox. She'd been left in the waiting room, sedated, with her hands bound behind her back by a handkerchief.

She was half Iranian and had a beautiful nose. She wore lots of cheap jewelry that turned her skin green. Her hair was so long it touched her ass.

She suffered severe withdrawal from heroin. Three days off the stuff and her hormones were raging.

Counselors at the rehab caught Susan trying to have sex with virtually all the rehab inmates, male and female. One day, Joe found her in his broom closet. With his mop. She was leaning forward against the Band-Aid colored wall. She had inserted the mop handle into herself from behind. She had her long black skirt bunched up over her ass.

When Joe walked in, she froze. Then she turned her head and looked at him. Her eyes were black hot coals and impossible to read. Joe slowly backed out of the closet. He went down the hall and into one of the counselor's offices, where he mechanically started emptying the trash, paying absolutely no mind to the counselor who was in there.

About ten minutes later, Joe went back into his broom closet. He knew she wouldn't be there anymore. He carefully picked the mop up and licked its handle. It tasted like sugar.

Joe had been raised in a motorcycle gang in Oregon. He was first laid at age twelve, by Martha, his half brother's common-law wife. She was four-feet eleven inches with kinky blond hair and facial tattoos. One night she just crawled inside Joe's sleeping bag and started sucking his dick. Once he was hard, she hoisted up her denim miniskirt, straddled him, and rode up and down on him so vigorously he was sure she was going to break his dick off. When Joe tried to kiss her, she slapped him so hard his lip bled. He was so afraid of her he couldn't come. But she did, making a horrible sound like a wounded moose. A few minutes later, as she was crawling out of Joe's sleeping bag, his half brother came over. He made a clucking sound in his throat and then laughed. Joe thought maybe his half brother would kill him. But he didn't.

The next day Martha fell off the back of Joe's half brother's bike and rolled under a truck on the highway.

"You killed her," Joe's half brother accused that night.

How Joe had killed her, he wasn't sure. And it was never mentioned again.

When Joe was 16, there was a massive raid of the motorcycle gang, and most of its members were indicted on murder and narcotics charges. Joe fled. He started hitchhiking East and got off in Chicago. Some guys jumped him and stole his shoes. One of them put his dick in Joe's mouth and came on his face. Joe went to a Salvation Army and slept there one night.

He ended up in a detox and was ultimately given a job as a janitor there. One night, he got picked up by a tiny stripper at a bar that some of the detox workers frequented. She wasn't stripping there, just getting drunk. She didn't even talk to Joe before putting her hand on his crotch. She took him home and told him to shut up and turn over, and she rammed stuff up his ass. First a finger. Then a hair brush handle. Then she ripped the arm off a smiling plastic doll and rammed it up his ass. Joe didn't protest. He watched her jerk off. She didn't put anything up her own ass.

Her name was Jolene.

He saw her a few times a week for several months. Then she was murdered. The cops never figured out who did it or why. She was found stabbed in the bathtub in her apartment.

Now Joe hadn't had sex in two years. Every time he fucked someone, they died.

The day after the mop incident, Joe found Susan in his broom closet again. She was completely naked but didn't have anything inserted inside herself.

"What are you doing?" Joe asked.

"Nothing," Susan said.

She stood up and turned her back to him. She was so skinny her shoulder blades poked out like razors, but she had a nice shape, hips rounding out slightly from a miniscule waist.

She bent forward and smashed her cheek against the Band-Aid colored wall. She had extremely long straight black pubic hairs that parted to reveal the pinkness between them. She turned her head and looked at Joe with hot coal eyes. Joe didn't move. He didn't even put his hand to his dick that was so hard and distended it hurt.

"That's a really bad idea," Joe said to her after eternal seconds.

"Yeah yeah yeah," Susan said and then arched her back and wiggled her hips slightly.

"Do you need a place to live?" he asked.

Susan straightened up and turned around and her face turned little girl.

"Yeah."

"Okay. You can live with me," Joe said.

An hour later, Susan had packed up her plastic bag of belongings: two pairs of panties, a black T-shirt and a bra.

The moment they set foot inside Joe's small two-room apartment, Susan lay down on the floor and fell asleep. After sitting there watching her sleep for a few hours, Joe gently scooped her up and put her on his twin bed. An hour later she woke up and went back to the floor. She was still asleep in the morning when the phone rang and one of the counselors from the rehab called to tell Joe he'd lost his job. Consorting with the patients was strictly against the rules. But Joe didn't care. He had Susan in his apartment.

When Susan woke up she was horny. She didn't even brush her teeth or take a piss, she sat up on the floor and reached for Joe, who was sitting in the only chair he owned, a plastic armchair the color of avocados. She put her hand on his crotch and Joe made a face.

"What, baby?" Susan said.

"Don't do that."

"What's the matter?"

"I don't wanna."

"Yes you do," Susan purred, feeling the big lump in his pants.

"No," Joe said.

Susan peeled off her shirt. She had an orange bra on.

"I got this in France at Tati," she said, running her hands over the bra. "Tati is this amazing cheapo store they got over there. Kind of like our K-Mart or something, only the underwear is nice cotton. You can't find nice cotton underwear at K-Mart," she said, defiantly, as if expecting Joe to contradict her.

"I realize that," Joe said, even though he didn't. "Why were you in France?"

"Come ON," the girl said, taking off the bra and teasing her dark brown nipples so they stood up like angry blueberries.

But Joe wouldn't do anything.

Over the next few weeks, Susan tried a lot of things. She got outfits. First just run-of-the mill things like vicious red teddies and garters and stockings and fuck-me pumps. She would dance in front of Joe in his tiny apartment and Joe would watch but he wouldn't touch. She got a nurse's outfit. It was starchy and hard when she rubbed up against Joe's skin while he tried to sleep. It gave him a hard-on but he still wouldn't fuck her. He didn't want Susan to die. He thought maybe even telling her about it, about the curse of the women he fucked, could kill her.

Then Susan got the clown outfit. It was the stupidest, craziest thing any girl had ever done to or for him The tenderness of that stupid crazy gesture almost melted his resolve. But not quite.

Not even when he came home from work one day—he'd gotten hired on as a housekeeping aide at the seedy Heart of Chicago Motor Court not too far away—and found Susan in bed with another girl, a chubby Spanish girl with a lascivious red mouth, and the two of them relentlessly ate each other and inserted fingers and vibrators into each other. Joe just made eggs. He and his hard on.

And then Susan started shooting dope again.

Pretty soon she had gone through all Joe's money buying dope. She would shoot up all over her body and Joe would just watch. He locked her in the bathroom one day to try and make her kick her habit but she just jumped out the third story window.

A few days after jumping out of Joe's bathroom window, Susan resurfaced.

She was at least ten pounds thinner and her eyes were huge and full of pain.

"I'm sorry, baby," she said when Joe opened the door and let her in, and he folded her into his arms and felt her bones poking into him.

"It's all okay," he reassured her, but after a minute she grew fidgety and then Joe went and sold his stereo to get her some dope.

In a week, Susan had pawned everything Joe had, which wasn't much. When his apartment was completely barren, Susan left. The next morning, Joe woke up with the headache.

After the surgery, as he lay in his hospital bed reflecting on what life would be like now that he'd had the grapefruit taken out of his head, Joe glanced at a newspaper and saw that the singer Carnie Wilson was having her stomach taken out and having a new one put in. This one would be the size of a peanut.

Carnie Wilson was quoted saying: "I am so obese I could die."

Maybe the grapefruit from Joe's head could try shoving itself inside the peanut in Carnie's stomach. Thinking about it gave Joe the first hard-on he'd had since Susan had left.

When Joe got out of the hospital he didn't want to go home. Home would remind him of Susan and of the grapefruit. He wandered the streets for nearly 24 hours straight and then, completely exhausted, he went home. There was an eviction notice taped to his door. He would have to find a job soon.

Two days later, when Joe was walking and wandering as he'd taken to doing, he bumped into a woman on Wilson Avenue whose hands were smeared with tattoos of the motorcycle gang who'd raised him. She was stocky with brassy blond hair. She had on a Black Sabbath concert T-shirt with the sleeves cut off. Her arms had loose meat hanging off them. She noticed Joe staring at her tattoos and she started talking to him.

"I ain't running with them anymore, though," she said after Joe asked her about the motorcycle gang's Chicago offshoot. I got a good job. I'm a lifeguard. Lotta old people come in there and dog paddle and I sit there. They let me smoke too. No one says shit. Sometimes my husband comes in and we sit there and get fucked up and the old people don't care," she said.

"I'll hook you up if you want," she told Joe after awhile.

"What's that?"

"They need a weekend lifeguard. I'll hook you up."

"I can't really swim."

"I'll teach you," she said.

A week later, the woman, who's name was Denise, let Joe pass the lifeguard test and then hired him as part-time lifeguard. Five days a week, Joe sat in his room watching the little black and white TV he'd found in a dumpster on Astor Street. On weekends he was a lifeguard.

Denise started hitting on Joe. One Saturday, when he came in for his shift and went into the tiny office where he was to sit for the next nine hours watching old people dog paddle, he found Denise sitting there, smoking a Kool. She was wearing cut-off shorts and a tank top. She had enormous breasts. They seemed to have a life of their own. He reflected that if Denise were to travel, a separate passport would have to be issued for her tits.

"You wanna come over tonight? Stewie's out of town," Denise said to Joe, taking a languorous pull on her Kool.

"Oh," he said, frightened.

"Oh? I make you and offer and 'Oh' is all you got for me?"

"I can't."

"You can't what, boy?" Denise hissed through her very small teeth.

Joe thought about how her teeth were so tiny and her tits so huge. Her maker had clearly been having a bad day when her number had come up.

To quell any more nastiness, Joe agreed to come by her place that night.

When he got there, she was wearing nothing but skimpy mesh underpants that rode up her strange flat ass. When Joe didn't instantly grab her and throw her down and fuck her, she flew into a rage. She looked horrible when she was angry.

Finally, as she was calling him a cocksucking pussy, Joe reached down inside the panties and put his finger inside her. She shut right up. He pushed her down to the floor. He moved the crotch of the panties aside and stuck his dick in her. She said: "Baby, baby, baby" and her hips wiggled and her eyes rolled back in her head. The moment Joe came, he pulled out of her, hoisted his pants back up, and left. He figured her death was imminent. He didn't want to see it.

The next day Joe didn't show up at the swimming pool. He didn't want to be hearing about Denise's death. He stayed in for a week straight.

He pulled the phone out of the wall. He cooked up a big batch of rice, the only thing in his cupboard, and subsisted on that.

On the eighth day, he went by the detox where he had once worked. The detox people agreed to hire him back. Patients came and went and sometimes Joe wondered if Susan would appear again.

One day, Joe was walking home from the detox when he saw Denise coming down the street. She was with another older woman. A short woman.

"Joe, babe, what's up?" Denise said.

"Hi," Joe said, and his heart stammered.

"You look pale, what's wrong?" Denise asked.

"Joe?" the other woman said, scrutinizing Joe.

Joe looked nervously from Denise to the other woman.

"Joe, did you used to live in Oregon?" the woman demanded.

"Yes," Joe said tightly. The woman was Martha, his half brother's common-law wife, the first woman whose death was on his head.

"I thought so. How you doin' kid?" Martha said, and she pressed her short squat body up to his.

Joe stood frozen.

He didn't understand.

Just a day later, watching a movie on TV, he saw the stripper, the ex-girlfriend who'd turned up murdered. She was playing a nurse on a TV movie that had been filmed just a few months earlier.

Joe consulted with one of the counselors at the detox, who then hooked him up with a shrink.

"I thought I killed everyone I slept with," Joe told the shrink, a small man with close cropped dark hair and an extraordinarily long nose.

The shrink was fascinated and told Joe he ought to come in three times a week. He then had many colleagues talk to Joe and take pictures of his brain. They concluded that the grapefruit's position inside Joe's brain had triggered an extreme sexual guilt complex. Now that it was gone, so was the complex. Joe needn't think he killed everyone he fucked anymore.

The detox hired Joe back. Eventually, Susan did come back through. At first he didn't recognize her. Her hair was shorn short and she was dressed in vivid colors. But she still wore the cheap jewelry that turned her skin green.

She pretended not to recognize Joe. He cornered her in the hall when she was heading to the bathroom.

"Come live with me. It'll be different this time, I promise you that."

Susan just laughed at him, a hollow lifeless laugh. She wordlessly walked ahead into the bathroom. Joe left her alone for the rest of the day. He tried again the following day.

She just laughed again though. She wouldn't speak.

One night, when all the other patients were in the TV room, catatonically staring at the big screen TV, Joe ran into Susan in the hallway. She was sadly shuffling down the hall. She was wearing a limp blue bathrobe.

"Susan," Joe said, planting himself in front of her.

"You sent me off the deep end, Joe," she said, looking up at him with her lifeless eyes.

"It's all a terrible mistake. I had a grapefruit in my head. I loved you. I didn't want to kill you."

"You're insane."

"No. It was the grapefruit."

"Joe, you need help."

"Let me show you," he said and he forcefully took hold of Susan's bony arm and led her towards the broom closet.

"You have to leave me alone," Susan protested when he'd gotten her in there.

"Look," Joe said, putting his hands to his head and parting the hair there to show her the scar. "There was a thing in my head. A tumor. I can explain everything."

She just looked at him with those hollow eyes. He put his hands on her shoulders and forcibly flipped her around. He leaned her forward so that her cheek pressed against the Band-Aid-colored wall and her ass arched out. He bunched her limp blue robe up over her hips. He parted the incredibly long straight black pubic hairs and kissed her and licked her. He put his fingers inside her. He rubbed his painfully-distended dick against her ass. She finally turned her head and looked at him and a fragment of life had come back into her eyes.

Olive Hershey

Dan the Tree Man

I want to tell you right away this is a mostly true story I made to celebrate my birthday. I know Dan the Tree Man and I've watched him work, so that part of the story I know for fact. Dan is real, and his boss, Triple T Tom, is real, and my cottonwood tree is real and precious. . . I treasure everyone in my story as I do in my life, especially the ones who work their way into my libido.

The made-up part is a birthday gift to myself, something more exciting than French underwear or a new pair of shoes. I guess you'll be able to tell where the character who is mostly me takes her first steps off the curb into that runaway street which is fantasy.

Dan is in his forties now. His hair is curly blonde and his eyes are crazy aquamarine blue, and his hands are large and bark-rough. His face and his arms and legs are tan from climbing up trees and amputating their limbs. Sometimes even entire trunks.

I don't remember what year I first met Dan. Sometime early in the rip-roaring eighties, when I was still in my forties, and Dan must've been in his late thirties the day he showed up with a crew from a tree service whose name I don't remember to trim dead limbs from an old cottonwood in my backyard.

Dan really stood out among the shorter, less comely guys on the crew because his lemon yellow hair swung down his broad back and he towered over the rest. When he smiled at me through the screen door all my teeth started aching and I had to hang on tight to the doorknob.

"Could you step out here and show us which limbs you want cut, ma'am?" he asked, and I nodded, speechless with shyness and weak with desire. I'd reached a time in my life when I'd begun to be invisible to anyone who wasn't trying to sell me something.

"Why do you want to trim this tree?" Dan asked. I walked out my door with a little lift of my heart. He was standing inside my backyard, a wild tangle of wisteria vines and weeds. His head was thrown back, and he was gazing up into shining heart-shaped leaves.

I was afraid a lot of the tree was dead, I told him, feared that rotten limbs were weighing down the healthy part of it. "What do you think?" I asked him, thankful that I'd washed my hair that morning. Thankful I'd worn my new red T-shirt.

Dan took a long time answering while he walked all around the yard, looking at my tree from every angle. I sat down on a bench and crossed my legs. "Let's see what the tree says," he said, glancing over at me and flashing a smile. He unfastened a thick rope from around his waist, tied a brick to the end of it, and threw that brick up over the lowest limb so it swung about twenty feet above his head. Then he hooked the brick on the curved blade of a long-handled saw, rigged up a canvas sling to sit in, and pulled himself hand over hand up that rope in about two minutes.

The muscles in his tanned calves strained against his skin while his feet walked his body up the tree trunk. Meanwhile his sinewy arms were pulling him higher with a robust exuberance that made me want to laugh in admiration. Watching him move naturally and skillfully about his business, I thought of whales I'd seen playing off Provincetown, leaping gracefully in the early morning light.

That day, before he left, we talked a few minutes. Dan told me he was writing a book about his life, and I said I'd like to read it when he'd finished. Then he asked me if I'd read *Oliver Twist,* and I said I had—a long time ago. "I thought you were a person who might've read that book," he said.

As I told you, I met Dan in the early eighties. Over the years I would spot him around town, usually hanging from his lifeline high in a tree. When I could, I'd stop my car for a few moments to watch him fling his rope, then throw himself out into space, and always I'd wish

I could climb up there with him, look around, get my bearings. Breathe clearer air.

By spring of this year, Dan was working with another company, Triple T Tree Service. Last week I phoned Tom, the proprietor, to escape being sued by tenants of forty-four new town homes sprouting like poisonous mushrooms across my back fence. One large limb on my beloved cottonwood had died since the last time Dan was here, and it seemed likely to smash somebody's roof one day soon.

And, suddenly, here was Dan again, suspended in my wrinkled old tree, twenty feet up on the lowest limb, his face in shadow, the sun falling behind him, and his eyes burning with a hot blue flame.

"Olive, is this the one you think you want cut?" he said.

First names. We were now on a new footing.

He pointed to the next limb up, whose bark was beginning to slough. "Looks bad, Dan, don't you think?"

"Yeah, but I want to listen to this tree first."

He had a small hammer with him, as well as the rope and a mountaineer's ax. His boots, laced to mid-calf, had long metal cleats in the soles that gripped the bark tight. From my position below, I admired the athletic tautness of his tanned inner thighs. He was just starting to ascend the main trunk of the tree, had actually sunk the blade of his ax into the bark and was headed higher when I took a leap.

"Hey, Dan, have you got another one of those sling seats?" My words hung there in all that crisp spring air between us. Mockingbirds and cardinals made love in the dark heart-shaped leaves. I held my breath. Stood there in the sun dressed only in an oversized tee shirt, my French bra and a transparent fantasy.

Dan didn't miss a beat, just performed a little pirouette up there on the branch and gazed down at me intently. "Take a look," he said calmly, "in that sack I left on the table there, and you might find one. Just tie it to the rope on the ground and we'll see how good your arm is."

In my teens I was a hunk. The first boy who ever invited me to dance at some eighth-grade party asked how much I bench pressed. Later, men would approach me on the beach to ask if I wanted them to train me as a lady wrestler.

Okay, okay, so I knew better, but life was passing me by. I had to put my hands all over this beautiful, gutsy man. Something seemed fated about our paths crossing again after ten years. . .

I tied the rope to the grommet on the canvas sling. Next I tied two sheepshank knots around a patio brick. Then I threw it underhanded just as high as I could in the direction of Dan the Tree Man, who was waiting for me on the branch.

There was a breathless hush. The only sound came from a southerly breeze shivering the shiny cottonwood leaves so they whispered like falling water. The hair on my arms stood up. The brick rose toward the branch Dan was standing on, and I crossed my fingers. He stretched out a brown arm and that brick smacked squarely into his right palm like a fast pitch nestling into a glove. Deftly, he tossed the rope around a limb above the one he was standing on, and, using it like a pulley, lowered the sling to me on the ground below.

"Okay, just say when you're ready," he called down to me. I'd been ready for about ten years.

I stepped into the sling, held its two ropes, and called up to Dan. "Okay."

Right away the ground fell away under my feet and I began to rise. My heart was rattling around in my chest as I climbed to a leafy house the color of granny apples. Cardinals darted among the leaves and doves moaned like lovers in ecstasy. Up here the wind blew strong and sweet against my skin. The hopeful smell of new green leaves dispelled every doubt. I was in the right place, that day and instant. I was going to make something happen with Dan the Tree Man that would be entirely new and interesting. At least to me, which was all that mattered.

I had reached the moment when in real life I usually blow it, the shimmering, lucent second when I wobble on the threshold of delight, so hungry for Dan's touch my knees and ankles were dissolving. He was reaching down to help me step from the sling to the branch and I said the very first thing that came into my mind.

"Your mama must be so proud." Young as he was, his face still got lines in it when he smiled at me and nestled me with one arm, close to his hip.

"Mama's been dead a long time," he said, "but I sure hope she would." He looked away from me off into the middle distance, and he had that wistful little boy look that gets me.

It turns out Dan knows the value of silence. He could endure a pause now and then, for which I am grateful. Then he looked me dead on and asked me a question. "What's that mean on your shirt?" I looked down, realizing I'd worn a shirt my therapist had given me that has "Hungry for Love" emblazoned on it in red letters. That's the title of a cookbook for lovers he's promoting.

"It means I'm starved for affection," I said, and I pulled my shrink's shirt off and dropped it to the ground. "You too," I said, tugging at the neck of his blue shirt. When he'd slipped out of it, I put my arms around him, stood on tiptoe, and kissed him, tasting the salt on his face. He already had one arm around my waist. That arm tightened and lifted me off the branch, bringing me up to meet him. The look on his face was confused but pleased, so I kissed his lips, wind-roughened but smooth inside. I didn't feel invisible.

"You ever spend the night in a tree?" I asked him.

"When some girl I'm with kicks me out and I can't find a better place to hide."

"Sometime you might just want to lie around in a tree somewhere. You could build a bed or hang a hammock that would rock when the tree moves in the wind. You know?"

He looked at me as if I'd spoken to him in Swahili. "You want to make it in a tree?" he said, slowly, as if savoring the taste of words in his mouth. While he spoke he was looking out over the raw-looking condominiums where once a grove of pecan trees grew to the age of sixty years.

I stopped and looked at him and smiled mysteriously. "I have a secret," I said.

"Nobody'll hear if you tell me." His eyes were blue agate marbles, sweet and guileless. For a second I thought I couldn't do this, shouldn't do it. It would be like stealing. I leaned closer to his freckled pink ear and whispered, "I've wanted to make love to you a long time." Saying the words made me feel even more visible.

"I can make us a bed out of a hundred feet of rope," he said. That's what I like about men like Dan. They know how to do things. In three minutes he'd woven his lifeline into a hammock so sweetly knit it could cradle my new grandbaby. We stretched the two ends between two old limbs and crawled in. The new green leaves made a wall around us, so we couldn't see the houses or the ground or Triple T Tom or the rest of the crew. The wind blew over the roofs of the houses bringing the salt scent of the gulf.

Dan looked admiringly at my new black bra. When he kissed the tops of my breasts and pushed my bangs back from my face, ah, very tenderly, I felt a warm tide rush through me and there I was, floating on the surface of my desire just waiting for Dan to throw me a life preserver.

Dan told me that day he'd finished his novel and asked if I'd read it. Then we talked about being a writer and what that meant about someone's life.

"All a writer wants is for someone to think she's smart and pretty and squeeze her tight," I told him. "It's not easy."

"What's so hard about loving you?" His big rough brown hand was making slow circles on my white belly, and his circles were moving south.

"I don't usually tell people how to do it," I said. "Would you mind moving your hand down a little lower?"

Being with a new man, making love, is like teaching English as a Second Language. One thing Dan knew thoroughly and well were verbs. He used a great number, all in the present tense, and not one of them was passive. We didn't have to worry about our shyness or our nakedness because we were both so busy learning new words. Under his weight my body curved like a supple young tree, moving with the wind, and none of our swayings, none of our sayings, was quite like any other.

And we rocked.

Lee Christopher

Lust After Fifty

Martin Baker was my husband for fifteen years. He left me for a younger, more attractive woman, his soul mate, the woman he couldn't live without.

My depression lasted for six months. But when Martin announced that he and Lynda were getting married as soon as the divorce became final, I felt a sudden sense of freedom. It was as though I woke from a bad dream. While it's true I was over fifty, I figured if I lived to be 100, I still had half my life to live. And if I didn't, I certainly wasn't dead yet. My clit reminded me I was healthy and alive every time I touched it.

The most difficult part about being single again was figuring out how to enter the dating scene after fifteen-plus years of abstinence. I had done my homework with regard to disease and equipment. I had copies of my health certificate made, and I had already purchased a few sex toys.

One advantage to being over fifty is I discovered I was no longer shy about going into adult bookstores. S/M toys didn't turn me on, but I did think I should have on hand one small pair of handcuffs, a new dildo, black garter belt, high heels, and an adequate supply of condoms.

Buying condoms proved to be an education in itself. I discovered there were as many different types of condoms as shades of lipstick. There were latex, regular, extra large, ribbed, smooth, reservoir-tipped, blunt-end, designer or generic, French tickler, French vanilla and a rainbow choice of colors including glow-in-the-dark ones. I opted for one box of regular size, natural colored, and one box of glow-in-the-dark for those kinky nights.

I had thought some of Martin's friends would ask me out, but I was wrong. Martin's friends, like him, all wanted young pussy. What they failed to realize, of course, is that age and maturity provide a woman with much more than wrinkles.

Billy, one of my students at the community college where I taught English Basics, had no age hang-ups. In fact, he said he preferred older women. Billy was twenty-three and wanted to learn how to properly lick a woman's cunt. I knew he would be a quick study and so we agreed to meet every Friday after class. Billy and I shared many wonderful orgasms together, but it had to end. Billy started wanting to talk. The last Friday I saw him, he said I was a real cool lady.

Although I didn't want to get fixed up, go on a blind date and all that, my friend Nancy insisted she had found the perfect match for me. He was fifty-five, a wealthy stockbroker, divorced with no children, had a sense of humor, Nancy said.

Edward and I dated the traditional three times before he kissed me and then asked me to come in for a drink. It had been six months since I had made love with a man my own age and was hungry to be in familiar territory. However, Edward wanted to make love with the lights on. As a woman grows older, she learns to appreciate fully the beauty and value of candlelight. The other problems with Edward were that he cracked his toes and drooled when he came. He apologized, saying orgasm made his lips numb, thus the drool. He said he cracked his toes because it gave him the feeling he was hearing the ticker tape, and nothing was more exciting to him than coming with the sound of making money in the background.

After several more bad blind date scenes, I became totally discouraged and fell into another deep depression. And then one morning after reading the *Rocky Mountain News* obituaries, my life took a 180-degree turn. I discovered the personals.

Since I was not looking for a meaningful relationship or developing a long-term friendship, my choices were limited, but once again I did have choices. I disregarded age requirements. Experience should count for something. The first ad I responded to read: "Passionate romantic male writer desires encounters with woman with a sense of adventure and spontaneity.

Enjoys music, museums, movies, and foreign travel. Answers all inquiries immediately. Signed, Mr.Smith." Well, Mr. Smith and I met at the library. I could tell he was disappointed when he saw I wasn't twenty, but then his male mind shifted and he gave me that look that says, "She can't be that bad in bed." We went directly to his apartment, exchanged health certificates, and I let him select a condom of his choice, but we never got it on because he couldn't even get his cock hard enough. He said he had never gone to bed with a woman who had gray pussy hair. I was devastated.

I left Mr. Smith's apartment, and I drove straight to a beauty supply house where I bought some dye, went home, and colored my cunt hair black.

Seeing my cunt hair black gave me hope. I continued to read the personals. Billy had left fond memories in my mind and so I answered Kevin's ad. Kevin was twenty-eight. Kevin's ad read: "Time for a real man! I can provide excitement, fun, and thrills. Signed, Box 482." Kevin was sweet, but he came before we could get the condom package open.

Making a vow to leave young men alone, I went for the more mature man. Alex from New York wrote: "If you want romance and roses with a man who is experienced, write to me. Signed, James T. Romantic." I wrote to Mr. Romantic. I discovered that as a man ages, he learns how to combine business with pleasure. I received a dozen red roses and a bill from the flower shop he owns.

One of the most interesting men I found in the personals was Larry from Kansas. Larry was a struggling artist with lots of potential and imagination. Larry did not want to meet in person. He wanted phone sex.

Let me digress for a moment. Here's a word of caution to women who use vibrators—if you want to try phone sex, use battery-operated ones. Once, my foot got caught in the cord, and I disconnected myself at a very crucial moment. The other piece of advice I have is to be sure to have an extra supply of batteries.

Now back to Larry.

I rather enjoyed phone sex with him. As I said, Larry was an artist and always inventing new ways for us to enjoy our bodies. One night he thought we should try multiple phone sex. He had three-way calling and so we had sex with a telemarketeer from Ohio who was selling Frisbees made by the same company that makes diaphragms.

Although Larry was an adventure, there is nothing greater than the touch and feel of a man's body next to you. And there is no dildo in the world that can take the place of a real penis.

I decided to sign up with a dating service. This is where I found Roberto. I knew Roberto and I were a possibility when we talked on the phone and he said, "Despite some of my faults, I have my pilot's license and would like to meet someone who enjoys flying." Adventure excited me.

Roberto and I met at the airport. I can't say that it was love at first sight, but it was certainly, for me, lust within five minutes. As Roberto talked, my mind raced with fantasies of making love with him at 35,000 feet and on sandy beaches in Mexico. I'm sorry to report, however, that Roberto did not have the same attraction to me. After talking with me for about ten minutes, he looked at his watch and said he had an emergency. He said he had to fly his mother to a town close by. This is when I became convinced that all men want women who are uninhibited, have *Penthouse* bodies, can cook, and are financially independent.

I took a vow of celibacy.

On my birthday in June, Martin, my now ex-husband, called to tell me he and Lynda had broken up and wanted to know if I'd let him take me to dinner. I said as politely and as dignified as possible, "Fuck you very much!" I hung up the phone, immediately took out the yellow pages and randomly let my finger fall on the list of plastic surgeons. After making an appointment with Dr. Andrew Bissell, I poured myself a cup of coffee and began once again reading the personals.

Jane Creighton

Jane Creighton

Soldiers and Girls

The list of names begins at the vertex of the walls below the date of the first casualty, and continues to the end of the east wall. It resumes at the tip of the west wall, ending at the vertex, above the date of the last death. With the meeting of the beginning and ending, a major epoch in American history is signified.

—National Park Service Brochure, Vietnam Veterans Memorial

Larry, I love you. I'm sorry you had to die. We tried to stand watch together. Christmas Day, 1967, was supposed to be a truce. I'm sorry. Love, Ron.

"Mom, where're these people buried at?"

"He was a real quiet boy."

Chain Howler   Dingleberry
          Messiah

Teofilo C. Rios   Erineo Mendez Mendez
          James P. Vadbunker

Don't Forget
Stephan Jarras
Michael Peterson
I won't
THE GREY GHOST
I've been dead so long trying to keep you alive.

—Scrap of paper left at the Wall
Overheard speech
Engraved names

I.

Two bad dreams. In one, someone's sister is raped; in the other, she is robbed and killed. The first dream occurs in a movie theater. There's a "we," an audience settled on one side of the line between what's real and what's been made up. The seats are reasonably plush. We sit in sight of the ordinary. Concrete floors, a carpeted aisle, no reason to think ill of the people next to you. From this place you fix a belief about your origin, and the sister, when she is on this side, she does so too, she fixes hers. When she is on this side, the theater can be freshened up, the carpet cleared of all but the most resistant stains. The old audience leaves and a new one shows up. The movie ends, and it begins again. We are content. We move on. But when she is on that side, time freezes: He rapes her and we do not move.

The mother who comes to you in the second dream does not look like the one you had. She is tall, thin, and gray-haired. Long in the teeth, an ex-smoker, a corrosive look about the eyes. This woman is commanded to be your mother by the dream. She is the mother who is a stranger, so that the child knows its distinct foreignness. The sister is implied rather than present.

Your uncle, the geneticist, expresses relief at the appearance of research indicating that dream images are randomly pulled from the memory bank and that there is no particular significance to their order. He worries about the way people fool themselves into a reliance on mystery, rather than on the application rational thought to an empirical world. So much for the interpretation of dreams, he says. So much for the pursuit of narrative behind the random discharge of sleep-induced memory. He thinks the need to shape a story from a dream is sentimental, a way to absolve the self from responsibility for the present. As if, "My mother came to me in a dream" might lend itself too much to the idea of fate.

Nevertheless, this is how she comes: Floating. She says, "Your sister has been robbed and killed."

In the first dream the sister is raped. When she is on this side, on your side, the room can be freshened up. But her position shifts at random. When she is on that side a man pushes her, belly to the floor. He is gaunt and pale, dressed in black. She is seven months pregnant. They have moved off the screen. He rapes her from behind. She screams but the audience can't hear her. We are horrified, but no one moves. "Stop! That's my. . . " and we see you form an O with your mouth but we can't hear you, don't see you get out of your chair. We are frozen to the spot, and, after a little while, entranced.

Your mother comes to you in the second dream but she does not look like the one you had. No one around but her and you. In this dream, the sister has already been killed. One dream, the other. One, the other.

"The worst thing a culture can do," Jack said to you—you were in bed, and he'd been telling you the story of his life—"is to train its young men to be killers."

Wrong, you thought to yourself. You're wrong about that, and although the hold this war had on him seemed often to be solely about what had been taken from him, you loved him and had been listening already, days and nights. You didn't know what to say. Didn't move.

Did you ever, I mean you yourself, kill anyone? The question drifts across years, attaching itself to one foolish moment or another, sometimes asked.

"How could I have told you?" In 1987 you're sitting with Fred in his back yard. You haven't seen him for some fifteen years, have tracked him down in your efforts to reconstruct who and where you had been. The two of you are reminiscing about the old days when you were both ostensibly in love, 1971, shortly after his return from two tours of duty as an army medic in Vietnam. You were nineteen then, your feminism at an early stage. You were ferocious about wanting to know everything, from all sides. It was your right to comment on the world.

You also wanted succor, and to give, to be graceful and strong in the relief of others. You, both of you, considered having a child for one fleeting moment in the sunset air of Berkeley. You wanted to be held. Your own mother had just died. Both your parents were gone. You desired to replace them with omniscience, the ability to be subject and object, the giver and receiver of adulation, to be as fecund as your mother but nowhere near as vulnerable to her particular self-effacement, that death.

"How could I have told you about it? You would've had to have been there," Fred says. "I wouldn't wish that nightmare on anybody." He's explaining to you how you were then, how you asked, begged to know what had happened to him in Vietnam. You were trying to understand him. You were working hard to be a good woman. You were also intent, he remembers, on the justice of the thing, almost frantic about your authority to judge a situation that, because you were a female and overtly against the war, you couldn't experience.

It's 100 degrees in the Napa Valley. Fred's wearing olive drab. When you arrived he was clearing the back yard to make way for the christening of his second adopted child. You recognized him immediately, of course, same clothes as the last time you saw him, the combat .boots laced up tight on a day when other citizens are wearing flip-flops or running shoes. He had one of those combustion engines strapped to his back with an extension that cuts weeds, replacing the old-time scythe—that beautifully named tool that lacks mechanical efficiency.

Seeing this, the thought brushed by you of chopping weeds in the back forty with your father the first day he trusted you with his scythe, how you pitched and swung in the vicinity of his muscular body, your sweat and his lifting into the summer air somewhere else, in another time. When Fred saw you he unstrapped himself and strode through the carport to embrace you.

This is how you could really tell: He stopped on a dime in front of you, spread his legs, and executed the same fervent, formal hold that used to make you wonder where his hips were, and how you might possibly manage to make his head and neck melt into the welcoming valley of your own shoulders. You never could. Perhaps you never finally wanted to.

You talk through the afternoon, painting histories, your own nomad existence against the turmoil he's had trying to stay in place. Jack figures faintly on your horizon, not yet present enough to acknowledge. And Fred is looking for work. Wants to get back into some health-related field, after years spent burning up in the wine business in the frigid grip of his remote father. He's been battling alcoholism, difficult lifelong rifts within his family, and of late, stuff about Vietnam. What stuff? He brings out his scrapbook. Says he hasn't touched it for years but found it again recently after his fourteen-year-old nephew came home gung-ho from some Nam movie.

There's the picture, newsprint. Heads and torsos on the ground, Hamburger Hill. Fred on his right elbow leaning over a man whose head is thrown back. Hands busy with something. Tablets. A syringe? The face of the man whose head is thrown back grimaces, a bent look, lush with pain. And Fred, steely in the picture, seems heroic. Is. Both like himself and unlike. How he could inhabit the figure of a man shaped to give solace and to protect. Even bent over a wound he is upright, uniform. The photo an instant of permanence rippled with memory; how he would disappear into dissonance, the room disintegrating, table and bed particled and wheeling. The wild nights he would try to crumble in your arms and, failing this, walk out the door, not come back.

You didn't understand it. You were nineteen and busy, you thought, trying to replace family. He said a few things—house, marriage, lifetime—and for a moment you thought that meant you, what you wanted, what he had. To live in a home the beloved would have you enter. The woman he marries instead of you manages to sit through the panic of his nightmares, the long absences. She is lovely. Strong as a rock, he says. Staying power. He always knows where to find her. Now he sits before you holding his first child, a severely palsied boy who lurches and gurgles, whose bright eyes drink in the landscape and you, a figure in it. The problem with you, you think, is your trickling desire to have doubled for him, for anyone else, to have tripped out to the perimeter and taken the shots yourself. Felt in your flesh the wound that might have kept them all alive as you, faint and spent, pressed your breasts and hips into the earth and bled.

II.

So, what I loved about Jack seemed to have less to do with his body than with standing next to him casing the terrain in Tilden Park, imagining the night air in the lowlands of Vietnam. How he sat backed up to a tree and listened to the discrete moans of a dying Vietnamese man out in the bush. I let him talk.

A buzz in the air, slow-moving insects drifted through sunlight. I would've been here, he said, and the guy just over that rise, maybe twenty yards away.

Phenomenally boring, he said. The waiting. Those soft moans. He said he was thinking, "Oh, let him die," and I waited to let the story, such as it was, wind down, pick up again, wind down, sunlight dappling the ground.

Jack was a medic, too, but different from Fred. Fred was a rich man's son, whereas his father had abandoned them when he was two, turned up later as a garbage collector in Pasadena but never wrote, and never sent money. Jack said he had to struggle for every damn thing he ever got, and the war sucked it all up, left a big hole gaping at the center of his life until he learned how to sandbag it, then fill it in. I met him much later in my life, both of us brilliant with suffering and loss. Fully ready, we'd say, to handle our casualties, caress them into the ground and move on.

"In sixty-eight," said Jack, "I got bounced out of college for beating up a narc, freshman year. So I was 1-A and it was either enlist, get drafted, or split to Canada . . .

"I was in a sweat, kind of desperate. I thought about Canada for a while, but couldn't, you know, see myself there. Nobody'd back me up. My family, my mother, she'd never fathom it. And people I knew were signing up. So I thought, I'll enlist, get a better chance to pick my position. Being a medic, maybe, I could help save lives. . .

"But also, by that time Kennedy had shifted his politics. He was campaigning on an anti-war platform, and for sure he was going to get elected and put an end to it, pronto. I knew I'd never get sent up. So I signed myself into the Army, went into training. Two months later, boom, he's dead. Oh Lord, sitting in those barracks, a bunch of nineteen-year-olds. . . .

"When that came over the wire. . . you can just imagine how I felt."

Jack spent a year in combat, but before being shipped to Vietnam he worked the paraplegic ward at Letterman. He had a routine. Every shift he would come into the ward and begin turning patients. Soldiers paralyzed below the neck by severed spinal cords were strapped into beds that rotated 360 degrees to facilitate a more equitable relationship between each soldier's body and gravity. That kept the blood flowing, helped reduce the possibility of bedsores."Once you got done rotating the last guy to a standing position," he said, "it was time to roll the first one face down. We did that all day."

"They'd line them up and ship them out of San Francisco," he said. "And every day they'd rain back down on us in pieces. Their skin would get real flaccid. You had to work their fingers so they wouldn't curl up."

He used to walk through my dreams, sometimes a sidekick, sometimes a mentor to my adventures. He'd show me how to load and unload trucks, guns. That was before we became lovers. When we were still friends, and I didn't, somehow, feel responsible for him, for all that time he'd spent in the Army.

He didn't ask me to feel that way.

He was tired of it, he often said. Just a kid when the war swept through his life. His own nearly grown children carried away early, he said, by a savage ex-wife who had plenty of money but still wanted child support. He took care of people all his life, he said. Couldn't save anybody anymore.

He had a kind of exuberance. He could curve himself and roll out of cadence on a walk, or back into it, sometimes play both ends against the middle. Take it or leave it, finally, after a lot of hard work. And he loved sex.

Who doesn't?

"The worst thing a culture can do," he said, sitting up in bed," is to turn its young men into killers." He was talking about himself, how hard his life had been.

The mother's there sometimes when I roll over, solitary. I'm sweating, I've just aroused myself over a memory, dip and thrust of someone's buttocks, the strokes I make cresting a wave, an arm flailing against the horizon. Momentary. Disappeared. She's always walking along a sidewalk. Looking at me, but not for me. She never says: Why haven't you had children?

I think of a man I met hitchhiking, 1973, British Columbia. That day we traveled through high country, near Kamloops? Through land Dan Blocker—"Hoss" on Bonanza—owned. Maybe he had just died. What was this guy's name? He wore platform shoes and bell-bottoms, regularly did sound for the Grateful Dead but was going for a four-month stint on some mining operation. Said he was an expert with explosives. Would put us up for the night. Long hair, tie-dye shirt, etc. I sat in the middle, sort of straddling the gearshift, my girlfriend on the passenger side. When he shifted gears it was a gesture, an invitation. Fuck authority. Want some?

He told the foreman we were friends of his wife's, then settled us on the floor in the front room of his cabin.

"Either of you feels more comfortable in a bed, just come on back," he said. "Plenty of room."

The strokes I make cresting a wave, an arm flailing against the horizon.

I went back and it was something like—I had my period but felt awkward about mentioning it until he said, after trying to thrust himself into me, "OK if we pull the plug?"

"Platforms? You fucked a guy who wears platforms?" she said to me the next morning, and I didn't answer. Too embarrassed. I heaved my pack on my back.

Did you come, huh? Did you come?

Boston University, 1970. The drawing room in the brownstone dorm set aside for scholarship students. We cook our own meals, learn to manage a limited budget. Preparation for life. Massive quantities of food after midnight. Cindy's got pelvic problems because her boyfriend weighs 300 pounds. Mary Beth does too much acid. Margaret's pre-med, scrubs her face with alcohol, is bulimic. Charlotte. Charlotte. Autism? She sits cross-legged on her bed, rocking for hours. We whisper behind her back, pity and contempt. I photograph myself in the drawing room mirror. I'm fat, can't wear the clothes from home. "They always bring too much the first year," says Mrs. Mahoney, dorm mother, who's talking to my brother about the quantity of baggage I've carried through the door. *Her mother's dead and she's got no home,* he thinks. *What the fuck is she supposed to do with it?*

Mrs. Mahoney screaming on the landing: "No boys after ten! What are you? Sluts?" Hundreds of people, mostly men, race down Bay State Road after slashing tires at the president's house. Invasion of Cambodia. I go to bed with a Guatemalan freshman in the middle of the student strike, but will not make love, and so we argue back and forth. Why not? I don't want to, let's be friends, the whole world's falling apart, why sleep alone? Why sleep at all? But I'm insistent, and sleep with him there, without dreaming.

We will meet again, fourteen years later, New York City. Romaldo will be in exile, speaking in various forums against the century of U.S. imperialism in Guatemala, and will come across my name on a list of Central America anti-intervention organizers. We will sit at my kitchen table and discuss old times, what has happened to us, the sweet luck of finding an old friend immersed in such work. I'll report my travels here and there, the incessant search for a way of life, the urgent clarity I felt among the friends I made in Nicaragua, how passionate they were, and optimistic, and how difficult that was to maintain back home. He'll tell me about study at the Sorbonne, the intellectual life of Latin Americans in France, his return to Guatemala, death lists, victories, life in Mexico, the murder of friends. Intent. Flirtatious. And I'll begin to feel, listening to him, the frayed edges of my narrative, its inchoate Americanness, what I can't make clear through stories, Romaldo, the years of sexual politics played out against a scale of militarist history too broad to sketch with ease, how I can't place myself with any certainty—

"No, really," he'll say, with a gesture cutting me off. "What have you been up to?"

And I'll try again, speaking about frustrating disappearances among some of my peers, which for me will mean a fading off of idealism, an inability to harbor in a complex present relatively simple lessons from a ferocious past. How myself I've avoided marriage, children, a straight career, how finally I've been unwilling to confuse myself with family ties or upward mobility.

He'll look amused. He has already written several novels. Been married and divorced, has a child in Mexico being raised by its mother.

"You were so neurotic then," he'll say easily. "You still are."

III.

Jeremias Roman   Edward W. Milan
Pelesasa S. Tauanuu

Bernell Taylor
Fred L. Thrift

Say them. Speak. Dead young men smiling toward home, in a picture propped against the hard reflecting surface of the Vietnam Veterans Memorial. I look, remembering everything. In 1979, I fell in love with a woman whose name I keep close to me. She was lovely and cheerful, militant. For years she organized with the United Farm Workers, until the patriarchalism became intolerable. Then, she rolled over into the feminist movement against violence against women, where I met her. At that time, all of it seemed so clear, a visible war we could fight. We'd wrestle our bodies back from billboards, magazines, Nazi porn scenarios, the fear of being out at night. It started circa 1978 with that *Hustler* cover of a woman's torso being fed headfirst into a meat grinder which—if you were standing in a bus station or corner store—you could see stacked next to local papers blandly detailing the night's disappearances, suspected rapes, murders. With a suddenness that raked your breath you might have felt—depending on who you were—that no matter what you said about yourself, no matter what progress you thought you were making, you were still meat, somebody's target, a naked bitch.

Who was the enemy? She moved to New York and joined a consciousness-raising campaign which included, among other things, organized tours of Times Square, in which groups of shirted and sweatered women familiarized themselves with the daily workings of the pornography industry. We went to movies, entered peep show booths, stared up into the crotch of a woman whose face we couldn't see, but who seemed angry by the way her hips swung away from the window. As if her hips could talk, muttering disgust, a grunt. Because we stood there frightened and appalled, and also, some of us, fascinated, and not likely to reach through the window to stick money in her cunt. Cunt.

The woman I loved was slight, had soft, blond hair. But you could see how firmly she planted her feet when she walked, how her hips swayed and filled the air around her with purpose. Once next to me in a biting, cold sun on 59th Street, she turned smiling and said, "Sometimes I think you're the man." An inside joke. How I leaned into her, my large hands playing across her body.

I watch myself leaning into her, how my hands played across her body, how I'm the woman being the man who blushes and laughs, pleased with this idea, resting my head for a moment on her hip, then going on.

I watch myself watch her, how I was sometimes the man moving over her and inside, then a woman looking down then up into her face, her sense of my approach, her skin, my hands. Uncertain. Immigrant. How she listened to me tell her about my mother. But I was talking about myself, how hard my life had been.

She died fighting cancer in 1984. I keep her name close. Her body, long before that, was lost to me in the ambiguity of my own sexual preference. The stripper's hips blur into hers, mine. Eventually, the movement's rage against violence turned to problems of correct sex, a rigorous self-policing. How could you continue to sleep with men? Women naturally prefer a gentle eroticism, egalitarian, give and take. No they don't. Not "naturally" anything. Yes they do, but they don't know it; they've been socialized to hate themselves, their bodies. Butch tops and femme bottoms are simply learned, oppressive behaviors. Uh huh. But.

I remember raw sex, a spindly guy whose name I kept forgetting, whose past I didn't care about, and who pleased me by not caring about mine. Part of a project to dismiss someone else, her, another man, the particular fence I'd been riding between gay and straight.

"I don't want to hear about your damn past," Jack spat out. Of course he didn't. He wanted things fixed and settled. He'd worked hard to make himself a man, singular, as hard as I'd worked to avoid being a woman caught in the perimeter, a target in stark light. Trying to double and multiply, hurl myself across continents, unlike my mother. Veterans take their tours along the wall, slow and easy. Graceful descent. Stop short, touch the wall here and there, maybe like feeling a body for its pulse, or like a lover. But maybe it's too soon to touch, maybe she won't yield, soft press of their hands reaching way overhead, the way the names pile up at the center, how the letters feel rough, constant, always there, background and subject, yet always a surface, prophylactic. The names a barrier you can't quite, can't—

The mother never says: Why haven't you had children?

So I don't answer: Maybe, Mother, because you were enough for me. And because your children leave you.

Then Jack wanted to spice things up. Years, anyway, since I'd seen one. Maybe I'd changed. Together, we got a couple of videos and retreated to a friend's house who was away for the weekend, since neither of us had a VCR. Our friend's TV was secluded in a shady, screened-in back porch. We sat upright on a wicker love seat, already beside ourselves trying to stretch our legs, get comfortable. Ten minutes into it, she was down on all fours in front of a roaring fireplace, having a party front and back, Muzak burbling in the background. She sucked one, the other fucked her, a kind of grammar. Body language. Raw redness in stark white flesh framed under the gaze. A certain uniformity about their bodies punctuated and defined Jack, then me.

Were we supposed to fuck now?

"Pretty boring," he said after awhile, and shut it off. We went to bed without touching each other. My silence, this time, called the shots.

Later, he tried to name the dissonance. "I guess you're kind of prudish, huh?"

We were driving the brushy hill into Sausalito, on our way to see my friends Simone and Etel. Etel had written a novella about the execution of a Lebanese teacher of deaf-mute children during the Lebanese Civil War. The teacher loved a Palestinian man, had joined the Palestinian resistance, and for that reason was captured and held at her school by the same Christian Phalangists who were her childhood playmates. They interrogated her in front of the children, lingering for hours over the fine points of her religious education, her youth, her loyalty, her betrayal. Then they tore her body apart, slowly and with purpose. The children could not ask: *Where, where did she go?*

But I was not thinking of that, at least not in any way I could name. I was thinking about bodily integrity in the silence that filled the air between him and me. My mother's, the paleness of her flesh glimpsed through the bedroom door in the last years of her life. Things that frightened her: silence, abandonment. A story she told about driving home alone one night, barely making it to the front door after being chased and nearly run off the road by a car filled of strange men. How she felt safe with my father who would never, she made clear, make her feel the way I do now. Caught in the glare, misread, reduced.

My life. Yours. My life has been so hard.

Once I tried talking with Jack—I was trying to be intimate—about the fantasy that both thrilled and shook my nights, all those working-class guys like people up and down the road I grew up on—out in the field fucking that woman. Somehow they at least had class status. She had none at all, she was naked except for that trench coat that fell away from her, and they were clothed. That's the way the images, first seen as photographs, work. They gradually embed themselves in memory, dropping details along the way, but from the first you know that the flat image has already become something other than a woman with a name, a body both like and unlike others, who lives in a house, maybe with a sister, step mom, kids. Works nights or doesn't, first shift at the rest home, cooking, cleaning. You can't really see her hands, if the nails are bitten off or manicured, how they might work a needle, pump gas, or even touch another's flesh because your eyes have erased any evidence of who she might be. What she might do with her hands has nothing to do with what is happening here.

So I told Jack, because I was unhappy that things weren't going well, and I couldn't figure the weave of the problem. Was it the sex? The fights about money? My fear of debt and his carelessness about it? We still might have married, had a child. But he had grown children already, whom he never saw unless they bought their own plane tickets and came to him. This bothered me, as did my own torpor. I'd have liked to shake it; it didn't feel like my best self. I was trying to learn how to say what I was thinking, instead of drifting in reticence.

I mean, I couldn't expect him to read my mind.

I said, sometimes, I felt myself leave, lift out and hover over the bed, and sometimes it was pleasurable to be released from who I was, to become thoroughly animal, though always still that "I," watching myself, us, him plunging into a body, me. But lately I'd been invaded, I said, by something abject, dissonant, a sense of myself disintegrating on a field. That somehow the fantasy had reverted to the photograph, too much like what was actually happening to a woman not given her name. I was quick to tell him: no, no, it's not about you.

Maybe it scared him. At first I didn't know what he felt. But he wrote it up, days later. It became his story, a working-class man in love with a middle-class woman who fundamentally saw working-class men as faceless, brutish in the night. And all this finally a legacy of his own oppression, how he was forced to be that soldier in an alien field, poring over bodies he couldn't patch or save. How the women he'd known who all have names couldn't love him enough. The idea became the measure for everything. How he never had anything growing up but a disappeared father and a mother who struggled to keep them all clothed. She did. She did that. They all worked hard. And when he got bounced out of college, she didn't back him up. "Your country's calling you," he said she said, but she worried for him, and prayed for him when he enlisted.

All that pain. What the culture did to working-class guys, and then women worrying him about debt, about where the money was going to come from. "And now you're telling me you have a problem?" His story for it, a true story. He worked hard for what he's got, so where's the payoff? What the war did, still does, a way to keep talking.

And a way to shut you up. Because I let him stay out there in the timeless muck, humping his burdens while I kept track. I loved him or I hated him. It didn't matter.

Oh let him die.

IV.

1990. Just bought cigarettes from Vietnamese man at local gas station around corner. He smiles always and calls me "Ma'am." Have got on black cowboy boots, stretch pants, brown leather simulated army bomber jacket from Banana Republic that Jack bought for me last year, not long before the end. Already holes in the sleeves. Have just come from Friday afternoon beer-drinking session with best girlfriends and am feeling surly. Have been talking body hair, how little nephew and nieces stare and whisper to each other when they get chance to see pubic hair pouring out of our bathing suits. Bush in the armpits. Wasn't supposed to be a problem after 1968. Am feeling surly but don't act it. Big part of self so very sorry, Mother, to be smoking still. Slide through transaction, nodding and smiling, try not to be apologetic. What does he care? With grin cover up various stances of self in apparent conflict: wholesome worldly fresh youth smile aging sweet femme crusty butch sarcastic academic androgyne? Anglo? Ma'am?

Hand on car, reach inside open window to pull handle on busted car door, just about everything breaking down, can't keep up funds to fix and replace. New war about to breach, banks failing, whole new wave, immigrant, uncertain. Door open, lift right leg to enter, spread of hips in the air, weathered hand cuffed by leather holding keys, am aware of old feeling.

Of being someone else, same but different. A boy, a young man. Jangle of keys stuck into hip pocket, scrape of soles on asphalt. Manly tug on the jacket, sweet thin hips. Don't worry, baby. I'll take care of you. A boy named Joe trembling at the barn door: I'm going to kiss you. Now.

Undo the buttons of her blouse, caress her neck and touch, just lightly touch her breasts, take her hand and pull her inside. The barn loaded with rusted tools, furniture, parts of an organ, a wicker baby carriage, an old Crosley only her father could fix. Lean her against it, push against her. Hold her head in my hands and kiss her eyes, her cheeks, her lips, run my hands down her neck, catch the blouse and peel it away from her shoulders, the bra, her breasts. Her breasts. Work my hips press into her, work my hand into her cutoffs, pull the zipper, take them down, off her, lay her down in the cramped and dirty back seat of the Crosley, lay her down naked and me still fully clothed tugging at my own belt because she is breathless and frightened, hardly moving but looking at me, wide, bright eyes waiting for me to pull it out and I do and say *I love you baby* and with my hand guide my cock through her pushing, and pushing split the cherry, sail into her all dark and exploding.

No, that's not what happened. He trembled, he kissed me. Then—I don't know why—he walked back up the field to his car, got in, drove away.

The strip of 35mm contact print I remember from a book of photographs by an American photographer. Floating in white space, just large enough to see exactly what happens but too small to read for the particularities of face. Eyes in focus or out? The set of the mouth? Somewhere out in the country, at the border of a grassy field, backgrounded by the dense undergrowth of a forest. In the first, a group of beefy men stand in a clump toward the left of the picture frame. Mostly their backs are to the camera, blue jeans and denim jackets, hair scraggly or parted and greased back, men in their thirties and forties. Bikers. Rednecks. Toward the right of the frame a woman wrapped in a trench coat lies curled on her side, her legs bare. High heels? Slender, her chin tucked down in her chest, an arm stretched out in the grass.

A jowly man, a giant, has entered the second frame. He has bent himself over her, has placed his hand on her knee and is pulling open her legs. He wears baggy chinos, which seem to broaden his already vast backside. Hindquarters. Butt. Ass. His body blocks most of her but there is a tip of breast, the coat dropping away from pale thighs, the turn of her face toward him. The other men talk among themselves. One or two turn their heads.

Third frame, on his knees, her legs frogged out to the sides, his head descending into her crotch. His hair—his hair is—her face slack, on her back, breasts falling slightly off to the side, his hair a buzz cut his short fat neck crinkled with effort, burrowing into her.

Fourth, side view, shot low, the men surrounding her pinch and pull her breasts. She fills the frame. See sky behind her. Face blocked out, her body arched? See his eyes, he is looking up at her face, breasts, his nose and mouth buried in her, cunt? Vagina? Beaver?

Fifth, somehow nothing of his flesh. He hoists himself elbows locked belt undone and zipper downed massive clothed weight meeting and sunk into the delicate rise, her flesh only.

The sixth frame pulling back, mostly broad grass, woods behind. Now she is left planted in the field while, one by one, each man fucks her, drifts away.

A mother moves about somewhere behind me.

It is the year 2000.

There is a certain uniformity. Is she you or me? Am I her, or doing it to her? In the distance, a figure in dark clothes cuts across a snow-blanketed field, heading this way. Over and over. Who is it?

duVergne Gaines

i want to fuck you like a man

I dream of breaking him. He is tall, six feet, three inches. Burning and always a bit tousled brown hair. Green eyes and rosy cheeks. His shoulders are broad as the sun. Long, thick, lean legs. A slightly cock-eyed flash of white grin. He dazzles. He's married. With children. I know them.

I want to take him. Violently. I can't stop thinking about it. At night my pussy clamors for him. I lick my fingers, lie on my back, slip my hands between my legs, part the lips of my cunt and lacquer the nub. At night, I become alive.

mottle the thrum brown
cock of his, inside out
grade school art project
push the lower intestines
back and up, scoot the liver
to the left, finger out
a uterus, butterfly droppings
for ovaries and drill out

vagina canal with pencil ends
so that my sink hole
closes up, labia fold in
snap wallet and clitoris
goes jack-the-beanstalk up
thick, hard and purple
i can lunge into him
feel his whimpers at first
i am thrilled electric by
snail horn rummaging in
warm pink i nudge up into his
gut my ass-muscles glisten
with each thrust his short
breaths trill trill like a
cicada his nipples glow
furious bright his lips
part his belly shakes his
thighs twist tight around me
i cum in a gush of leaves

Her legs curl wide at the thought of light, soft on his bare chest. The girth of his waist. She goes to him. Wraps her arms around his neck. Pushes her groin into his cock. Breathes deep the musk of his body. Her mouth fastens on his. Deep and desperate. She tongues his ear, tunnels the veins in his neck. Grinds her pussy up into his hip. Takes one hand and gropes his cock. His size makes her sopping wet. She groans, his legs quiver. His cock grows.

She kneels in ecstatic service. Nuzzles his swelling sack through his pants like a colt searching for a nipple. She mouths the shaft with hot breath from outside. He tries to stand. She reaches up and torques his nipples. She unfastens his belt. Unzips his pants with her teeth. Nuzzles the impatient mound. Pulls the boxers down. This man larger than life. This man like a God, he trembles as a child. The sight of his cock erect, swelling effusive is like a drug. The head glistening moist with resin. First, she cups his testicles. Licks his inner thighs. Exhales on the furry, straining nut sack. His hands are winding in her hair. Touching her face, her lips, her mouth. He shudders and whispers. Begs for a mouth, a cunt, a touch.

She puts her mouth rich with saliva on his ruby red shaft. He bucks into her mouth. She caresses his nuts and buttocks as she tunnels the length of his cock. She shuttles her tongue over his cock pushing it deeper and deeper into her throat. The shaft nudges her tonsils. She gorges on his cock. The deep thrusts satisfy like deep thrusts into her cunt. She requires it. She requires him. His cock swells like a blood-filled hot bullet popsicle. She pulls her mouth off, laps at the tip. She lathers and licks his pulsing blue king cock vein like a cat.

His legs start to buckle. He pulls her head up. Takes his mouth and kisses her with such force. Mouths mash and lock. He sweeps his arms about her. Wraps her to him. Grinds his cock into her. Twines and tugs at her hair and buttocks. Ferociously kissing her eyes and mouth and face and neck and ears. He pulls at her clothes. She shoves him away. Looks at him.

Slowly takes her shirt off, her skirt, her shoes, her panties. He comes to her. Bends down and sucks on her nipple like a hungry baby. His hands travel down to her cunt. He shudders at her wetness. His fingers circle her clit and then push into the hot field of her cunt. She is silky and sweet. She lives for this. She is supple and light.

He falls to his knees and scoots his tongue into her cunt. He roulettes around and around her jeweled clit and darts his tongue into her vagina, in and out and in and out. Then in a flash he stands and grabs and lifts her up and straddles her legs about his waist and thrusts his cock deep, deep, deep into her klatch. She feels him as she has never felt another man in her entire life. Her entire pussy is electric. The firm girth of his cock overwhelms her. As he thrusts in and out of her she yelps and whinnies. Her whole being becomes the mouth of her cunt. And the sensation of the passage of his cock through it over and over again. She is knotted about him. Her face tornadoed into his. Her arms feeling his arm and back muscles and buttock muscles as they lunge into her. Her clit rubs up against the nub of his pelvis with each thrust. She is going mad. He lunges more and more deeply. Her clit swells and swims with pleasure. She can feel it coming on. She can feel it start to ride. She is so hot and wet and full and mad. She is completely penetrated in that place. The lips of her cunt stretch and contract around him. Each time his prick fires into her, his hands holding her ass, her clit is illuminated like an act of fucking God. Sweat is pouring off of them. Until it fully comes and something is summoned forth. A yell so deep and guttural, animal and rich. That they both laugh. Laugh like hyenas and fall onto the bed in hysterics.

For a moment. Until he looks at her so hard it scares her. Kisses her with a gentle fury. And grabs her from behind. Pushes her onto her knees. And at first just touches her buttocks from behind, roving fingers all about each fleshy half moon. And then leans over her from behind cupping her breasts. Licking his fingers, pinching her teats, tugging. His pungent smell alters her brain. Her loins are famished. He drives her crazy hunched over her, not pene-trating. Then he licks her buttocks. Breathes on them softly. Finds the nub of her cherry asshole and licks. Then down further to her cunt. Into her cunt. Then her blossomed clit. He lathers her clit and asshole with his tongue. Then leans over her again. Breathing deeply from behind. She feels his cock rub up against her. She beseeches him to fuck her. He kisses the nape of her neck. And asks her if she wants it. She says, Yes, yes, a thousand times yes. Fuck me, you bad fucking mongrel. Fuck me. He teases the mouth of her cunt with his rock hard moist cock. He says she is like a god to him. He says she is all he desires. He wants to die inside of her. He says he wants to fuck her every moment. He says he wants to have a dozen children with her and fuck her pregnant and drink her milk.

He lightly penetrates her. Just a touch. In a bit and out a bit. She is going mad. He says he wants to grow sagging old with her. He says he wants to fuck her when they are both old and dry and crotchety. He wants her forever. He is hot like a fever. She can feel his heart slamming through her back. She reaches one hand under her to her clit. He reaches one hand to join her clit. The fingers circle her clit divine. He cuts into her fiercely, suddenly now. She gasps and fucks for the universe. Juts her ass up into his loins. Feels like she was born to do this, born for this moment. Born to encompass this man. He rams into her with total desperation. His entire body arching into her cunt. She toggles her clit with her fingers and his fingers. She can feel his cock swell ever more within her. It feels enormous. It catches some ecstatic hook within. She can not breathe as the pleasure sublime begins to roll from deep within her gut and cunt and heart. He bucks in and out of her and starts to say her name and Oh my God, Oh my God, Oh my fucking God and violently shakes as he cums repeatedly inside of her. She is moaning wild. She can feel the semen fire into her loins, a gift like water on dry, cracked soil. It is almost enough.

They collapse. They are drenched. Each feels the other's heart ricochet. They nip. Smile messy. Starried blue to green, green to blue. The sublime sweat of sex.

But she wants more, she wants to fuck him. She wants a cock. She wants to plunge into his asshole like a man and have him like a girl. She wants him to feel her inside of him and surrender and clench. She wants his legs wrapped around her neck as she drives into him. She wants to break into his body. She wants this God of a man to know what it is like to crave complete domination. What it is like to feel only appeased by her cum. What it is like to see her face as she mounts him. How it feels to want to bear a child of her from his balls to his cock to his stomach to his throat. And know the reckless thrill of her growing and thrusting and exploding inside of him.

Mary McGrath

Matthew

Matthew was 14, barely old enough to know women, let alone men. Hell, he barely even knew his own body, overgrown and awkward, like a puppy with its wide feet and unmanageable body, too small to be effectual, too large to be under control.

Sometimes Matthew noticed his classmates staring at him—girls and boys. He didn't know what to make of it. Was something amiss? His shirt untucked? A button missing? Maybe his fly was open? What Matthew didn't know was that others were in awe of him; not just of his Adonis good looks, or the wry smile that could mesmerize strangers, but also at his style—a wanton style that made him seem almost shy.

He liked track and the solitary victories that surrounded the sport. He could command the turf to create magic beneath his feet. At first, he was attracted to the 100-yard dash. Sprinting, the dirt would fly, and the win would be ten seconds away. It was immediate and blame could be cast upon no one but himself.

But before long, the greater distances began calling him. Cross-country allowed his mind to abandon the trivia that circled on the school yard, minutiae that bored him, but still required his attention. On the track, he could focus on the larger issues that rendered him sleepless, wrestling with things he was afraid to question. Running gave him a temporary relief. He could condense his energy and, with rehearsed rhythm, pick off his opponents one by one, the thrill of the tape stretched taut before him.

Fall practice was already underway. Coach Barnes executed the first of many routines: ten laps around the track. Matthew was bored by the request. After all, he had defeated both Tom and Paul last Saturday in their meet against Battle Creek. Why should he have to run again? After two laps, Matthew fell behind to plot his escape and get a jump on the showers. It was bad enough never getting enough hot water, let alone tolerating a bunch of guys whooping and hollering all the time. Matthew was quite well-endowed for his age as well, and all the guys liked giving him a hard time.

He found their jests irritating and embarrassing. No doubt most of them thought he'd gotten laid by now, but Matthew wasn't that sort of guy. Sure, he had his fantasies, especially in the mornings, when he couldn't contain himself.

Slowly, he would wake to the pounding of his impatient penis. He'd start on his back, massaging his thighs, pretending his palms belonged to someone, anyone else. Then, with rehearsed expertise, he'd begin, his right hand grasping his cock, moving up and down to the pulse of his stereo. Matthew would arch his back, his head buried among the pillows that were still damp from dreaming. With his left hand he'd wipe the hair from his forehead as he wrestled with guilt, delight, and confusion. Soon it would be too late to think as his ass tightened and he took aim, his juice spraying like a ripe beer on a hot summer day. Relieved, he'd rise, pretending that nothing had happened as he sat down at breakfast with his parents, wolfing down his usual cereal, toast and juice.

Fortified, he'd head for the shower, and begin all over again, first lathering up the soap in his hands like a sculptor, spreading it like warm clay all over his parts. This time he'd take the shaft in both hands, massaging it like a pump, trying to hold back his excitement. Thankfully the radio was always blaring, its screeching guitar rifts muffling his whimpering cries. Thighs still quivering, he'd rinse off, and would begin his routine for school.

Back at the track, it was time for Matthew to make a quick exit from his dull practice. The coach liked him well enough, and with his legs already aching from Saturday's meet, he figured it was OK to take part of the day off. Besides, he really was tired of being last in the showers. His legs hurt. He deserved a reprieve. He headed for the locker room.

Matthew started peeling off his shorts, but was having difficulty taking his jockeys down.

"Great timing," he thought. Matthew knew he had little control over himself, but why was he getting a hard-on right now, right in front of all the guys who would soon to be coming into the showers with their Cherokee yells and shallow tales of victory?

He tried covering himself with a towel as he headed toward the corner of the gym, but the harder he tried, the larger it grew. He felt stupid, so he finally dropped the towel and picked up his gait. On his way over, he caught a glimpse of another member of his team, Erik. Erik was a freshman with promise, and the quickness of a jackrabbit. Looking over, Matthew noticed Erik's gaze upon him. An uneasy flow of tension started from his abdomen and crawled up his torso, like warm lava flowing over dry earth. The sensation puzzled and excited him. He had never felt quite like this, except while reading dirty magazines or watching the freshman girls bounce during cheerleading practice.

He dismissed the feeling and turned his concentration toward standing under the hot pulse of the shower, and his aching thighs. Blasting the faucet, he ducked his head beneath the spray and began massaging his legs and buttocks. Erik, who had made his way toward the showers as well, liked how well Matthew seemed to know his body, much larger and more formed than his own, which still hinted at prepubescent boyishness.

Erik couldn't help noticing Matthew's erection, and wondered if he should turn away, or continue watching. He backed up slightly, so that he was partially hidden by one of the lockers, and continued looking on. Matthew's hard-on was growing larger, which seemed odd, since he didn't really seem to be doing anything to encourage it. Erik noticed that he himself was suddenly getting excited by this observation. In Sweden, where he came from, things like this were perfectly normal. It was not uncommon for boys to wander into puberty with a variety of experiences, and experimentation with other boys was not unusual.

He wondered if Matthew might be so inclined, so he ventured into the stall right next to him. Dropping his towel, he turned the knob and was immediately doused with a spray of cold water. Matthew started howling at Erik's misfortune.

"Gee, I thought if I got in here early, I could at least get a few minutes of hot water," Erik exclaimed.

Matthew, noticing Erik's hard on, found himself at a loss for words.

"I. . . I thought the same thing myself," he stammered, trying to keep his eyes off Erik's erect penis. "It's tough, always trying to shower with cold water." He felt stupid, grasping for words in front of this freshman who seemed to be looking right through him.

"Especially when we know what cold showers are really for," Erik teased, nodding at Matthew's groin.

"Yeah, right," Matthew said, obviously self-conscious at his body's disobedience.

An awkward silence hung between them. Matthew shuffled, his gaze dropping to the ground. Quickly he turned off the shower and grabbed his towel. As he headed for the lockers, he felt Erik's stare etching itself into his back. He could feel himself flush, with that uneasy flow of lava creeping up his abdomen again. Hurriedly, he donned his T-shirt and jeans, and headed for the bookstore, where he worked.

Bookmark was a Michigan chain, known for a fair sampling of the classics, topical volumes, and a wide variety of magazines. Matthew worked there three times a week to help his parents, whose means were not nearly as pronounced as many of his classmates. Coming from a family of six kids, things were lean. Matthew couldn't compete with the rowdiness of his older brothers, whose tales of wild women and drinking alienated him. They belittled him for not really being "one of the guys," despite his natural athletic abilities, and boyish good looks. Somehow Matthew suspected they were jealous, since school came very easily for him, while they had to scramble to make C's. His mother saw his natural abilities, and in between track meets, she encouraged him to follow the classics, especially art. Matthew loved to draw; a pastime he rarely shared with his fellow members of the track team. Boys at fourteen were too quick to judge any pursuit that went beyond the usual parameters of sport, girls and drinking. Drawing was a definite promise of chastisement from his other team members.

At school, between algebra and English classes, Matthew would pull out his tablet and begin his pencil drawings—usually of nudes, both men and women. He exercised his skills by taking the photos he found in fashion magazines, rearranging the figures by posing them in reclining positions with their clothes off. Sometimes he liked putting two men together, embracing, Herb Ritts style. At night he'd continue with the drawings while he did his homework. This was dangerous though, for his mother liked to come upstairs and interrupt his studies. Hearing her footsteps on the stairs, he'd shove his tablet between the mattress and placate her until she was satisfied she had helped him. After she left, he'd pull out his tablet and continue.

Tonight was no different. After work, he took out his tablet and began to sketch. Dressed in baggy trousers, he leaned back and slowly began to unzip. Oddly enough, one of the faces he drew looked surprisingly like Erik on the track team. Matthew dismissed the thought and tried to concentrate on the face of Mary Ann instead, and what it would be like to slip his hand down her panties. Soon he was back to completing his algebra.

The next day, Matthew noticed Erik watching him as he sprinted around the track. That uneasy feeling spread through him again. He decided to run faster, hoping to outpace the sensation. When he completed the lap, Erik was still staring at him.

"Wanna race?" Matthew ventured. Maybe Erik would stop staring at him if he left him in the dust.

"Sure," Erik replied, trotting toward the starting area.

"You want inside or outside?" Matthew thought he'd give Erik any advantage, since defeat was inevitable.

"I'll take outside," Erik said, dropping a few yards behind Matthew to take his position.

Matthew lined up, certain of his victory. Maybe he'd slow his pace so Erik wouldn't be too discouraged.

"Once around? OK ready, on your mark, get set, go!"

Matthew took off, feeling the comfort of his stride as he sensed his lead on Erik. He so enjoyed running. It made him feel as though he could escape all that plagued him. Then half way around the track, Matthew saw the blond blur to his right. "He's creeping up on me, the little shit," he thought. Suddenly, he decided not to be a nice guy anymore, and quickened his pace. He had underestimated the freshman, and Erik started gaining on him. Matthew tried to cut loose, but for whatever reason, couldn't keep up with this young bolt of energy. Fifty yards before the finish, Erik passed him, winning by three lengths. "I. . . I guess I must be tired," Matthew explained. "Had to work last night at the bookstore. . . "

Erik just smiled. "Race you to the showers!" He let Matthew win.

Once inside, while they were peeling off their trunks, that uneasy feeling began to flow over Matthew again.

"You know, maybe I'll just shower at home today," he said. "There's never enough hot

Mary McGrath

water here anyway," he feebly continued.

Erik sensed his discomfort and said, "I've got a better idea. C'mon!" He jogged down the aisle to a door at the far end of the locker room. Matthew followed. "Ever been in here?" he asked. Matthew shook his head. "It's the coach's shower, and they always have enough hot water."

Matthew noticed there was only one stall. "C'mon, we can both get in. Besides it will save on hot water, and they'll never suspect a thing!" Matthew complied, slipping off his tank top and shorts, and stood outside the shower, waiting for Erik to take the lead. He adjusted the knobs so the temperature was agreeable to both of them, and stepped in. Matthew was a bit reluctant at first, but the water was much warmer than what he usually got in the locker room, so he couldn't resist.

"Not bad, eh? And no one knows about it, well, except you and me," Erik beamed. "How're your legs doing? Still sore?" Matthew nodded.

"In Sweden, we practice certain massage techniques which work great. They're a lot better than heat and ice. You Americans are so provincial at times. Can I show you? You place your palms on your thighs like this. . . " Erik put his hands on Matthew's thighs and rubbed.

Matthew tried to mimic Erik's massage techniques, but couldn't seem to follow what he was doing. He also felt confused being in the shower with this beautiful boy. He thought he should feel guilty, but in a way it seemed like the most natural feeling in the world—none of that strange awkwardness he'd felt going to the movies with Mary Ann.

"You're bright, but you don't follow directions very well," Erik teased. "Here, you do it like this." Erik placed his palms on one of Matthew's thighs and began squeezing the muscles between his hands. Slowly he crept his way up the leg until he was about three inches from his crotch.

"Feels good, huh?" Erik beamed at him. Kneeling, he couldn't help but notice that Matthew was starting to get hard. He gazed down at Erik, but said nothing. Erik took his palms further up Matthew's thigh, slowly reached around until he had one of Matthew's butt cheeks in his fist. Matthew's legs began to tremble, but he said nothing as Erik continued, sliding his right hand between the cheeks, and the other hand now cupped beneath his cock. Matthew closed his eyes, and leaned back, bracing his weight against the stall of the shower. Erik moved his face closer to Matthew's body, and began licking the pubic hair around his loins. His right hand slid deeper into Matthew's crack, groping for his asshole. Matthew began to squirm. Erik grasped him tighter. Licking his middle finger quickly, Erik slid inside Matthew, and dug in deep. Matthew gasped, throwing back his head, the shower blasting his face. Erik's finger began circling inside Matthew's ass, as he took his penis into his mouth, toward the back of his throat. Slowly he slid up and down the shaft, feeling the pulse of Matthew's pleasure pounding inside him. He quickened his strokes, plunging his finger deeper in Matthew, until he could no longer hold on. Matthew let out a cry, his cream driving its way into Erik's mouth. Matthew shuddered, a look of disbelief clouding his face as he grabbed his towel, and quickly headed toward his locker. Erik slowly turned off the shower, and began drying off, dismayed by the young flushed man who was obviously in a panic to leave.

Trish Herrera

The Ride

He was driving, while she sat slouched down in the passenger seat, one foot clad in a riding boot and perched on the leather dashboard. He looked over at her, eyes closed, her muscular thigh lit by the sunlight streaming into the car. Her large breasts poked through the tight jersey shirt and draped over her fitted jeans. He loved to watch her when she was still and resting.

He pulled up to the stable near the barn. The little dog Judy ran toward the wheels of the car barking wildly. "We are here," he said gently. She opened her eyes and smiled, leaned over and gave him a soft kiss. His lips felt like velvet to her.

"Goodie," she said. Childlike. Excited. She opened the car door and got out. He watched her move, her hips bobbing as she sauntered toward the stable. He had called ahead and the horses, Ginger and Pepper, the spicy Tennessee Walkers, were saddled and ready to run. The animals snorted as they approached.

He didn't give her a whip today, but carried his favorite riding crop and a long dressage whip. They mounted and started down the path. Neither horse had been trained as a show walker, so the ride was not perfectly smooth. She, on Pepper, was in front, her beautiful ass cheeks freshly spanked from the morning's play and bouncing up and down. A delight for his eyes. With her head back and her hair flying around her face, she had a wild look as if she had been set free.

Yet he knew he would soon bind her. Hands overhead softly cuffed and restrained. Her back arching and accepting each lash of his crop. He never made a mark on her beautiful skin. The tingly red blood merely rose to the top of her hide. He was a genius with whips, giving her the edge of pleasure before she came, letting her go wildly into his control. His touch extended to her through the leather. He slapped Pepper's haunches and the horse lurched forward, carrying her up the hill of the trail. She sunk her knees into the sides of his belly. Her legs spread wide over Pepper's back, wetting the saddle with her juices through her jeans.

Pepper was a large horse. Strong. Her baby. She leaned over and hugged his mane and neck. The dog Judy yipped and ran alongside them. The man and Ginger followed in pursuit.

The air was soft and cool this morning in the park. The Southern California weather had turned into a gentle autumn. He waved her to follow him into a small thicket opening, away from any public eye. She turned Pepper off the trail and obediently followed. Earlier she had drunk his cum, and as he dripped deeply into her mouth she could feel his restlessness. He dismounted and told her to stay on the horse. Judy sniffed around the trees, digging holes to cool her belly in. "Give me the reins," he said. She obeyed and sat up very still, her back straight and her eyes staring straight ahead. "Remove your shirt." She pulled the little jersey shirt over her head, her breasts held by a soft, half-cup, lacy bra. He had chosen it for her in a French lingerie shop.

"And the bra," he ordered. She reached back, still mounted on Pepper, legs holding her tight, and unsnapped the garment. Her large breasts fell loose, skin soft, nipples erect. She was already hot and wet from the ride and the smell of the animal and the leather saddle and whips, and the feel of his eyes on her rump.

"Your nipples," he said. "Touch them for me." She put her long finger tips on her nipples and twisted, not blinking until her eyes burned from the intensity. "Now suck one for me, baby." She could see him out of the corner of her eye. He was stroking his crop and watching her. She cupped her hand around her breast and lifted its heaviness to her bowed head. She could reach her nipple with her full lips and began to lick and lightly suck the brown nipple. "Now, the other one." She obeyed, and when she was finished, hot and wet in her saddle, he instructed her to lift her hands above her head and clasp them.

She looked incredibly beautiful, clad only in her boots and pants, mounted on the dark back of Pepper, arms held obediently above her head. She was tanned and sweaty. "Look straight ahead and do not move unless commanded," he whispered. She felt the warm soft end of the riding crop brush the center of her back, all the way down to her waist, then lightly upon her shoulders and around her neck. She moaned. The intensity of waiting for his first touch was excruciating. "Yes. I know you want this," he said.

The leather touched her hip lightly, but she did not look down. She was transfixed, her eyes straight ahead. "Close your eyes," he said, and she felt his breath near her back. Moments which seemed like hours passed. And then the sting of the whip across her back, sending a shiver down into her cunt, a shiver so deep, so filled with longing.

Again the lashing, over and over, until her back and tits were stung red. When she reached her limit, a small sound came from her lips. "Stop," she said. And he stopped immediately, gently brushing her skin with the tip of the whip.

"You can put your hands down and open your eyes," he said. She could see he was holding her bra out to her on the end of the whip.

It had grown dark and the stable was deserted. They rode into the barn and began to dismount and unsaddle the horses and brush them down. He watched her strong upper body while she brushed Pepper's back and guided him into his stall for the night. As she came out, he stopped her and pulled her to him. She could feel the hardness of his cock against her leg. He stroked her body gently and began to unzip her jeans, pulling her panties to her knees. He stroked her tight ass. "Turn around," he commanded. He bent her over and inserted his fingers into her mouth. "Get them really wet for me. Get my fingers nice and wet for your asshole." She licked and sucked his fingers until they were dripping wet, and she felt him insert one, then two, fingers into her pussy and then into her tight rear hole. When his four fingers had opened her he said, "You're ready for me now." Then he unzipped his pants and turned her towards him and told her to get his cock wet. She licked and spit all over his cock, knowing the pleasure that would soon be hers. She loved his big cock in her ass. He turned her again, his cock glistening from her mouth, and bent her over, telling her to hold her ankles. Her tight little asshole opened up like a flower for him and he dove in, pulling her onto the shaft of his cock.

The smell of hay, sweet from the horses, and the cool fall night filled her. He pumped strongly and evenly into her asshole. Long, slow pumps, each one deep into her sweet ass. He held her by her hip bones, pulling her up to him as she held onto her ankles, her pounding tits banging against her thighs. When he came he moaned, pulling her to him like a heavy weight into his groin. Her body twitched, wanting more. He released her, putting her gently on the ground and pulling out his cock, which shone with cum. She pulled up her panties and jeans, then placed his beautiful immense member back into his underwear and jeans, zipped him, and knelt before him. Her cunt desperately wanted to come, but she knew he would make her wait for him now. He kissed the top of her head. "That's a good baby. Let's go now."

In the car she began to get restless. He listened to the radio, the news. She fidgeted in her seat and looked out the window. Her cunt and tits ached with desire.

They drove through the gates and pulled up at home. They got out of the car and went through the front door and up the stairs, to their bedroom. It was cozy and warm. She peeled off her clothes, drank a glass of water, and ran a bath. The water felt good on her ass, still hot with desire. She closed her eyes and drifted off in the bubbles and bath oil. When she was finished she wrapped herself in a fluffy bath sheet and headed off to bed. He was downstairs. She could hear his voice and the television, the news. She closed her eyes and slept.

The sun streamed into the room and little lights of day warmed her skin. She moaned, and tried to roll over. Her hands had been tied to the bed above her head while she was sleeping. Soft, fur-lined leather cuffs kept her firmly in place. "Good morning my love," he called to her as he entered the room. He was dressed for work in a nicely cut suit and tie and smelled freshly groomed.

His lips came down softly on hers, and she hungrily responded. "I just want to get a good taste of you before work today," he said, opening her legs and sitting on the bed. "But first a little gift." And in his hand were two nipple clips, held together by a delicate golden chain. The clips were designed to be worn around the nipples as jewelry. He applied them until he saw her wince. "I want you to wear this for me today and when you think of me, gently pull this chain. Very gently, my love. As gently as I have kissed your lips this morning." She smiled as he caressed her brown nipples, making them stand on end for his pleasure.

Her pleasure. Their pleasure.

He had a soft look on his face, was smiling sweetly. He sat back on the bed between her legs. "Now lift that cunt up for me to taste this morning." She opened her self out to him like a breakfast table. The first feel of his soft tongue on her clit exploded into instant orgasm. She began to convulse and push her cunt toward his freshly shaved face. "Yes. . . yes baby. . . mmm. . . good." He dove deeply into her cunt, covering his nose and face, sucking her clit.

Her tied arms stretched up, her gold-bound nipples danced for him. She came until she exhausted herself on the bed. Calm and satisfied, she lay back. His face glistened, and he smiled as he freed her hands, rolling her over onto his lap. He began spanking her. When her bottom was nice and red he released her.

"On your knees, my baby." She obeyed. "Now unzip my pants." She knew this meant she could only use her teeth. His cock was very hard. She managed to get it out. He pinched her little nipples, already tight and firm from the clips. She wrapped her lips around the tip of his penis and began to suck. She sucked until he came, and she swallowed and licked up every drop. He bent down to kiss her. "Zip me." She stood as she zipped him up gently, and he took her into his arms and kissed her passionately.

"Be ready to ride at six. And no panties."

He smacked her ass and left for work.

Gwynne Garfinkle

Data Entry

When I wake after a few hours of fitful sleep—too distracted by his warm body next to me to get much rest—it's around noon. I have work to do, so I let him sleep. Shower, coffee, breakfast, then I sit at the computer in my living room with a pile of scientific summaries to transcribe. I'm quickly accurately typing, Czech titles replete with haceks, lengthy broken-English paragraphs written by Czechs, full of technical jargon and chemical formulas.

Eventually I hear him stir, move around in the bedroom. Then he appears, wearing black T-shirt, black boxer briefs, we say hi. He goes into the bathroom, water splashes in the sink. When he comes back out, I don't turn, lulled by the even clacking of the keys. Suddenly I sense his nearness, turn and he has pulled up a chair, is sitting just behind me, watching me. "Keep working," he says, so I do, excited by his watching presence. His fingers steal over my right nipple, I sigh, stop typing, turn, I want to kiss him, but quietly he says, "Keep typing." As his fingers play me my fingers lightly caress the keys, slipping over them, typos proliferate as I heat beneath his unerring fingers on my nipples, first over then under my T-shirt.

Then lightly his fingers circle and circle between my legs, over the light material of my black leggings, my thighs full against the chair—I part my legs ever wider as he begins to rub me with his whole hand and I can barely bring myself to keep typing, though somehow it only excites me more, this effort to concentrate on something besides his hand between my legs, his fingers on my nipple, I imagine myself typing the words FUCK ME FUCK ME imagine typing I want to suck your cock instead I type words like electron reorganization non-isothermal flow reactor all words are starting to sound dirty, again and again I have to stop typing, drowsy with pleasure, my fingers resting on the keyboard. I'm moving my pelvis against his hand. "Keep typing," he murmurs and as I force myself to begin typing again the effort the words his voice send me over the top and my fingers rain upon the keys jioeraiathparekopweatqkoperaioaekopwef'pkwegi'kw gejo;wgajogwioiiojiiwfiaerio'jojiaajt-gaulahtekafds

Afterwards I see my orgasm on the screen a burst of letters.

Miriam R. Sachs Martín

Miriam R. Sachs Martin

First

I am her first.

oh, she's had other women, has taken them with the careless, butch angle of her legs, the powerful jut of her hands, her limpid, cruel eyes.

but I am her first.

she's had girlfriends, kept them night after night, year after year, alternately hurt and loved them, I would imagine, but still, I am her first.

the first night we got together, it was all about me on my back, arms wrenched up behind my head, her hips against my cunt, her tongue down my throat, her body invading mine, tormenting, ratcheting me up against an unbelievable, inevitable climax. the heat and the breath in her red truck took up *all* of the oxygen, and—sure—I'm a twenty-six-year-old homeowner today, but for the night, I felt back at sixteen with no place to go, an unbearable wet cunt, stiff sore nipples, panting lungs, saying no but meaning anything but; saying no but meaning yes, yes, it's true I said no, but I wanted her to hear "capture me, fuck me, hurt me."

but she wouldn't let me touch her, no, not her, because She Doesn't Do That, because I hadn't yet become the first. I reached for her breast, tried time and again to slide my hand down her pants to the cunt I knew had to be eager and gasping, and was met with iron resistance; ferocious, negating strength.

"Don't you ever take your clothes off during sex?" I asked.
"Nope, not really," she said. Quick. Proud.
"And your lovers put up with that?!"

I was incredulous. and this girl, this beautiful, fierce, don't-yet-know-how-to-be-vulnerable girl, this girl who had, till that minute, never quite met her match, had never met a lover whose desire could batter down butch walls, just looked at me, impressed, that someone might even try.

well, she never went home after that date, was all. she came and she stayed, and has been staying ever since. and tomorrow we go to get her furniture and make it official. and becoming her first has been one of the most glorious fights I've ever had the pleasure to take part in, and let me tell you, I *love* fighting.

she is a deer caught in headlights, she is a teenage boy imprisoned by his own hormones, she is my little fuck-toy, my slave, her face belongs to my hand cracking across it, her breasts belong to my mouth punishing, tormenting, owning them, her hips belong to my hands sliding around them, her wrists and ankles belong to the restraints I choose to bind them with, and
her cunt

her cunt

her cunt

her cunt belongs to me. *she* belongs to me. *she* belongs to being pinned down, tied down, and force-fed my fist, my hand; she needs to be wrestled into submission and given what is good for her, and good for her is what I am.

I am so good for her.

and we have graduated from tenuous touches of one finger

to two fingers

three fingers, four.

and each time her hips buck wildly, eagerly, under my hands, but her eyes cry out in terror.

and it is my job to stay present and to stay mean enough so that she keeps a toehold on this earth.

and it is my joy to rape her, to fill her—cunt, mouth, ass, mind, eyes, hands—with me, with my love, my come, my desire—it's mine, all mine, to spear into her with the hard salivating thrust of my need. It's my pleasure to take her when she didn't know she wanted to be taken, and it's my job to give her herself back, when she didn't even know that was possible.

like I said, I am her first. and having taken her now, my aim is to be her last.

Tammy M. Gómez

Tammy M.Gómez

I Want to Feel it Deeply

I really love Mark. It hits me often tonight as I lay in bed watching a movie on TV. I'm distracted by thoughts of him; I cannot focus on the world apart from him. All my mind wants is to reminisce and dream. I want to capture or re-capture the passion as I remember him. I say his name over and over, "Mark, Mark." I spread my legs, jutting my breasts out, wanting his touch. I walk from one room to another, always thinking, "I want you, Mark."

This weekend was so good; he was so loving, romantic, sexy, soft, inventive.

After my gig, we drove home to Aspen, stopping first at McDonald's for me to pee and for Mark to buy a Happy Meal. At home, we climbed tiredly upstairs to do a steam. It was Mark's idea. We undressed, first him, then me—and stepped into the steaming cubicle. I could feel Mark's eyes on my body, especially on my breasts. He was melting; his eyes spoke soft silent passion and desire. I was basking in this feeling and didn't push for anything. I wanted to be passive, to be an object—of his desire. I wanted to feel his lust become thick and heavy like the hot moist air that embraced us. We were slick and wet with our own oils and perspiration. It was primal in a very serene, elegant way, because we were slow-moving and silent. Mark finally spoke his desire to suck my breasts.

He moved outside the cubicle to dim the lights for better effect, which made me shudder inside with anticipation, and the pleasure of being there with so beautiful and exacting a man, a man who sought the same sense of aesthetic completion that I enjoy so much.

I deliberately moved very little and, when it was necessary, moved only with liquid fluidity, soft and slow. Prior to sexual consummation, the attitude and physical bearing of the participant/lover should be almost sacred in its elegance and posture. Mark had gone outside the cubicle, presumably to cool down, but gradually he became purposeful.

He stared at me through the glass, and I felt myself becoming a human jewel in a showcase, or perhaps a hunted animal in a cage—sensing the desire to be possessed by another, stronger than me. He pressed his body against the cubicle, then his mouth moved against it, and I felt his tongue through the glass, pressing towards me. Towards my mouth, my tongue, my breasts, my wet fire, my vagina. I met his presses with my own. It was desperate, we were pushing towards each other, with the glass in between. The passion rose. I wanted him so much. I was gyrating and raging inside, but my body maintained a dignified slowness. It was beautiful seeing his lust build. His perfect penis was engorged and pink, the most satisfying color I know. It engaged and captivated me.

He was seemingly serene and open, open to exposing his cock, his desire, his passion. I loved him more for this. This opening up, this fresh vulnerability. I will not exploit it, nor mock it. It made me happy to have him as a partner.

The night unfolded deliberately, with hardly a word spoken between the two of us.

The towels we spread on the living room floor absorbed our moisture, and the dimly lit space swathed us in an arousing glow. "I want you." "You are sexy." Whispered homages inspired me to melt completely for him. To unlock the tight holding spaces, to abandon restraint. To throw myself open. I invite the invitation to do so. Again. Again. I love Mark's gentleness and forcefulness. There are perfect moments with him. I love him because they happen and will again happen. I love him. I love Mark. I want to feel it deeply, as I walk, as I sit, as I breathe.

Tammy M.Gómez

Lap the Lap

Tomorrow morning. . .

I'm gonna yawn at the dawn an'
see the early morning light, all right!

I grab a sandal to slap the alarm from
the on to off position, you say you

wanna go fishin'? Tiptoe yourself to the
kitchen, slip some slices in the holes, grab

the jam and some ham, 'cause the burner's
gonna burn, the burner's gonna burn,

the burner's gonna burn. But I don't get

worked up, 'cause my toast just jerked up, and

it's crunchy—like I wanted, like I wanted,
like I wanted. Like I said, it is the A.M.

and I believe that I will lay him, after crunching
toast. After crunching toast, it's the most, now

I know how he will boast, 'bout the headsnap
and the toe tap that he does when I got my

tongue in his jelly lap. I lap the lap, I lap the
lap, I lap the lap, I lap his lap. Like I wanted.

Like I wanted. And afta awhile *he* gets worked
up, *his* toast gets jerked up, and he wants to slip

his slices in the holes. Slip his slices in the holes,
where the burner's gonna burn, the burner's gonna

burn, my burner's gonna burn, and the flames—
they don't never go out.

Pia Pico

Daddy Dearest

To: marquisv@aol.com
From: analog@chickmail.com
Subject: Collars
Date: 5-3-00

Dear Master,

I went to Walgreen's today and bought stuff for the trip to Italy—travel bottles, toothbrush, antacid, ziploc bags, the slim red dog collar you ordered me to get. I didn't want to test the collar in the store to see if it fit because there was a lady with her two kids in the same aisle looking at dog stuff, so I waited until the drive home to try it on, and sure enough, it was too small. It barely wraps around my wrist twice, and my wrists are tiny! So I'm going to use a different collar tonight, the one I bought for myself—the red leather one? I know it's not exactly following your instructions, but just for tonight? xoxo, anna

p.s. I did find a nice leash!

To: daddyo@msn.com
From: analog@chickmail.com
Subject: sis's birthday
Date: 5-4-00

Dear Dad,

I can't come to sis's b-day bbq, but I'm going to Italy for two weeks. Sis says you're checking your sugar levels every morning. She also says you don't exercise enough. I told you, even a walk down the hill to the stop sign is better than no walk at all. Go out the door, down the driveway, down the hill, and stop when you see red. When I get there, we're walking everyday. Prepare yourself.
Love, anna

To: marquisv@aol.com
From: mailto:analog@chickmail.com
Subject: Prudence is an ugly old maid. . .
Date: 5-5-00

Dear Master,

Its 3 A.M. I can't sleep. Been staring at the TV for three hours. Soon I'll go to bed, even though I can't sleep. My mom used to say that resting was as good as sleep. But I don't dream when I'm resting.
I went to the bathroom, sat down on the toilet (it needs serious cleaning), pulled my black dress over my head and threw it on the floor. So I'm naked except for my black lacy bra, which makes my tits look bigger and creamier (wish you were sucking them) than they actually are. Sitting there peeing, I reach into my bra, pinch one of my nipples hard, as if you were clamping it with a stainless steel clothes

pin. I can't even feel it, so I twist my clit between my thumb and forefinger, but I can't get a good grip. I need your tongue, I need your mouth, your teeth. A week before I get to see you is way too long.

So I'm in my bedroom, I secure the red leather collar (I still can't find the kind you asked for, but mine is red, sturdy and comfortable), I sit down on the edge of my bed. In the vanity mirror, my shoulders look frail, bony. Relax, baby, you say. In the mirror, it's not me watching me, it's you.

I stand and rest my knee on the bed so that my ass (take a big bite) faces you. The red collar lays on my nape like a necklace of blood. You move around and sit down on the edge of my bed. Suck my nipples, maul them with your lips, Bite me, tear me open. Your kisses are cool and your hands are firm around my waist.

Good little slut, you say. You're a good little bitch, aren't you?

Yes, daddy, I say. I'm your whore, your slut, your fuck toy. That's a girl, you say. Suck daddy's cock.

So I suck your cock, draw on it, let you shove the whole thing into my hungry mouth.

That's my little cocksucker, you say. You are divine, you say as you come.

Thank you. Thank you for letting me suck you off. I can sleep now, I think.

Loving you, anna

To: daddyo@msn.com
From: analog@chickmail.com
Re: Re: Sis's birthday
Date: 5-6-00

Dear Dad,

No. The Chevron card is not a good idea for sis's b-day. Remember what happened when you gave me one? You scrutinized every single charge, then called me up and cursed me out over the phone for using the damn thing. I think you gave it to me so that you could spy on me. Jewelry is better. At least she'll be able to wear it.

Love, anna

To: daddyo@msn.com
From: analog@chickmail.com
Subject: yes you did
Date: 5-6-00

You did too curse me out. You told me to "go fuck myself" and then you slammed the phone down on me. I wouldn't be surprised if you blocked it out. I would have had I said it to MY daughter. anna

To: daddyo@msn.com
From: analog@chickmail.com
Subject: (no subject)
Date: 5-6-00

What do you mean you hope I die in the airport on my way to Italy? What is wrong with you?

To: marquisv@aol.com
From: analog@chickmail.com
Subject: The cut worm forgives the plow
Date: 5-7-00

I had a fight with my dad yesterday so I didn't write you, but I'm better now. I think his diabetes is getting worse, and maybe he's worried about dying. I'm not sure what do about him, whether to relegate him to crazy status or what. I love him, madly. I wish he would let me love him the way I'm good at.

Where are you? What are you doing? Do you have any instructions for me? Three days left.

To: marquisv@aol.com
From: analog@chickmail.com
Subject: Prudence is an ugly old maid
Date: 5-8-00

Fuck! I've come so deeply, I've gone deaf.

Hit me HARDER, dearest. I've been a bad girl. I need the snapping sting of your leather belt, the flat of your palm packing heat on my ass. Bruise me. Give me kisses so hard my blood rises up, stays visible for days. My skin craves your punishing kiss, the nasty asp-lash of your cane.

I remember being prostrate over my father's lap, my pants and underwear down around my ankles. He has folded his thick leather belt in two, so that he could whip my twelve-year-old butt five times because I sassed him.

On my bed, yearning for you, I slide my legs wider, stretch my knees as far apart as they will go. My whole cunt drips and my fingers whisk around it like tiny birds. Take me flying. Tie me down to the bed in a big X with a pillow beneath my pelvis, and make me surrender. I want to flame out, shining like shook foil.

Please, dearest, cleave the halves of my ass in two with your

cock. Kiss my asshole, my cracks. Mend me. Snug and wrapped around you, I'm your gift, your present, past and future. Let me come for you daddy. I praise your good name, your devotion, your good mastery over me.
your slave, anna

To: daddyo@msn.com
From: analog@chickmail.com
Subject: Re: Italy companion
Date: 5-8-00

None of your business. A friend. Male. Love, me.

5-08-00
Houston, TX
6:30 p.m.
I haven't heard from the master today. I got to record this weird dream I had during my nap.
I am walking down the hill near where I grew up. Some boys are playing T-ball in Stone Field. One of the boys wearing a yellow hat bats a ball all the way to the pepper tree. I stop to pick it up, and I see my father lying on the ground covered in dirt and leaves. "What are you doing here dad?" I ask. But he doesn't say anything. He just looks at me with these weird eyes, like he's in pain or something. He asks me to give him my hand so I do, and he pulls me under the pepper tree curtain, which shades us from the view of the boys playing T-ball. And then he begins to kiss my neck, and I feel myself getting turned on, even though I am thinking "Eew, this is my actual dad." (I'm thinking this in the dream.) He wants to make love to me, and I let him remove my

shorts and pull off my v-neck T-shirt, and when he settles me down beside him, I see that he is crying a little, but I am not sure why. He holds me and rocks me for a few minutes, and when he finally slides into me, it is like a snake, like an eighteen-feet long greenish blue snake, and he snakes all the way through me, up my cunt, through my intestines, stomach and heart, through my esophagus and throat, out my mouth. Then I woke up.

Weird. I need to go to Walgreen's and get some padlocks.

To: Marquisv@aol.com
From: analog@chickmail.com
Subject: Dreaming of Mercy Street
Date: 5-8-00

You ask about my daddy thing. How it developed? I didn't get enough of him when I was young. Cliché, but true. For whatever reason. So I swore I'd never be with anyone like my dad, and thus began the sad parade of men in my life who were exactly like my father, in one bad way or another. In hiding from my fear of meeting a man like my father, I blinded myself to his presence at every crossroads.

It's ok. Now I know that I'm looking for a man exactly like my father, only better for me, because NOT my father.

So, what follows is one of my attempts to seduce myself into loving my father so that when I met him again, I'd be prepared:

thinking about sex but I was thinking about it before, too perhaps I should go back to bed get naked part my legs like the red sea cup my breasts whisper to the ceiling

Suck me, Daddy

Daddy comes down from where he is, comes down to fuck me.

Daddy can do it to me like no other man. He hates me because he wants me and I'm hard to have. He has to work to get my attention. Sometimes, my mother says I'm going to hell for all the bad I do to this world, but Daddy's been to hell and back and he tells me it's not too bad there.

When Daddy and I are alone together in the hills near the river, he will step back and watch me move through space and time, and he will accept me exactly the way I am. Then I approach him, remove my clothes piece by piece, prolonging the spectacle so that we both get weak with lust, and when I take off my bra, my breasts swell and blush. I stop before he can envelop me, slide off my underwear, inch them down over my thighs, my pink knees, my size-seven feet. I poke my middle finger inside my pussy, just enough so that a juicy bead of me sticks to my fuck finger. I show Daddy this bit of essence, my essence which comes from his essence. His skin shimmies and slackens, and I can see the boy he was, the way he was, and I imagine we are father and daughter, girlfriend and boyfriend, husband and wife all at once.

He takes me to the river and cleanses me. I reach for his cock, saying "Thank you, Daddy, thank you for making me, for letting me be alive." Daddy cups my ass, just like he did when I was his baby, and he pulls me out of the water, lifts me dripping so that I can wrap my legs around him, so that he can carry me to a place where he can lay me down and change me.

He spreads my legs and sticks his mouth on my cunt and sucks the girl in me right out. I arch my back and giggle, take a fistful of his curly hair and pull, first softly then more firmly, so that he has to come up and give me some of myself from his own mouth. I see my warm cunt spunk on daddy's lips, and with one of my hands, I pull his mouth to me and suck myself from his tongue. With my other hand, I grab his ass and position my cunt so that he can slam his cock into my fuck hole.

As we fuck, my love for him grows and grows. It blooms and grows. And blooms again. Uhhhhhh. Afterwards, he pulls his spent cock out of me and rubs it over my belly, marking me. And he tells me, softly in my ear, so that if I blink I might miss it: I am made whole in him, perfect, complete.

Am I disgusting to you?

To: marquisv@aol.com
From: analog@chickmail.com
Re: without contraries there is no progression
Date: 5-07-00

Dear Master,
Well. I don't believe you.
But it's more than just incest. Sex, Drugs & Rock & Roll is fucking over. Give me Sex & Violence.

I long for a deep searing lash to repair me. Split me open with your rod. Don't spare me. Inside there are more of me waiting to be born. Rip me open and let them out.

Let me tell you about violence. When I was little, I carried around this image of myself standing behind our dining room door holding a hot iron. As if for protection. Because whenever I was bad, my daddy hit me good and hard and long. I deserved it. Daddy could see into all the bad I did: the pinching strange babies feet until they wailed, the coveted Barbies I stole from my cousins, the lies I told everyone about my life, the secret shame I had for being alive. Daddy whacked me with his leather belt. Made my bottom burn like a big bee sting. Made it redder than Rudolph's nose. Then of course he wanted to hump me. And I wanted to fuck him.

Once he held a kitchen barstool above my head, threatening to crack my skull with it, and I looked at him defiantly, duly noting the beet red blood rushing around his face, said, "Go ahead and hit me. I hate your fucking guts."
He didn't want me to grow up. He didn't want me to leave him. Now, I play his little girl; I've become her again. In my fantasy, I give him all my love I didn't give him as a little girl, and I give it to him as the woman I am. He needs me to do this, and I need him, too, because when I am happy and grateful, I feel too big for my body, too big for my mind, larger than my surroundings even. I can be too full of light, music, love and gratitude. I can carry the whole Pacific Ocean inside me and the sky, too. But this feeling, if you understand me, scares me sometimes. What if, with this hugeness, I crush someone? Drown them? Crack my heart through their skull?

I need you, master, my governor, to help me become the woman I am, and not the one the culture would have me become, whoever she is. In this process of becoming, if I do hurt someone, I need to be reprimanded. Please help me stay humane.
love, anna

To: daddyo@msn.com

From: analog@chickmail.com
Subject: over & out
Date: 5-08-00

Dearest Dad,
I'm off to Italy. Please take care of yourself while I'm
gone. Walk down to the hill to the stop sign. Or, a little
past it. I want you to be there when I return.
love, anna

Public Display

Thot evening fell cold and quickly; still, we walked to the club instead of taking a taxi. Anna and I clomped ahead of Chico, our arms interlocked, our steps coincident with one another. Chico smoked behind us, humming a Coltrane tune.

They were my best friends in San Francisco. Several nights a week the three of us sat around one of our apartments, talked of our dreams—someday, Chico would be a famous painter, I a stage actress, Anna, our ultimate fan, which was what she wanted to be, admiring us to the best of her ability. She was talented at worshipping us, but that wasn't why we loved her. We loved her for her agile tenderness, her sensual intelligence, her pliancy. I had introduced the two of them, after Chico and I tried our best to be lovers and failed. She and Chico were in love, and they put up with my ranginess, my inability to settle on any one boyfriend. That evening, we were on our way to an industrial music club where Jack, the man I'd been obsessed with for over a year, was headlining a show with his band Grotus.

"Are you excited?" Anna asked.

"I'm nervous," I said.

"Will he talk to you?"

"Perhaps."

Chico drew up behind us on the sidewalk, draped his arms around our shoulders, kissed my ear, then Anna's. His lips were cold, and they sent a shiver through my torso.

Inside the industrial music club, the large room was filling up and close with smoke and steam rising from wool-clad bodies. Winter coats were piled over the tops of stools around high cocktail tables. We found a table, set our coats on one of the bar stools, and sat down, surveying the stage over the heads of fans.

"There he is," I said to Anna, who nodded and gave Chico a twenty for drinks. Chico left for the bar, pushing his way through the throng.

"Just what about him do you like?" she leaned and asked.

"I like the way we fuck," I said and stared at Jack on stage, setting up.

"When was the last time you were fucked?"

"Nine months," I answered.

"Nine months?" she crowed. "What the hell are we doing here?" I felt her squinting at me, but when I turned, her eyes softened, "Poor baby," she whispered. She smoothed the peach fuzz on my cheek with her palm and kissed me lightly. She slid her fingers around my ears, up the back of my neck and played with my hair, caught up in a long red braid. She pulled my face toward her and kissed me again.

Chico came back with our whiskeys. "What's this?" he said.

"Girl talk," Anna answered, smiling at me.

"I'm here for you, too," Chico said. He set the whiskeys down on the table and leaned over to kiss my cheek. He reached across me to kiss Anna's lips. I watched them kiss each other tenderly and felt an ache in my heart.

Chico sat down on the barstool to my right. Anna was on my left. As the band started, Chico reached his arm around me to stroke Anna's hair. Then he reached up under my braid and massaged my neck. He alternated between her neck and mine during the first song. By the end of it, from the whiskey and the neck massage, I could begin to relax my shoulders.

"How you feeling, doll?" Chico asked.

"Better," I said.

"You two want another drink?"

"Umhum," Anna and I hummed. I handed Chico a twenty.

"These are on me," he said, waving the twenty away.

I turned to Anna, "Do you know how much I love the two of you?" I asked, feeling the warmth of the whiskey between my shoulder blades and breasts.

"Do you know how much we love you?" Anna said. I smiled at her as she leaned to kiss me, and I was surprised when it wasn't the quick kiss we usually gave one another. This kiss lingered, hinted a yearning, an incipient hunger. I didn't pull away, but when we parted lips, I struggled to appear calm. Anna grinned at me through her mild whiskey bliss and leaned her head against my shoulder. Her hand fell easily onto my thigh, and when she sat back upright, she kept it there. I placed my hand over the back of hers, traced her veins with the tips my fingers and watched the stage. I found stroking her hand like this increasingly erotic, and by the time Chico came back with our drinks, my breath was heavy and my cunt beginning to swell inside my underwear.

"To exquisite friends," Chico said, raising his glass. Anna and I lifted our glasses and clinked them with Chico's. As we sipped, our eyes met over our glasses, and I noticed her pupils were dilated, her white cheeks flushed. She set her glass down, took mine from me and set it down, too; then reaching beneath the hem of my skirt, she found my bare calves and slid her fingertips up the smooth skin to the tops of my knees. My chest rose and fell rapidly, my nipples strained against my flimsy bra.

"Hey, hey girls," Chico said, "we're in public."

She dropped her hands but only so that she could move her stool closer to mine. Using one hand to take another sip of whiskey, she dropped her other hand and clasped my socked ankle with her fingers.

"What are you doing?" I said, my voice loud enough to be heard over the industrial music but slow enough to indicate to her my intrigue.

"Nothing," she said, running her warm palm around my knee and up under my thick crepe dress, stopping only when her hand met the nexus between my thigh and cunt.

"Anna!" I moaned, "People will see." She repositioned herself so that our barstools were side by side, our hips adjacent to one another, blocking out any view of us from the crowd behind us and screening views from the side.

Chico, having caught on to the erotic development between Anna and me, pressed himself against our backs and placed his free hand on my right shoulder, teasing it with the tips of his fingers. Anyone looking might have thought that we were merely affectionate friends.

Then Anna, softly at first but with increasing firmness, fluttered her index finger over the cotton crotch of my panties. I eased up to the edge of the stool to allow her better access to my cunt. Having moved forward on my stool, Chico took the opportunity to sit down behind me. I could feel the press of his cock against the small of my back. The club was crowded enough so that no one seemed to notice when Chico began massaging my belly, then raised his left hand and cupped my breast. He discreetly massaged me there, pulled at my nipple through my dress, causing me to wince.

Suddenly, my cunt shuddered, swelled, and leaked a large pearl of moisture against the cotton panel of my underwear. Anna turned and flicked her tongue in my ear, and the warmth of her mouth contrasted with the pain of Chico's fingers on my nipple sent me into a brief paroxysm. I gasped and instinctively spread my legs wider, rocked my pelvis back and forth on the edge of my barstool. Anna's finger was still outside my underwear, but taking my sudden abandon as her cue, she moved the flap of my panties to the side and tucked in her finger, nuzzling my clit with her knuckle. I looked around, but it appeared that no one was noticing us. My cunt oozed over Anna's fingers and palm, my breath came in short pants. As the waves of pleasure continued gripping my body, I looked toward the stage, remembering Jack. The thought of him on stage, oblivious to my drenched cunt not even 100 feet in front of him, amplified my titillation. I spread my legs wider. Balancing myself, I held still, so that Anna could slide her finger inside me. She rotated her hand and plunged one finger inside my slick lips, slipping in and out as the rest of her palm mas-saged the skin between my legs and ass. I clutched her finger with my vaginal walls, and she, using another finger, opened my labia wider and slid her pointer finger in me, too. I moaned, rocking my pelvis back and forth on the edge of my stool. Chico continued his subtle but sharp tweaks on my nipple, while he worked his lips over the sensitive skin under my braid. I turned my head to the right wanting, to reach Chico's mouth with my lips, but his head was too far behind me.

Before turning back, I saw a couple—a man and woman—on our right, staring at us with puzzled expressions. I sucked in my breath and turned to whisper in Anna's ear, "We're being watched."

"Good," she groaned back into my ear. "Should we give them something X-rated to watch?"

Anna leaned back and whispered in Chico's ear. Chico moved his right hand down my stomach, pressing it full and hard against my belly. I felt a delirium approaching, and tensed when I realized what was about to happen, but Anna and Chico had me firmly in their thrall.

"Come on, baby," Chico breathed in my ear. "Come on."

"Wait," I said, "people are watching."

"It's all right," he murmured in my ear. The squall of the music on the stage was reaching full volume and force when Chico reached down and lifted my skirt so that he had access to my clitoris. With Anna's fingers plumbing my cunt, Chico rubbed his index and middle finger in quick, firm circles over my clit. I felt my juices surging and a climax growing all the way from the bottom of my toes. As my orgasm swelled, I turned toward Anna and met her mouth with mine, pulling on her lips and tongue as if I were trying to take her whole body into me. As we made out, her fingers continued to slide in and out of me; Chico continued to rub me. I had no idea what the couple on the right were seeing and I didn't care. The entire room—the stage, the tables, the smoke and screaming music all disappeared the moment I started to come over Anna's fingers. I heard myself screaming over the music, and I was sure that Jack must have heard me, too. My cum shot out of my cunt with tremendous force, spurting in quick, liquid pearls over Anna's fingers. Chico's breath was hot and labored against the fine hair on the back of my nape, his hips undulating rhythmically against my ass and lower back, and I could tell he was close to coming himself. Shuddering, my inhalations and exhalations came in quickening breaths through my mouth. Anna looked at me, and I sighed and covered her mouth with kisses. Her kisses were hot and searching, and as we kissed, I visualized what Chico and I would do with her once we were home.

Chico's hands were back on my belly and he pulled me into him. "Let's get out of here," he announced so that both of us could hear. Disentangling ourselves, we stood, sighed, smoothed our clothing, and finished our drinks in a few gulps. I noticed that the couple on the right was gone and a group of four women had taken their table. We walked past them on our way out and they didn't look at us once. I glanced back at Jack as we exited the club.

Outside, Anna sidled me up against the club wall, probing my mouth with her hot tongue.

I put my hands inside her long coat, pulled on her ass, pressing her pelvis into mine, imagining her white supple body spread out naked on the futon at her apartment. I kissed her mouth as if it were her cunt. And when I let her go, she could barely breathe.

"Jesus," Chico said from the curb where he stood, trying to hail a cab. "Good thing this is San Francisco and not Omaha, Nebraska." We laughed, and a taxi swooped toward the curb. The three of us jumped in and Chico gave the driver the address.

"Please hurry," Anna said.

Exemplar

Anna didn't think she could bear the rain anymore. From the living room chair, in the green afternoon dark of a summer monsoon, she watched the lemon-sized raindrops pour down outside. It had been raining hard for twenty-eight hours. Anna sat and smoked and stared out the window. Henry was in New Hampshire, at a writer's conference for three weeks. Dead Loaf, she muttered to herself, exhaling yellow-brown smoke. The phone rang in the back room, and she let it continue to ring without leaving her chair to answer it. It was probably Henry, calling from New Hampshire, full of particular details about the workshop that day, what the famous writer had said about his story, what funny thing he'd said at dinner, how many people laughed. He would leave out the blond writer woman from Virginia, the half-Swedish half-Mexican nymph everyone was trying to fuck, even the women.

The night before, Henry had called late, Anna answered, half asleep. "It seems as if I've raised you from a dream," he said. "Perhaps I should've called earlier."

"No, no," she mumbled. "It's okay."

"Do you want me to help you wake up?" he whispered.

"Sure," she said, rubbing her forehead.

"Imagine I'm there," he began.

Anna listened while Henry described how he was pinning her down, refusing to let her move, holding her neck firmly in his teeth, his hands clamping her hips beneath him so that she couldn't even wriggle. Anna sighed a little, to let him know she was listening. While she listened, she stroked her clit and cunt a few times, curious to see if she could actually find the thrill of him inside her, but through the phone she couldn't imagine his skin, the slap of his thick hipbones, the rough suck of his mouth on her nipples. When he got to the part about his rock-hard cock ramming into her wet pussy, Anna stifled the wrong genre of groan. Before he could ask if she'd come, she told him to lie back and relax, and began describing what she would do to him were she there. She would take his cock into her wet, warm mouth, cradle his balls in her palms, licking the space between them and his ass, her mouth and hands tight and wet on his cock again, sliding it up and down, taking all of him inside her, all of him, until he came hard and deep against the back of her throat. And she swallowed.

Henry shuddered against his sheets. Anna hummed ambiguously.

"That was great, baby," he said. "Did it turn you on?"

"Did you have a good day?"

"Yeah, can I tell you about it? But, wait, did you come?"

"Sort of," Anna lied.

"Oh. Okay. Today in workshop. . . ." he began.

Sitting in the living room as the rain continued, Anna fantasized about monasteries and convents, contemplating the direction of her life since the second grade, when she'd decided to become a nun. She was still a nun, though a nun in a whore's body. What else could explain the loveless affairs with other men? Her dislike of sex with Henry? Her dislike, she assumed, of sex in general.

The doorbell roused Anna from her melancholy. She pushed out of her chair and crossed the dark room to the big wood-and-glass door. Flicking on the porch light, she squinted through the glass at a young, drenched man who stood hunched against the locked gate with a clip-board swathed in clear plastic. She unlocked and opened the door and stepped out onto the porch, assessing the wet man on the other side of the locked gate.

"Can I help you?" she asked through the rain and wrought iron.

"Hey," the young man laughed above the deluge. "How are you."

"Better than you, I think," Anna said. "What do you want?"

"I work for the Sierra Club, and I'm canvassing the neighborhood for memberships and donations. Can I come onto the porch for a moment?"

"I don't think so, I'm not interested," Anna said. Just then a huge bold of lightning cracked over the house across the street. "Can I ask why you're canvassing in a storm?" Anna yelled over the rain.

"My quota deadline is tomorrow, and I really need the money. I've got to turn in fifty signatures by noon tomorrow to get paid this week."

"How many do you have?"

"Three. Four if you sign," he said, sticking the clipboard through the wrought iron. Anna smiled, opened the gate, and let him in.

Two weeks later, the rain had stopped, but the boy was still there. He and Anna left her house only to buy groceries and to get his guitar from his girlfriend's house. They had stocked the kitchen with foods he liked: tofu, brown rice, spinach, leeks, butternut squash, Brown Cow yogurt, tiger milk bars. He cooked for Anna, hearty macrobiotic meals which filled her stomach but kept her body light and buoyant. After meals, before making love, he played for her. He was a jazz musician, trying to support himself solely on his music, hence the canvassing job at the end of the month when he realized he wouldn't be able to make rent. "Day in, Day out," "Night and Day," "Body and Soul," "All or Nothing at All," he played for her while she sat naked in her chair, her bare legs draped over the sides, her hands caressing her smooth, white stomach, the swell of her breasts. He would play and watch her as she stroked her clit and smiled at him, dipping her finger into her pussy, sliding it in and out, lifting it to her lips, licking her own sweet juices from the tips. He didn't stop playing while she pleased herself and him with her display; he made love back to her, working his fingers over the fretboard assertively, then tenderly, always attuned to the center of the song, while his colors and tones expanded and contracted, creating spacious meadows of sound and silence inside of Anna.

Because of the rain, everything outside bloomed new and surprising. The azaleas screamed their fuchsia imperatives, the wisteria weighted the air, the honeysuckle dripped. With the boy, Anna felt a lack of division, a calm presence of moment-to-momentness. It felt like the way jazz could take a series of opposites and make them one unified story. He would slide inside her and search or every possible centimeter of her interior skin. As he moved, Anna gathered his body around her, wrapped her legs tightly against the back of his, massaged his supple ass with her hands. When his tip bumped up against her cervix, she gasped more with awe than pain: each deeper thrust was a discovery of just how far she could feel him inside her.

Each evening he spent hours tasting her skin with his tongue, licking, pulling and biting, not just the nipples or the earlobe, but also the rim of the jawbone, the area beneath the breasts, the inside of the thighs, the back of the ankles. He bit softly at first, but sustained his bites so that with time they grew harder and he suspended Anna between the place of pleasure and pain, taught her that the two were not separate, but capable of producing the same flown thrill. Anna loved to feel her full belly pressed flat against his. With him inside her, she rolled him over and stretched out on top of him, moving back and forth slowly, her clit slipping firmly against the top of his cock. Before she could climax, he'd turn her over and enter her from behind, and while he pulled and pushed her hips toward and away from his cock, Anna's fingers found her clit, massaged it in circles, and moaning, she felt her juices slip and drip over her fingers, onto the cool sheets.

Anna felt as if the boy were everywhere inside her at once: while they fucked, she felt him in her cunt, her ass, her mouth, between her breasts. The pleasure felt unlike anything she understood before, and she relished each smooth wet millimeter of their sex. Kissing each other deeply, their tongues became like another genital, probing, searching, exploring the entirety of the mouth. Like they were feeding on and off one another, and with this new nourishment, becoming one sex—not male and female, but something different, more original.

"Open yourself wider," he'd say, and Anna would, not thinking she could get any wider, surprised by how much more of her there was to open.

One evening, when the boy was rehearsing at another musician's house, the phone rang. This time, knowing well it was Henry, as it had been Henry every other night before, Anna picked up.

"Hello?" she said to a crackling static on the other end.

"Hello? Anna? Anna, where have you been?" Henry sounded frantic.

"I've been here," she said calmly.

"I've been worried dead about you," he said. "It's been raining here for days, and we've all been cooped up going crazy. I thought maybe the phone lines were down because of the storm there and all, but I reached my mom, and she said—"

"No," Anna interrupted, "The rain's stopped for a while now. Everything here is good."

"It is? Are you okay?" he said, his voice thinned with worry and suspicion.

"Oh, Henry," she said, "The whole world is in bloom."

"It is?" he said.

"I am," she said.

Henry was silent on the other end of the phone.

"Henry?" she said.

"Yeah?" he whispered.

"Can I tell you about it, please?"

"OK," he said, "I guess."

"Two weeks ago, during the storm. . . " she began.

Ammi Emergency

Relationship

I make a list of things to tell you the next time I see you. Not on paper, of course, but in my head.

1) I almost cried last time while we were fucking. I'd like to cry sometime. Would that freak you out?

2) Linda calls my new haircut (the short and rumpled mess) "after-sex hair."

3) I should have asked you to gag me with my underwear.

We did it like a porno, but we did it right. When you put the knife to my throat and said, "If you scream, I'll kill you," I felt it all: the scream ricocheting inside my closed mouth, the terror of the knife, and the anticipation of the blood below it.

You pressed hard. I felt the tip and the stiffness of your wrist. If I'd spoken I would have been cut so I lay soundless and shaking as you climbed on top of me. Your cheek was rough. Your jacket smelled like leather. I caught the fierce green of your eyes—unforgiving and full of fear—before you slammed a hand over my chin, forcing my face sideways and my eyes shut. The knife sloughed, cool and ribbony, over the loose flesh of my earlobe.

"Please don't. Don't. . . ."

I meant it, but in the larger sense of refusing something I could not name, not in the framework of the scene. This had been planned. I was wearing a throwaway blouse but my trust in you was delicate and site-specific. I didn't think you would hurt me any worse than I could handle, but I was anxious to meet the person inside you who would. If he kills me, I reasoned, he'll never be able to hide the body in time. I assumed you knew this, and found the thought both comforting and titillating.

"If you do everything I tell you to, you'll live. If not—" Here your hand snaked flat along the side of my body, up over my breast, the thumb and forefinger rooting out the nipple. You grabbed the hard nub and twisted. "If I don't cum, I'm going to kill you."

You lay still over me with your ears up, deciding what to do. My whole front slate tingled. I charted the points of your body—hipbones, knees, cock, chest, belly—and where they fell against me. I wanted you inside me all at once and as quickly as possible, like a shot in the spine. I wanted to absorb the penetration with more than just my cunt. Ass, legs, back, teeth. I wanted to feel your presence under my fingernails and up against my gag reflex. Your hand continued down the fold where our ribs met. I held my breath.

"No panties." Your tone was neutral, your fingertips barely grazing my swollen lips. I was wetter than I'd ever been when you parted me and traced a finger along the slit. "You little whore."

Your fingers in my hair. All at once. Yanking me up off the bed and shoving my face down towards the floor. I was too stunned to remember my limbs, let alone order them. My knees hit first, then my forearms. I skittered into a ball as you kicked, once, the back of my leg.

"Please!"

The wood was cool and sticky with dust. I realized my skirt was up, the bottom of my ass exposed, before I became aware of my throbbing joints. The pain started a tally in my brain labeled only "SENSATION." All tactile input raised the bar. And all of it spiraled in towards my center, luring my clit out of its casing and up towards my heart.

Thud.

Center of my back.

So hard my lungs made a noise like speech.

Your hand moved from where it had fallen, pulling my shirt up over my ribs and following it with the knife. It was a more intensely illicit sensation than I expected, becoming familiar with the part of the blade one's not supposed to feel. I felt the squirm of watery chicken and limp greens. I felt the relief of separating from myself.

You groaned low and pulled me into you, the rough weave of your pants against the back of my thighs. Your teeth were hot glass between my shoulder blades. The veins of your fingers stood and went blue as you raised my skirt, crumpling it into a ball above my mons. I spread my knees and dug my nails in along the grain of the floor, but instead you stood, shuddering out a breath.

"Get on the bed."

I think sometimes about what I want from you and I boil it down to:

1) Recognition

2) Absolution

3) Kinship

One, as in, I want you to recognize yourself in me and to find the part of yourself you had no name for before. I want you to call this part by my name. Two, simply, I want the forgiveness of someone who's done worse. And three, I want the depth of emotion only children feel. I want something that reverberates in the soft tissue with the immediacy of mother is leaving on a train *and she's never coming back.*

I was walking through the top floor of an office building today, carrying a red convection bag filled with hot take-out food, when I came to a corner where a mirror should have been. This was the design of the place; my brain only expected what was suggested by its internal symmetry. So I turned, anticipating my own reflection, and instead found a hallway. Where I thought I was about to catch the canary blur of my T-shirt, the brown of a furtive glance, the red leather sack of steaming pizza, I found only the long tapering gray and sloping ceiling of distance accumulating. And at the end a blank white wall. For a second, before I realized what had happened, I thought I was that wall. Thought that the colorful tomboy in other mirrors must be someone else. And I wasn't surprised. I sometimes think my body is a territory shaped, in negative space, by the lies I tell myself.

I remember an argument we had in Nevada. You were wearing overalls stained with desert dust from the ankles to the crooks of the armpits. The lines of your face held its thin grains and your lips were white and still. You were nothing I knew how to speak to. But then you explained yourself, I answered, we touched, and suddenly you were me again. Myself as a strange, sad man in pale, splattered overalls, searching the dead white desert. Searching for and finally finding me—between the black peaks of August mountains, the air heavy with talc, the bloody pink of the far horizon—with my own eyes.

That isn't all I have to say about recognition. That isn't even the half of it. Do you know that sometimes when I masturbate, I imagine I'm you, fucking myself? Make sense of that. Please. Tell me where you end and I begin. Because if you know me, maybe you can for-give me.

Absolution. I don't believe in original sin. I do believe I have always been deficient some-how—unfair, unwashed, selfish, empty of remorse. I worry that I'm not a full human being. Sometimes I eat the last piece of bread and think nothing of it. In the war, in the concentration camps, when the apocalypse comes, I might eat the last piece of bread. I might hide it in my pocket, crumble it down so the others won't notice.

With you, I haven't any doubts. Your pockets are already full of bread and condoms. A thirty-five-year-old man with twenty-year-old lovers. In New York, you visited me while on tour with your band. Experimental jazz: I thought you were so smart. My place was white and boxy, left over from college. Dressers were piled with textbooks, walls broken up by posters. A thirteen- inch television, my roommate's model figurines. These are transitional trappings. I'm sure you noticed.

We drank imported beer on the roof and talked about art. The Empire State Building was in front of us, lit up red, and below it the skyline in creams and blues. I felt my life squat and brace itself, preparing to sprint. I stood up and told you the truth. The next day you tied me to my college-student bunk bed, saying the rest of the band would kill you if they knew. Saying you were old enough to be my father.

I was wearing a minidress and knee-high Doc Martens. My breasts were high and full, the blood beneath tremulous, present in the sharp beats and slippery spaces between. We'd gotten stuck in the rain that afternoon, lost in SoHo and Tribeca. You were dripping from the ears and scowling. I was blissful: amazed to have you timing your steps to mine, amazed at the dark wet stain my body made inside my clothes. Suddenly I was no longer an empty place bordered on all sides by the dry crush of the city. I took your hand and the rain on my arms was already warm from the heat of my skin. It is only through becoming your lover that I learned, for the first time since adolescence, how to sit inside my own body and fill it completely.

Absolution. You have no idea. We stop at twelve, spend the rest of our lives running from junior high school. I had a fuzzy pink sweatshirt and one pair of acid-washed jeans. Buck teeth, baby fat, hair in foam curlers at night. I took long walks in the narrow spoon of forest between my apartment building and the highway, shoplifted trial-size styling gel from the CVS on the corner. I had no words for what I wanted—no words for the wanting itself—only the crest of unmistakable longing, breaking over and over on the hard contours of strangers faces. I remember watching sitcoms, taping posters of Johnny Depp to the wall, masturbating with the buzzing razor, the electric toothbrush. I remember that first time, when my hands petted the new hair at my mons, then pressed tepidly against the side of my clit. My hands immediately knew everything about speed and distance that I didn't, so I continued touching myself, dizzy with insufficiency and resignation. Nothing else so neatly bound together the love and rage that had been denied me.

This is how I have been obsessed with you since I learned to think. You were an archetype in my mind before you were flesh above me. You were gigantic and miserable, a shadow on my childhood, a bruise on the endless white flesh of suburban sexuality. I found you in a sixth-grade bully, in a cartoon super-villain. When I was eleven, I dreamt that you were inserting a tape measure, inch by inch, into my vagina. Of course, I wouldn't actually meet you for another ten years. But it might as well have been you. In memory, the man in the dream becomes you.

I showed you a picture of myself from that time. I'm wearing a gigantic lavender B.U.M. sweatshirt and my hair is long, shiny with oil. I'm skinny, no breasts, standing in my best friend's living room. There are Indonesian statues, rocks her family found in Tanzania, crackpot exercise equipment at my feet.

"You were cute in eighth grade."

You were twenty-five when the picture was taken. Working twelve-hour days, playing a cherry red guitar. You had thicker hair then. The purse of your lips was more arrogant (I've seen pictures) but I'm sure you had the same hands. You could have seen me in a mall, with that same girlfriend, pricing Champion sweatshirts or Arthur Treacher's meals. You could have taken my hand and walked me through the second-level exit, across the dank parking garage and into the rest of my life. I might have followed. With terror and bliss I can imagine putting myself against you, breaking myself for you even then. Especially then. This is only one unanswered image in the blurry and unclean fable that is my sexuality.

On February 16th, I take inventory. I keep the list in the same place as the others, that tally for the things we just don't write down.

1) Three cuts from clothespins, one on my stomach, two on my right breast.

2) A round brown bruise above my right nipple.

3) A spray of purple dots (broken blood vessels?) next to my left nipple.

4) Two bite marks, one on each thigh. The left one was higher and had a yellowed oval inside it: the hollow of the mouth.

The red snaps of the whip faded, so they don't count. And my ass might still be pink for all I know. But I can't see it in this mirror so I forget it, focusing instead on the spots that radiate color or sensitivity.

I look at my eyes and at my breasts, then at the clefts around my biceps. I flex, grit my teeth, curl my wrist so that the cords of my forearm plump above my battered trunk. I don't know. I don't know how it all fits together. All I know is that I just get to feeling so strong sometimes it scares me. My legs swell with balloon animals of new muscle, my neck takes root in the hard soil of my shoulder blades, my back expands like a cobra's hood. I do fifty push-ups without breaking a sweat. Who is this person and what relationship does she have to the weakling on her hands and knees?

I sometimes blow off S/M sex to run self-defense workshops. And vice versa. Other days, I get untied in time for open sparring night at the dojo. Facing partner after partner—the skin on my knuckles lizard-like under the gloves—all I can think about is attack and defense. Their vulnerability and my impenetrability. It is not about a kick or punch landed, parried. It's about who controls the fight. Speed, rhythm, positioning. I want to dominate at every level. I don't want to respond and react but suggest, entrap, or outright bulldoze my opponent. The greatest pleasure is knowing the move I will use to win before even stepping onto the mat.

You must notice. You must notice the change in me when I've just gotten back from karate, all sweaty and arrogant, wanting to be massaged and called tough. I know you do because I feel you slowly taking me down again, watching and waiting until I'm soft and exhausted enough to be pulled back underneath you. Waiting until I can again doubt the directives of my body, can mute my limbs and scramble my reflexes. Waiting until I am no longer the tomboy but the blank white wall. It splits me to think that outside the bedroom my muscles are a point of pride, a reaffirmation of my values and identity, while in the bedroom they become a meaningless factor, heavy like an overcoat and just as impersonal.

Martial arts and S/M are the halves of me I doubt I'll be able to reconcile. I can sometimes almost feel myself separating, the dueling urges staking out physical space in my brain, my right hand contorting into a fist while the left lays limp, expectant. Sometimes I look to who I was when I met you (when I sought you on street corners, quilted you from the loose threads of dreams) in the hopes that this woman can tell me about the two women I feel like today.

And I remember. I remember being twenty: New York, that tiny television, boots that never quite got broken in. I remember when dislike of myself and fear of myself were the only two components of my personality that reacted like living things, both urgent and indulgent.

When I was twenty everything that mattered appeared to me as a scream, off a bridge, into the yellow industrial lights of Brooklyn at night. It didn't matter so much what I was screaming about so long as it held the promise of catharsis. Sex never promised me comfort or even fun. Instead it offered death and rebirth in one encounter, the potential energy of the body released brilliantly, the tension that approached me always from within and without expended in a rush of joy and terror before I would have had to decide what to do with it.

I think of sex when:

1) I see your fingers bluing with tension over the yellowed keys of the antique piano.

2) I find pieces of your clothing in other people's homes.

3) I can tell you're lying to me. You're so smug, so unblinkingly entitled. It thrills me to be one of those things to which you feel entitled.

I climbed up on the mattress and waited on my knees, my skirt wrinkled, little black T-shirt pulled up over one stiff brown-rose nipple. Sweat dried, my forehead and armpits cooling. You sat in a chair, legs crossed, and folded the knife in the crook of your arm. Not a threatening pose, but I could feel the coiled tension in your calves and shoulders, the way you might spring forward at any moment across the short space between us. The possibility waxed and waned. You looked like a hunching gay man, you looked like a bird of prey.

You asked me questions, your mouth deliberate, jaws clasping and then tossing each word. Have I ever been fucked before. Have I ever had my pussy eaten. Have I ever sucked a man's cock. *I'm going to lick your pussy. I'm going to make you swallow my cock.* I couldn't see your teeth. I thrilled with the severity of your arousal.

"I want to see you touch yourself."

I pushed two fingers against my clit, face low and shoulders rounded. I actually did find this humiliating, having to put on a show while you stared, your eyes full of contempt and only mildly curious. I could have gone about it real slow—held myself open, pulled the pink crest of an areola up to my tongue—but this isn't what I do when I'm alone. I close my eyes, use mannish movements; I assume I look desperate and bored.

But you smiled, bemused, I suppose, to see me blushing and uncomfortable. You stood and stepped heavily towards me, lifted the hem of my shirt up over the other breast with the hook of one finger. Sweat tickled the inside of my knees and the shadows below my ass.

"Keep going."

You were close now, so close I could feel your breath on my face and the worn cotton of your T-shirt against my shivering bicep. It was quiet and dark behind my eyes. I heard my throat cluck; I heard myself swallow. Your fingertips traced a line over each swollen breast and in to the bead of nipple at their centers. I gasped. Nerves crackled as you moved slowly up, your fingertips velvet over my collarbone and windpipe. As I pushed two fingers up inside myself, I tasted your thumb parting my teeth.

Ooooom. My tongue angled itself against the ridges of your fingerprint as my dripping cunt seized around my fingers. I could disappear in that feeling—sucking—the way my body realigns itself completely around the object. I forgot myself and tensed my thighs against my fist. Then my tongue skipped over something asymmetrical and all at once I could taste the trauma of the digit you'd broken in childhood, the meshed bone buzzing with the chemical lemon aura of X-ray film. I saw the white lump in relief between my teeth and opened myself to you in a rush of sympathy. You grinned and pulled back your hand, watching as my face fell upwards, bewildered and expectant.

"Now suck on your fingers."

I raised my hand. My index and middle finger were glistening, balled with moisture. I ran the tips over the outside of my lips then fed them to myself. You leaned in, pressed your cock up against my hip, gently licked the stem of my hand. I swallowed and the taste of me coated my gullet and the roof of my mouth. You then opened me like a hinge, using my hair as a handle. I emptied myself of breath and you exhaled into me, the air from your stomach and lower lungs (tinged with digestion and tuba oil, the skins of other women) making my cells swollen and dizzy. You made me do it again and it was like dipping my fingers into a well. This time you sucked more of the juice out of my mouth, let out a low purr as you sipped at the cracks of my hands.

I forgot.

I forgot you intended to hurt me when you suddenly tore at the cords of my neck, shoved me back down so hard the wind off your violence cooled and calmed me. *Don't move. Don't cry, don't scream, don't moan. If you make a sound, I'll beat you.*

The mattress squealed. The sheet rose and was kicked to the edge of the bed where it wound round my ankles, purple and vaguely moist as a tug of intestine. You pulled me backwards by my hips, spread my legs—pushing aside the muscular flanks of my hamstrings and the stringy tug of the bed sheet—and met me in the cave of my body. Tongue, nose, upper lip, chin; all inside me, moving high and then low. Sucking, grinding with your jaws, seeming to swallow whole folds with all their associated nerves. Your tongue wound down my seam, flickered over my asshole.

"Uh." Faint, barely more than a gasp. I couldn't help it but you stood immediately. The lower part of your face was wet and your hair stood on end. You walked casually to the base of the bed, your erection bobbing in front of you, and made a fist of my hair. You shook me and I felt my neck bones spark. Light burst in shivering columns through my blurred vision, cracked electric stars with black centers down my spine. My clit seemed to cover an area halfway to my belly button. You slapped me again, harder, and the whole front of my body stung, then tingled. Organs purred, pleading in their little isolated voices to be hit again, to be given the delicious stillness that follows any act of terror.

The list of things I do not tell you the next time I see you:
1) When I see myself through your eyes, I realize how much I hate myself.
2) I hate the things about myself that I have in common with your other lovers.
3) Your hands on my rib cage hate me, the hot wash of your breath hates me, you can never give me the forgiveness I crave from touch.

I picked you up outside the jail. Lohn, Texas; nothing could have been uglier. You were standing in the yellow dust on a gravel road with no street sign, hand in your pocket, jacket draped over that same wrist. Behind you was the compound, fence shaped by coil upon coil of razor-tipped fencing. I could barely see through the weave of the wire; I had the urge to accelerate rather than brake when you reached for the handle of the passenger door.

You were wearing silver sunglasses and your posture was over-casual. You looked like a criminal, and it made me realize that you have always looked like a criminal.

"God," you said, "you're a sight for sore eyes."

I looked across the seat at you but saw only myself, reflected in your sunglasses. A sight for sore eyes. I don't know why I was so anxious to pick you up at the jail. Maybe I thought that if my face was the first thing you saw after a night in a holding cell, you'd imprint to it completely.

"That's an image I'll probably keep in my mind for a long time," you said after the last time we made love. You were talking about when you had me tied to the door, my wrists raised and knotted together with a bicycle inner tube. I was naked except for a parochial-school skirt I'd found in the trash, plaid and still ribbed with iron creases. Duct tape over my mouth. The room was dark and your shadow was all around me, hot because in Texas even the shadows bulge with blue heat.

I remember the sound of my breathing, then the crack of your hand against the side of my face. My whole body gasped, then surged as I took it in. As you moved to light a candle, I realized the bottom of my nose was gathering moisture. Sweat? I prayed for it to be sweat. But it kept coming, the drops soon tracing a warm, vaguely moist line over my gag. The blood had weight, it pressed against my lips and chin like a small salamander.

My eyes burned; my heart leapt at the promise of catharsis. I wanted to cry as much as I wanted to cum. Then the wick caught and at the same time we both looked down at middle of my chest, where the dim brown liquid had cut me in half. It curved, swelling magenta between my breasts, dribbling to a point an inch above the waist of my skirt.

"Damn," you breathed. I admired the contrast. Brown blood, gray-white skin. I never knew my body could oppose itself so completely. "Damn," you said again, a low growl that reverberated in the hollow of my throat and the walls of my cunt.

You dropped your voice and eyed me carefully.

"Do you want to stop?"

I shook my head and you lifted my skirt, grazing me silently with the tips of your fingers. The tears evaporated. Visual poetry, I thought, proud to have been a part. I liked the idea of you keeping the bound and bleeding me in your mind better than your keeping the smiling me outside Lohn, Texas. Sometimes when you don't want that image, it must appear, demanding and terrifying, a horror movie on endless loop in your crotch.

"Take off your glasses," I said when I found you at the jail. Below them your skin was parched and your eyes stony. Your hair stood spidery and sparse. I need to clarify something: when I wanted to keep driving, it was because, for a moment, I wanted you to suffer. Simple. I wanted you, cold, in your thin shirt, to face the legacy of pain and discomfort that is bondage. I wanted you to know deprivation and fear. I wanted you to know endless waiting. Out of love or spite (I don't know which), I wanted to give you these gifts, and I wanted to watch you unwrap them.

When we're not having sex we:

1) Build things, cook vegetables, and talk about history.

2) Drink too much.

3) Argue about books.

"How was your day?"

"Fine." But it wasn't fine at all. I'd fallen asleep on Janey's wicker couch and woke feeling I'd missed something tremendously valuable. My face was itchy and checkered. My hands didn't recognize one another. And that floating regret: it had something to do with you.

Then I remembered.

The whole reason I fell asleep was that I was fantasizing about you beating me. No sex even, just rage. I wanted you to hate me but still want me. I wanted you to hate yourself for wanting me. I wanted you to blame me, which you already do. You gave me a Gabriel Garcia Marquez book and a pair of nipple clips for my birthday. That meant something; S/M gear is expensive and you don't have any shoes without holes. I get stuck on the way both your shoes and boots are split just above the ball of the foot, imagine duct tape sealing and unsealing the rifts. Walking next to you on the street, I look down and feel a rush of loyalty and tenderness: someone should sponsor your fetishes.

I have this new fantasy. In it we are strangers. You pull up next to me on the side of the highway, driving some rusty, grumbly American car. I have my thumb out, the strap of one of my shoes is undone. I admit I'm running away from West Virginia, toss my bag in the back seat, and stick with the new identity. All you see is someone without a past, someone whose future is still far away. At first you are casual, pleasant. Then you swerve for a sudden, unlikely exit, and soon the roads are smaller and more crumpled. You pull over (I picture an apple orchard gone white with disease; Saratoga, New York) and make me give you head below the steering wheel. The idea of flight is now impossible. That door has closed and a new door has opened up onto the vista of a kidnapping. It is still a day's drive to your cabin in the mountains.

On the way, you threaten and yank at the radio. You grope my thigh and the leg band of my underwear without swerving. When you turn to examine me, I recoil; I'm grateful for the approaching road. There is a comfort to being in motion. When we stop my tongue swells dry and hot with hunger and anticipation.

You take me to a rest stop and order me to sit in an orange linoleum booth while you bring me a Whopper, medium fries, a Coca-Cola. I languidly scrape a slim-cut french fry through the ketchup, revealing streaks of white grease paper, and pretend not to notice that people are staring. Other travelers, older couples with tan hats and nubby shoes, whose RVs are parked in the truck zone.

A man with a John Deere cap says, "You all right, miss?" and I say, *Fine, sir thank you for asking*, with a look of such withering incomprehension that I know he will think of me— and of you, approaching with crisp, unforgiving boot steps, carrying the tray—for days. My clothes will be off-center and too young for me, my legs longer for lack of socks and for the peach and raspberry splotches fruiting all along the white calves. You'll eat without talking to me, touch my shoulder to indicate it's time to go.

Once at the cabin, I see a rug scraggly with dog hair, a broken television with red, blue, and green circles on the dial. Bent antenna and shellacked yellow cereal bowls. I see you leaving me tied for hours, then fastening a collar around my neck and hooking it to the thick leather leash you found on Market Street. I imagine being led to the living room in a ball, my hands tied behind my back, and being fed from a pet's dish. Chocolate ice cream— Häagen Daz—in three clean scoops. After, I nuzzle your crotch with my nose still sticky and you cane me, then lock me in a closet. I have no idea what I want. Only perhaps to wake in the middle of the night and feel first the heartswell of being next to you, then the dull throb of the handcuff on the bone of my right wrist.

It is important that people—other travelers—see us on our way to the cabin, in those anxious public spaces where everyone has left somewhere and not yet arrived somewhere else. I want them to see us and think of nowhere, to taste the lurid satisfaction that comes from being without a home and without allegiances. I want them to catch the trail of frenzied sex and closeted ambition that winds behind us, and I want them loosened from gut to groin.

"That's good. I'm glad you had a good day," you said. There was a three-inch cockroach on the floor in front of us, crumpled on its front legs, ass in the air, struggling with something insurmountable between my shoes and my T-shirt. "Are you naked under there?"

"No." But I was.

You sat down on the bed and laid a hand over each of my ears. Then you kissed my forehead and started talking about robots.

"Locomotion. With pedals," I added. "We could make ones that move like giant kangaroos! Thirty feet to the hop." I giggled, folding my arms across the cool sheet at my belly.

You nodded, twisting a sprig of your sideburn, at once devious and innocent and preternaturally calm.

When we found ourselves staring at that line of blood you could have:

1) Taken a picture. I would have told CVS Photo Developing that we were making a movie.

2) Picked up a paint brush and decorated my body with the watery crimson.

3) Pressed your fist to my sternum and commanded, "Lick your blood off my knuckles, bitch."

Oh, the poetry of cocksucking. I feel I can say that, having read poems on the subject, and having started, with the tip of my tongue, at the base of your shaft. I traced a vein and instantly felt you falling, the infrastructure of your resistance crumbling around me, the tenderness in the newly exposed palms of your hands.

I arched my face and began licking the shadows around the head, winding at last to that secret spot, the spade of skin where all the inarticulated and crisscrossing lines of pleasure in the male organ converge. Outside, the sun was setting, the windowpane glowing rose. Your fingertips on my cheek were lighter than pollen when I took you whole into my mouth.

You moaned, your thighs white, nearly hairless and shivering. I stroked the underside of your balls with my fingertips, felt them grow stiffer as your cock arched higher inside my mouth. Below you my body gleamed on the bare bed, the nipples ragged, the pubic bush budding gray steam.

I felt like a fish laid on a platter, still and cold at the surface but pink-hot at the center. Gasping, barely alive, cells crying out and dying for something so all-important I'd never thought to name it before. My cunt throbbed and welled, filling my lower abdomen with slickness and longing. I felt myself hollowing to the specifications of your body.

You put your palms on either side of my ears, pushed my head back and climbed on top of me. The sun was almost gone now, the light full purple. Your weight pressed the sizzling at my extremities in towards the center of my body. I felt pleasure absorb through the skin, burrow into deep tissue. The faint smell of watery beer hovered at each of your pores and mine drank off it, my belly tremulous below yours, my palate heavy with the ferrous, salty carve of your tongue.

"Do you want me to fuck you?"

Nodded: yes.

"Say it."

"Fuck me."

You peeled a translucent condom over yourself and held the tip at the base of my body. Then you leaned in and, with a ripple of your hips, were inside me. I gasped/breathed/moaned. The sound was expelled from my lungs rather than spoken, forced up from below as you filled me with a pressure that seemed larger than my trunk. I arched against you, my breasts swollen to the thin brush of your chest, my thighs locking around the flanks of your ass.

In the beginning, you were too big for me. It hurt every time. I remember watching you up above me on your elbows, face glistening in the darkness, while I tried to exhale. Organs displaced themselves to make way for each thrust, and afterwards an acid presence bit at me for days. You knew I was in pain but went so hard. I thought you were a monster. I heard you laugh once while inside me, a crinkly sound that filled me with exhilaration and horror. I thought I was a monster too.

In time my body adapted to yours and soon demanded you. Not just your cock but the way you moved. Your tongue in your mouth, your eyes left open, the way you raised my legs to strum the dove-gray bottoms of my feet. Now, with you inside me again, I realized afresh how pure the union was. I pulsed against you and bleated softly. I was nearly wild with tenderness.

"I want you to hit me."

You paused. I felt the distraction in your right arm, the paralysis and then the crack of your palm striking my cheekbone.

Uh!

I cried out. My eyes unfocused and my jaw fell slack. Blood raced to my face and neck, driven by your cock up my belly and then down again to my swollen clit. The world went black and white and red all over, and what remained were my hips, bucking against you hotter and slicker.

"Why is that such a turn-on?" you asked, not of me but of yourself. You were shaking now—close to real anger—but I knew you'd do it again.

Again?

I asked with my eyes and you responded in a rage, peeling back my hair, contorting my neck and shoulders against the curve of my spine. Tears flew to my eyes as sensation ricocheted from limb to throat to cunt. I punched you in the ribs (slow, leverageless swoops) partially to free myself, partially to provoke you. My fists thudded soddenly against your body until you grabbed the wrists, grinding the bones together and taking them roughly to the mattress. You took both of my hands in one of yours, slammed the other down across my mouth and nose.

"You want to be hit? You want to be hurt? Well, you'd better want this because now I'm going to hurt you."

I squealed beneath your hand in an effort to get a breath, twisted to raise your hips, but you just slid in tighter. Then you hit me. Once, twice, in the face, then on the sides of my body, breasts and belly. You leaned back in and bit my neck, sucking on the scream that reverberated beneath your teeth. I shook, gnashed my teeth against the wet meat of your palm. I tasted salt and iron and the resin of my own crumpled bangs. You then threw my face sideways, grasping at my hair to yank yourself forward, to press inside me to the pubic bone.

Too much! I wanted to cry, but my mouth was covered and besides, too much is really just right sometimes. I was rocked by torrents of blood and fear, saliva and sweat and sexiness. If I'd been standing right then, my legs would not have held me. That cry curled up in my throat like a dead bird and I gave myself over fully to the pulse of my clit.

I dug my nails into your back and neck as you raised up on your arms, pinning me to the bed with your cock, riding me harder and harder until neither of us could tell yelps of pain from those of pleasure. I tore at your shoulders as you bit my earlobe, then pushed my face down as though to drown me in the bed, the heel of your hand folding my eyelashes inside my eye.

I couldn't see. Your body was a wet heat that formed the boundary to my range of motion and imagination. I thought of days when the air is near white, the sky thick with human intentions and ridiculously low to the earth. Soon our mouths found each other and soon we were kissing. Not fighting with our faces but kissing—heady, tremulous, devotional. Your sweat trickled into corners of my mouth. My tongue found yours and lost its anchor between my teeth.

You jerked abruptly, and another rain of slaps broke over my cheeks and neck. This time a low shiver ran down me, as though a dark bird had swooped along the length of my body and would return with my sex in its mouth. Everything followed this path—brain, lungs, oceans of blood and lymph—until I felt my cunt arch then break below the cave of liquid.

I'm cumming.

My body contracted around you, my legs clenching, my teeth clamping around the loose skin of your throat. I felt my head rocking, the waves of vertigo as my hair ground against the mattress, the delicious spike and release as my chest thrust open to allow the bird flight. I rose then, finally free of the weight of wanting.

"Girl. . . "

At some point I started to emerge from my private darkness and realized you had joined me, the base of your cock pulsing against my vulva, your back arched and your hips low, the papery sound of your breath flowing in a hiss down my neck and back.

Then silence.

When did our clothes come off? Where did the sheet go? Always, it is like this afterwards, when we become aware all at once of the universe outside our bodies. Our lips find each other, slowly, like people who have never met, and then you retreat back into your life, I into mine. Sometimes, while the air is still warm and we don't yet need an excuse to touch one another, I let my fingertips have the back of your neck. I want the chance to thumb your soul before it recedes, as it always does, from the surface of your skin.

"Do you know, Linda thinks of this haircut"—I fluffed myself—"as 'after sex hair.'"

"I didn't know," you said with an incriminating little grin. Your chin was so sharp; you were sure you'd gotten away with something. You raised your fingers to pet my bangs, delicately, conversationally, as though being introduced for the first time.

As your hand traveled over my ear, then down the cooling bulb of my belly, I felt myself turn to you. Despite everything, I found my pelvis mirroring yours, my gaze absorbed by eyes murky and impenetrable as river stones. Without meaning to I held my breath, keeping myself taut, waiting with tiny flickering muscles for the first shadow of your intentions and for my response. For the keening of your body that I have been listening to always, listening, expecting, waiting for the truth.

Contributors

Nancy Agabian is a writer and a performance artist. An Armenian-American originally from Walpole, Massachusetts, she made art in LA for nine years before currently attending the MFA Writing Program in Nonfiction at Columbia University. Her first book, *Princess Freak: Poems and Performance Texts* was recently published by Beyond Baroque Books. She also makes funny songs with her friend Ann Perich as the guitar-less boy-less folk/punk duo Guitar Boy.

L.J. Albertano has unleashed her spoken word performances at every major venue in Los Angeles including the LA Theater Center, the Wadsworth and the John Anson Ford Theater. She's been featured frequently at Beyond Baroque, the Knitting Factory, Highways, London's October Gallery and other literary/spoken word meccas around the US and in Great Britain. Recognized "Best Female Performer-Poet" by the *LA Weekly*, she was one of five poets chosen to represent Los Angeles in Amsterdam's One World Poetry Festival. Her CD *Skin* is available on New Alliance Records.

Liz Belile created her first pornography in the fifth grade, when she drew naked lady magazines—"miniature *Playboys*"—and sold them to the boys for a quarter. Since then, she earned an MFA in Poetics from the Naropa Institute, has performed and published widely, has a book out, *Polishing the Bayonet* (Incommunicado) and a CD, *Your Only Other Option Is Surgery* (New Alliance). She has focused mostly on Gynomite and on her lit art site, www.bodyofwords.com—both paying bills and getting her thrills by editing and creating interesting content for the web—since 1995. She lives in Texas and plays music with her talented partner/boyfriend, studies holistic medicine, and teaches yoga as well as workshops for women who want to write and perform their own pornographic texts.

Lee Christopher is a writer, poet, teacher, and editor. She is the executive editor of *The New Censorship*. Her latest CD is *Jaded Love* with Bobbie Louise Hawkins and the Al

Hermann Quartet. Her latest chapbook is *The Hunt.* Her work has been published in *Bombay Gin, The New Censorship, Associated Writing Programs Chronicle,* and other journals. She recently received a lectureship at Metropolitan State College of Denver for one year, and is also an MSCD Technology Fellow. In addition to MSCD, she teaches at Naropa University, Regis University, and Denver University. She is completing a biography of jazz musician Haywood Henry.

Jane Creighton teaches creative writing and American literature at the University of Houston-Downtown. Her work has been anthologized in *Close to the Bone: Memoirs of Hurt, Rage, and Desire and Unwinding the Vietnam War.* Her journal publications include *Ploughshares, The American Voice,* and *Gulf Coast.*

tatiana de la tierra thundered down the mountains of Colombia in a fierce sexplosion of lightning and landed in Mayami, Florida at the tender age of seven. Doomed en el norte, she became an angry girl, a roquera pothead, a bearded lady, a spoken and broken escritora, and a Generación Ñ sinvergüenza pornographer. She has a MFA in creative writing from the University of Tejas at El Paso and a Master of Library Science from State University of New York at Buffalo. de la tierra currently spends her time casting spells, riding horses in the sky, and writing songs to her many muses.

Shaila Dewan is an award-winning journalist. Originally from Houston, Texas, she now covers fires, hijackings, and escaped cattle in New York. Dewan has been performing with Gynomite since the first reading in Houston, in April 1999.

Ammi Emergency lives in New Orleans and publishes *Emergency,* a zine.

Maggie Estep's first novel, *Diary of an Emotional Idiot* was published in the US in 1997 and in Germany and Italy in 1999. Her second book, *Soft Maniacs,* came out through Simon and Schuster in 1999. She has made two spoken word CDs, *No More Mr. Nice Girl* (Imago, 1994) and *Love is a Dog From Hell* (Mercury, 1997). Her writing has appeared in various magazines including *Spin, Harper's Bazaar, The Village Voice, Black Book, Shout—* and German *Elle* and *Die Zeit* in Germany. She lives in Brooklyn.

duVergne Gaines lives in Los Angeles and in Tucson. She is a Flaming Virago, one of the original producers of Gynomite. She is also the former director of the Fund for the Feminist Majority's "Rock for Choice" project and is on the board of directors at Beyond Baroque Literary Arts Center in Venice, California. A woman who consistently puts her money where her mouth is, duVergne is currently studying to become a lawyer.

Gwynne Garfinkle lives in Los Angeles. Her poetry, fiction, essays, and music reviews have appeared in numerous publications, including *Exquisite Corpse, Big Bridge, The American Voice, Loca, Paramour,* and the *New Times*. She is the author of a book of poetry, *New Year's Eve* (Typical Girls Press), and has just completed a novel, *She Wandered Through the Garden Fence*.

Amber Gayle is the writing half of Evil Twin Publications, a project she does with her twin sister, designer/book artist Stacy Wakefield. Recent work includes *Mud In My Veins, Grass in My Feet, Blood in the Sky, Cows in the Creek,* a book of poems and photos; *Ramble Right (My Evil Twin Sister #3,)* a novella; and soon to be released *My Evil Twin Sister # 4: Notta Lotta Love Stories.* Amber lives around western Oregon, mainly Portland at present, and is currently studying psychology via Goddard College.

Michelle Glaw likes to play in her band, The Vulgarians. She is a huge bookworm and she loves to write. When it comes to fashion and clothing, Glaw has her own twisted view of the spectrum. Originally from the Midwest, she has settled in Houston but is still roaming in her mind. She is a Pentecostal atheist, having lived in a bohemian commune where she curated occasional, quirky art shows and subjected people to her couture disasters. She has been performing with Gynomite since the Spring of '99. She is a Virgo on the Libra cusp—which makes her "a little more jazzy" than most Virgos.

Tammy Gómez writes and teaches in Fort Worth, Texas. She is an activist, a dancer, a mover and a shaker. She's hosted radio shows, organized book drives for prisoners, climbed mountains and been all over the world reading her luscious poems.

Trish Herrera Texas-born 1954. Subversive, irreverent fiction writer. No apparent reason for bliss.

Olive Hershey was born bad in the 1940's in Houston, Texas. After a misspent youth she made the mistake of marrying the first man who'd have her (since she'd wrecked her reputation, she figured her life was over). After seven years of frigid connubial bliss in beautiful Buffalo, New York, she returned to Texas where she blazed a wide path to Austin and points west. She got a Ph.D. in English from the University of Texas and a MA in Creative Writing at the University of Houston. Hershey has written plays, poems, and a novel, *Truck Dance* (Harper & Row, 1989). At present she is working on a memoir, a novel, and a lot more dirty stories.

Born and bored in Houston, Texas, **Melissa Hung** fled her hometown to pursue a creative writing major and a journalism degree at Northwestern University. Her work (creative and non-fiction) has been published here and there in journals and zines like *dis*Orient* and *A Magazine*. She has worked (briefly) as a day-care teacher, telemarketer, waitress, assistant to a crude oil pricing analyst, and newspaper intern—all before graduating college. Melissa currently writes news and features for the *Houston Press*, an alternative newsweekly.

Sassy Johnson, a performance artist/writer/director who lives in Houston, is originally from a God-fearing small town in Mississippi. She was a member of the former Queer Artist Collective (QuAC). While with QuAC, she led performance workshops for the Houston Area Teen Coalition of Homosexuals (HATCH). Sassy has been performing with Gynomite since the first show in Houston. She is also working on *On Hot Dogs, Beauty, and Sex*—a collection of essays on growing up as a lesbian in the South.

Miriam R. Sachs Martín has been published in *Paginas Tortilleras, Free to Be, Gertrude,* the *Santa Clara Review, New to North America,* and *Latino Heretics.* She's got two fabulous chapbooks: *Early Spring Flowers,* and *Show Me The Way To Montana,* and produces FIERCE WORDS TENDER, a twice-monthly Women's open-mike that's hotter than flamin' hot Cheetos, and wetter than the Lexington Reservoir. She lives in San José with her cat bundle of love and her beautiful, amazing girlfriend.

Mary McGrath's first book of poetry *Trespassing Stoplights and Attitudes* was published through Mudborn Press. Her piece "How to Exercise with Your Computer" appeared on the cover of the *National Lampoon.* An avid photographer, she is a monthly contributor to *Petersen's Photographic Magazine.* Her work has also appeared in the *Herald Examiner,* AIDS Project LA, Borders Books and Music, Santa Monica College, photoalley.com and is viewable on awesomegalleries.com. Currently she resides in Culver City, California, the "Heart of Screenland."

Pia Pico is a writer, a teacher and the leader of her own alt.rock band. In 1994, she received an MFA from the University of Houston. She works with a bad-ass theater company, for whom she is seeking a home, and is currently writing/producing her own original show: *Future Girl Hosts.* Originally a Southern Cali girl, for the past ten years she has made Houston her home.

Writer, journalist, poet, thinker, essayist, communications consultant and future expatriate, Vassar grad **Andrea Roberts'** physical body resides in Houston, Texas. Her work can be found on the written page, cyberspace, the back of napkins, and worn Mead notebooks— as well as at open-mike poetry readings in Houston. She has written for numerous alternative publications and cultural monthlies, illuminating political and social issues for over four years.

Carlisle Vandervoort is a visual artist and a writer. When she is not creating trouble as a fierce, out lesbian and yogi she can be found fishing, riding her bike, cooking dinner for friends, and digging in the dirt. Her interests in ritual, spirituality, water activities, and landscape design have found their way into both her writing and her three-dimensional work. She lives in Houston and Los Angeles.

Pam Ward lives in Los Angeles. She is a writer and a graphic designer. She has a book out through Incommunicado and was included in the *Gynomite* CD anthology.

Diana Wolfe, a writer, teacher, and mother of two, received her MFA from the University of Washington, Seattle. Her fiction has won several prizes and her story, "Bad Man, Funny Man," appeared in *Emeralds in the Ash*. Diana has also written columns on love advice and motherhood for various websites, and is a long way from home now, in Texas.

About Gynomite

Begun as a reading series in Los Angeles in 1994, Gynomite was the brainchild of writer/performer Liz Belile. The readings were collectively produced by Belile, filthy-minded poet duVergne Gaines (former director of the Feminist Majority Foundation's Rock for Choice project), and recording artist/activist Weba Garretson. Together, they formed The Flaming Viragos.

In June of '94, Gynomite sold out "the Lenny Bruce room" in the basement of Luna Park in Los Angeles—and just kept going, performing at a variety of venues and bookstores, as well as on the radio. The Flaming Viragos recorded and produced a CD (released on Garretson's label, Catasonic) from two nights of readings, then hit the road, packing the house with a CD release party at South by Southwest in Austin, Texas, 1995.

By September of 1997, The Viragos parted company (with love) to follow their own creative paths, and Gynomite lay dormant until April of '99, when Belile, who had been back in Texas for two years, realized that Gynomite was just what was needed most right below the Bible Belt. Texas, after all, is home of the Bush family, a far-too-popular execution chamber, and ridiculous penal codes surrounding sexual behavior and the sale and use of sex toys—which are not *nearly* as available as, say, firearms.

In Houston, Gynomite sold out theaters, was proclaimed "Best Reading Series" by the *Houston Press*, and invigorated the literati and arts communities. Belile co-curated two sold-out screenings with artist and film maven Andrea Grover for Grover's microcinema The Aurora Picture Show. Titled *Through Her Eyes: Stimulating Chick Cinema*, the screenings were part of the *Hot and Bothered: SexFest '99* events organized for Diverseworks artspace—which also featured a Gynomite reading. In New Orleans, Gynomite drew drunken acclaim at a jazz-club housed in a former brothel.

The dream is to take Gynomite on the road, throughout the South and beyond, liberating anyone who crosses its path.

Belile also leads a workshop for women to write and perform their own pornographic texts called *Breaking the Cherry*, drawing inspiration from her own training in literature with Allen Ginsberg, Diane di Prima and Anne Waldman, as well as Susie Bright's sexual manifestos, Betty Dodson's "self-loving" tapes and workshops, Natalie Goldberg's *Writing Down the Bones*, Candida Royalle's video work, Annie Sprinkle's fearless creativity, and Nancy Friday's *Women On Top*—plus the many amazing artists who are pushing the sexual envelope through literature and film to answer that age-old question: "What do women really want?"

What do women really want, indeed.

Click our lit at www.gynomite.com.

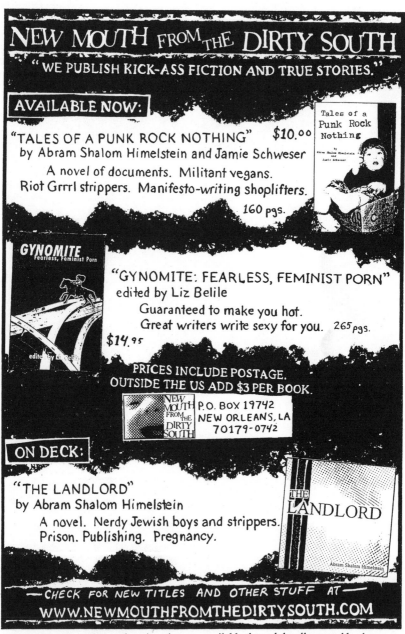